THE LAST FOUR

C.J. PETIT

Printed in the United States of America

First Printing, 2017

ASIN: B071ZYBKTW

TABLE OF CONTENTS

PROLOGUE

"But, Joe, ten years is so long away!" exclaimed Danny.

"We gotta wait until we're grownups, Danny. Maybe you or me could get away before that, but Jo and Caroline won't be able to 'cause they're girls. They can't go anywhere on their own. So, ten years from today we meet at the train station in Salina at noon. I don't know how far away I'm gonna be, but I'll be there."

Caroline looked at the boy she now considered her boyfriend, smiled and said, "I'll be there, Joe."

"Me, too," agreed Joe's sister, Josephine.

"Alright, then I guess I'll be there, too," Danny grudgingly replied.

Joe then said, "Now, if none of us gets chosen at this stop, then we'll keep moving the place that we're gonna meet until the first of us is picked."

"Which of us will get picked next?" asked Josephine, the dread of the upcoming choosing in her voice.

"I don't know," answered Joe, "The big kids and smallest kids went first. I understand why that happens, too. Folks want big kids to put 'em right to work. Other folks want the little ones 'cause they're cute and they can treat 'em like their own. We're kinda stuck in the middle, so nobody wants us that bad, I guess. All we can do is eat their food, and they gotta send us to school, too. We're bigger problems 'cause we're both brothers and sisters, and that's harder. Either they don't wanna break us up or they don't wanna take both of us. I think that the girls will be adopted first, though. I'll probably go last, 'cause I'm a little bigger and they'll figure I'll eat too much."

"Joe, I don't want to go," said Caroline, her teary eyes focused on him.

Joe took Caroline's hands, looked into her sad blue eyes and said, "Caroline, none of us want to go, but they just didn't want us back in Philadelphia. It's gonna take some time, but if you can't make it to the reunion in ten years, I'll come and find you. I promise. You have to trust me."

"I trust you, Joe," said Caroline as she squeezed his hands tightly.

Twenty minutes later, the train slowed to a stop in Junction City, Kansas. The four children were ushered from the train, carrying the bags that had been issued to them in Philadelphia and were led down the street to the church where the adults would be waiting to examine them. Normally, the choosing was held in a small theater where the children could be seen to better advantage, but with only the four children remaining, they used the church.

Danny and Caroline Stevens, Joe and Josephine Carlisle were escorted by their chaperone down the main street to the church where there were only four couples inside as prospective parents or guardians.

The youngsters had been instructed to smile to their possible new parents, to be polite and say how lucky they would be to become part of a new family, but Joe could never manage it. He tried it the first stop five days ago but had failed miserably. Now he just tried not to look so angry, but even that was no longer possible. Joe never could get past the anger of being tossed away like trash. It burned inside, and he presented a poor appearance to prospective parents.

Joe was angry at his birth parents, angry at leaving his school and friends, and just angry at the world. The only ones that could moderate that anger were his sister and Caroline. Danny was just there.

He and Josephine had been tossed out of their home in Philadelphia like three-day old fish. Their parents told them that they couldn't afford to keep them any longer, dropped them off at the local church and just walked away without even a handshake.

He wasn't overly fond of his parents anyway, but to be suddenly uprooted from his friends and the neighborhood he grew up in to be sent halfway across the country was just mean. He'd never forgive them for that, not that he expected to ever see them again. He was even angrier that they had sent Josephine packing as well. He was a boy and he was tough, but Josephine had cried for hours after she was told of their fate.

Unlike most boys, Joe was very fond of his little sister, even though she was only two years younger than he was. He was taller and much stronger and thought of himself as her protector, so he never let anyone, boy or girl, hurt Josephine. But it was their parents who hurt her the most and his inability to protect her on that horrible day had added frustration to his anger.

He had spent the first week before they boarded the train trying to console her, trying to convince her that it would be a great adventure, just like in the stories she loved to read, where she'd meet her Prince Charming out West, and he'd be riding a big white charger. But Josephine was nine and couldn't be fooled, so she remained terrified of the incomprehensible change in her and her brother's young lives. All she had now was Joe, and Joe didn't think he was doing enough for her.

But after they boarded the train and met Danny and Caroline Stevens, Josephine seemed to do better. The two blonde-haired Stevens children were from the same part of Philadelphia but had never met Joe and Josephine. They were in a similar circumstance, but not quite the same. At least Joe's parents had taken him and Josephine to the church. Danny and Caroline had returned home from school one Tuesday afternoon and found their parents gone. The apartment they had been renting had already been rented to a new family, who were in the process of moving in. It had been the new tenants who had taken them to a different church and left them.

Joe wasn't sure if it wasn't better for them than watching his parents cold, unsmiling faces as they just walked away.

Now they were on the train with Joe and Josephine. Danny was ten, a year younger than Joe, and Caroline was just two weeks younger than Josephine. They became fast friends as the train rolled westward and having new friends was better than having none at all. But each of them knew that their new friends would soon leave the train and would be friends no more, and they most likely would never see each other again.

Then the trainload of children began making stops in Missouri. The children would be lined up on the train platform, then be led like a circus parade from the train station, down the boardwalks to whichever location had been advertised on the flyers announcing the arrival of the train carrying free children for the taking.

They'd be marched onto a stage and large groups of adults would examine them like produce at the market. They would ask questions of the children, and if the adults wanted to take them home, they would tell their chaperone of their selection, sign a contract making promises that few of them would keep because they knew that follow-up inspections were rare, and off they would go with their new child or worker.

The number of children returning to board the train would diminish at each stop, and Joe had been surprised at first that neither Josephine nor Caroline had been chosen, especially Caroline. She was very pretty, with her blonde hair and blue eyes and could smile with the best of them, too. But she hadn't been chosen, even in Kansas City or Topeka, where large numbers were selected. His sister, Josephine, was almost as pretty, but with her brown eyes and hair, she wasn't as noticeable. She had a hard time smiling, too.

But with each stop, the bond between the four children grew and Joe decided that these new friends would not be abandoned, and he began to plan for a reunion. Now, with only four of them remaining on the train, the pact had been made, and all that was needed was to set the location for the reunion.

Now they were standing on the raised dais of the First Congregational Church in Junction City, Kansas while the chaperone gave a short description of each of the remaining four children to the couples watching, making each of them sound like brilliant, hard-working angels with small appetites.

As Joe almost scowled at the four adults before him, one man asked, "Do we have to take both the boy and his sister?"

"No. Generally, we do try to keep siblings together, but we recognize that it isn't always possible."

The man turned to his wife and they began to discuss the children loudly enough for the four youngsters to hear every word as if they couldn't. They were talking about Caroline, so when the man said they would take Caroline with them, none of them were surprised, but Joe glanced over at her and could see her already beginning to cry, so he just touched her hand and smiled. Not at the four adults, but only for Caroline. The other couple had already gone anyway.

While Caroline and Joe looked at each other, Danny asked if he could write to his sister, so the matron said she would give him the name after the new guardians completed the agreement. The standard agreement would require them to treat the child as one of their own, send the child to school, and upon his or her eighteenth birthday, provide the child with one hundred dollars.

As Caroline's new parents were filling out the form, he whispered to her, "Caroline, remember my promise. I'll come back when we're grownups and no matter what, I'll find you."

Caroline managed a weak smile and replied, "I'll remember, Joe."

The matron then wrote the information about Caroline's new guardians on the back of one of the agreement forms and gave the sheet of paper to Danny. Danny showed it to Joe, who burned the name into memory…Draper. Caroline was going to the home of the Drapers in Junction City.

The remaining three children were ushered from the church, all three looking back at Caroline. She had tears in her bright blue eyes as she caught Joe's eyes and waved.

Joe waved, then grew even angrier as he was returned to the train after losing his sad girlfriend.

Joe had been angry for years now. Neglect by his parents, then culminated by being cast off had turned him into a perpetually hostile boy. It seemed the only time he wasn't angry was when he was talking to Josephine and then, after they'd met on the train, Caroline. But now Caroline was gone, and he felt sure that Josephine would be next.

When the train made its next stop at Abilene, he was proven wrong when Danny was chosen by a local millowner. Joe had listened intently and caught the name of the selecting adults…Abernathy. He added it to his memory along with Caroline's new guardians, the Drapers. Abernathy in Abilene for Danny, Drapers in Junction City for Caroline.

The chaperone, Mary Little, was getting annoyed with Joe's inability to smile, but said nothing. She'd try to talk him up a bit at the next stop, Salina, the town where they had agreed to meet in ten years.

Joe and his sister were marched to the playhouse at Salina. It was a bit ridiculous to have that big stage for just two children, but they were paraded out onto the enormous space. Jo was taken almost immediately by a couple named Schmidt and Joe heard Miss Little say that he was a banker. Joe remembered, spelling out each of the adoptive parents' names over and over in his mind: Schmidt, Draper, and Abernathy.

Josephine cried openly when she was separated from her older brother, her protector, and Joe wondered what kind of cold heart could stand to do that. How could anyone take a crying, nine-year old girl from her brother? His last words to Jo were, "Ten years, Jo. Ten years."

She nodded and was led away, her new mother holding her hand as she looked back at Joe, tears still rolling down her cheeks, making Joe's anger reach volcanic levels.

Despite Mary Little's sales pitch in Salina, because that was what it sounded like, Joe was led back to the train and Mary wondered what she had to do to get rid of him. Joe began to wonder if she'd just shove him off the train at the next stop and actually hoped that she would. He'd be better off on his own and could go back to find Jo.

THE LAST FOUR

The train began rolling again as Joe sat alone with the chaperone in the long, empty passenger car. He didn't know the rules about how much longer the train would go with only a single child left, but it didn't matter. Joe's recent thoughts about being thrown from the train gave him the idea of just leaving at the next stop whether he was chosen or not and was slipping deeper into the pervasive anger about life, being turned out from his home, sent across the country, and now losing his sister, the only part of his family that he had ever cherished.

As angry as Joe had been for as long as he could recall, there was an interesting aspect to his anger in that he had never unleashed it on anyone. He had never even shouted at anyone, much less struck another person, but simply bottled it all inside him and if he needed to release any of the contained rage, he would do it in a controlled, easily understood manner that made even the fiercest bully back away. Twice before he'd channeled that anger to protect Jo from bigger boys that had scared her, and even she had told him how scary it was.

Now that same angry face had made him the last one to be selected and he knew that he wasn't about to be chosen at the next stop, which he vowed would be his last.

When the train stopped in Tescott, Joe remained on board with Miss Little as no one was waiting to even look at him. The next stop was Lincoln, Kansas. It wasn't some big city, so there was almost no point in Mary taking her lone piece of merchandise to the church, but she had to follow procedure, having been told that there were people waiting in the small town. When they arrived, there were only two couples present in the small place of worship.

"We only have one child available," said Mary as she stood beside him, "Joe Carlisle is a strong, smart boy in excellent health. He may seem out of sorts somewhat because his sister was recently selected, so don't hold that against him."

Joe simply stood next to her, feeling as if he should dance like a trained monkey or something but knew it didn't matter. No one wanted him, and he could understand the reason why. Besides, he didn't want anybody to select him either. He knew he had an angry face on, but it was just too bad. If they didn't like it, they should just leave him alone. He'd walk out of the church and when Miss Little was walking in front of him, he'd turn and run. Where he went was unimportant, he just didn't want to get on that train again.

One of the two men approached Joe and examined his sullen face. He was an older man, probably almost forty and his wife stood behind him, looking at Joe curiously.

"Son, you had a bad day," said the man.

"Yes, sir," Joe replied, courteously, as instructed, but still angry.

"I imagine life hasn't been too kind to you either."

"No, sir," Joe answered, wanting to tell him to go away.

Then he said, "Now, my wife Clara always wanted to have a child of her own, but we were never blessed. I'll be honest with you, son. She was kind of hoping to get a small child, so she could hold him and all those other things that mamas do to their children, but I imagine that you don't cotton to being hugged and kissed much."

"Never have been before, sir, so I couldn't tell," Joe replied honestly.

The man turned to his wife, who must have been touched by his answer, because she just smiled and nodded her head.

“Son, this is your lucky day. Would you like to come and live with us? I’m not as ornery as I make out.”

Joe looked at the man and thought his brown eyes were far from ornery. They were laughing eyes and not at all what he had expected.

Despite himself, Joe smiled and said, “I don’t think you’re ornery at all, sir.”

The man reached out with his right hand and Joe took it in his much smaller hand and shook it slowly.

“I’m Will Hennessey. Come on down and we’ll meet your new mother.”

Joe may have been surprised, the Hennesseys may have been happy, but Mary Little was ecstatic. She hurriedly made up the contract, then each of Joe’s new parents signed and she shook both of their hands while wearing a huge grin before taking her papers and almost dancing out of the church.

Will looked down at Joe, smiled and said, “Let’s go home, son.”

Joe nodded, and left the church with his new parents, Sheriff Will Hennessey and his wife, Clara.

CHAPTER 1

"But, Joe, I didn't mean nothin'!" shouted Ralph Wilkins.

"Ralph, it doesn't matter if you meant it or not. You cold-cocked Reverend Coolidge. Why did you do it in the first place?"

"He was preachin' at me for my drinkin', but it was in the saloon, Joe. He was preachin' at me in the saloon! Now, I don't pay no mind to some of it, but he just wouldn't let go! He was goin' on and on about me drinkin' myself into damnation and I finally got my fill of it, Joe. I had to shut him up. I didn't mean to hit him so hard, though."

Joe suppressed a laugh as he said, "Well, you did and he's pressing charges, Ralph. I'll toss you in jail and see if I can't talk him out of it, okay?"

"You'd do that for me, Joe?"

Joe leaned forward but stayed far enough away from Ralph's paint-peeling breath as he replied, "To tell the truth, there are quite a few citizens around here that wouldn't mind laying into Reverend Coolidge themselves, included yours truly."

Ralph grinned and went willingly with Joe to the jailhouse. After Joe had put him in an unlocked cell, he left the jail and headed to the church. He found Reverend Willard Coolidge in the presbytery with the door left open to get some fresh air. His wife was pressing a cold cloth against his jaw.

The reverend looked at Joe and his wife turned, removing the cloth.

“Did you arrest that heathen?” he demanded.

“I did. He’s in jail awaiting trial.”

“Good. I want to see him punished.”

“You know, Reverend, I’m not sure you want to go to trial on this,” Joe said as he scratched his chin.

“And why not? The man assaulted me!”

“Well, a trial means he’s going to have to get a unanimous decision from twelve local men to convict him. Now, I’ve been to quite a few trials, and it’s amazing how the defense attorney can get the jury to blame the victim. He only needs to convince one of them that the victim deserved what he had coming to him.”

“Are you saying that you think it was acceptable what he did to me?” asked the offended minister.

“No, Reverend, not at all. I’m just telling you how the system works. Now, if you’re convinced that twelve men from this town will convict a man for punching a minister for chastising him for drinking while he was in a saloon, then I’ll be happy to write it up for you.”

“But he struck me without warning!”

“It’s the power of the whiskey, Reverend. It addles the mind. As a man who’s spent a few years now breaking up barfights, I’ve got to tell you that you always have to expect them to take a shot when you’re not looking. I’m not saying that what he did was justified but getting a conviction would be difficult. You may just have to do the Christian thing, turn the other cheek and just forgive him.”

The reverend was caught between his anger and the logic of what Joe was saying. He knew the odds of finding twelve non-drinkers in the town was nigh on impossible.

"Alright, I'll drop the charges. After all, I am a man of God and can forgive his transgressions."

'Thank you, Reverend Coolidge. I'll see that Ralph appreciates what you've done."

"And tell him to stop his drinking and start coming to church, too!" the reverend shouted as Joe turned to leave.

"I'll tell him, Reverend," Joe replied, then thought, "and I'm sure he'll do both."

Joe walked out of the presbytery, returned to the jail, opened the door, walked inside and found the sheriff sitting at the desk smiling at his son.

"Well, Joe. Is he still pressing charges?"

"No, sir. He's decided to turn the other cheek and forgive Ralph for his sin," he replied as he grinned at the sheriff.

"I figured you'd be able to talk him out of it."

Joe walked past the desk and leaned against the bars at the sleeping Ralph.

"Ralph! Wake up. You're free to go."

Ralph continued to snore loudly enough to make the iron bars vibrate.

Joe turned back to his adoptive father and said, "Looks like we've got a guest for a little while."

“It’ll take Ralph a while to sleep this one off, I guess.”

“Reverend Coolidge instructed me to tell Ralph to stop his drinking and start going to church, so if I’m not here when he wakes up, could you let him know?”

His father laughed and said, “And I’m sure he’ll fall all over himself complying with the good reverend’s recommendations.”

“What recommendations?” asked Clara as she appeared at the door with a cloth-covered tray.

“Mama! Let me get that,” Joe offered as he turned and took the tray of food.

Clara smiled at Joe and said, “Thank you, Joe. I’m getting too old, I think. Either that, or that tray is getting heavier.”

“I think I eat too much, Mama. And you’re not getting too old, either. You’re just as pretty as the first day I saw you.”

Clara smiled, knowing Joe would say something like that. He always did.

“Are you still going, Joe?” she asked.

“Yes, Mama. I made a promise ten years ago and I’ll keep it. Like papa says, once you fail in a promise, all of the others are worthless.”

“Do you think you’ll be able to find them all? After all, it’s been a long time.”

“Folks don’t usually travel that far from where they started, Mama. The ones that don’t make it to the reunion, I’ll find.”

“You are quite a way from where you began, Joe,” she said softly.

"That's true, and it turned out pretty well for me, but it was all because of you and papa. I hope it turned out as well for my sister, Danny, and especially Caroline."

"You know, girls change a lot over the years, Joe. She may not even remember you."

"I remember her, Mama. If she doesn't remember me, then I can live with that. As long as she's safe and happy, then I'll be happy too. I still remember the face of the man that selected her, and I didn't like it. He had lying eyes. My sister should be living sixty miles away in Salina. That'll only take me a couple of days to get there."

"I never understood why you have never written to her, Joe. I never brought it up, but I may as well now."

"I was so angry at the time, I totally forgot to ask for the address. All I had was the last name, and it was pretty common. It'll take me some time if I have to find her, but I don't think it'll take me as long with the other two."

Will said, "I'm gonna miss having you around, son. Keeps me from having to stop all those problem children that call themselves adults from being bigger problems."

"I know, Papa. But it's as quiet now as I have ever seen it. I think I can be gone for a few weeks without anything serious showing up."

"It's quiet because you're here, Joe, but I'll be able to handle it. I'm kind of curious about what happened to those young folks anyway."

"It's quiet, Papa, because you taught me everything a man needs to be a good lawman: how to shoot, track and use my fists, but most importantly, you've taught me how to read people. Who's the one who's going to cause trouble and who's going to back away. Who's lying and who's telling the truth. It's what made you the man I respect more than any other I've ever met, Papa."

Will Hennessey fought back the inclination to a sniffle or two as he looked at Joe. When he and Clara had formally adopted Joe, it didn't take long for them to realize what an exceptional boy he was. How he had wound up as the last boy on that train was beyond him. He had been showing Joe the law-keeping business since he was thirteen and had him appointed as a deputy when he was only seventeen. The town fathers were very pleased with the appointment and grew more appreciative as Joe filled out and became a strong law presence in the community.

"Well, let's eat before we forget that the food's there," he finally said.

"You boys make sure to remember to bring that tray home this time," Clara said as she wagged her index finger at them.

"I won't forget this time, Mama," Joe answered before giving his mother a kiss on the cheek.

Clara smiled at her men and left the office.

"When will you be leaving, Joe?" his father asked as they ate.

"I'll leave early in the morning, the day after tomorrow. I'll get there early on the 26th and meet everyone at the train station. I just hope they all make it. It's possible they'll forget, but I don't think so. We were all very close before we were separated, but we were just kids. I'm sure that Josephine will be there, but if she's not, it will be for some serious problem and I'll have to find her quickly."

"Well, your mother and I wish you well, Joe."

That evening, Joe returned the tray to the house, had dinner with his parents, then returned to the office as he usually did. He'd make late rounds again before returning home to sleep.

Tonight, he sat in the office and wrote out his list of supplies he'd need on the trip. He wouldn't need much in the way of food. Tescott was halfway, so he could stay there the first night, and stay in a hotel in Salina when he arrived on the evening before the reunion. Then he'd be at the train station earlier than necessary, hoping they might show up earlier than their agreed upon time of noon. He knew that he would be anxious and expected they would be too, especially Jo. He wasn't as sure about Caroline, and he wouldn't be all that surprised if Danny didn't show at all.

He'd carry his badge, and even though anything beyond Lincoln's boundaries was out of his jurisdiction, he knew it did give him a measure of authority. He'd had to go outside of the jurisdiction a few times in the last four years, usually chasing after escaping outlaws, and he looked at the badge as another weapon in his arsenal.

He'd bring his twelve-gauge shotgun, his Winchester '76 chambered for the .45 caliber cartridge and his Colt which also used a .45 caliber round, but neither cartridge would work in the other gun. He'd bring two changes of clothes and his toiletry items too, as his mother had instilled a need for cleanliness into him that he never possessed in Philadelphia.

He'd take out a significant amount of his bank account because he didn't know where he might have to go if they weren't there. He'd been paid thirty dollars per month as a deputy for four years, but had spent little, as he still lived at home with his parents. He may have felt a bit guilty for not moving out, but not that much, because he enjoyed the time that he spent with them. Besides, the café's food wasn't close to what his mother could make.

He had almost nine hundred dollars in his account and withdrew two hundred. Luckily, what could have been his greatest expense, his ammunition, was paid for by the town. He and his father went through a lot of ammunition over the years, but it wasn't until he was eighteen that he began besting his father in target practice.

So, clothes, money, ammunition and guns were set, and he couldn't think of anything else.

He put down the pencil and folded the sheet before sliding it into his vest pocket, then leaned the chair back on its hind legs and balanced it as he thought of what his friends might look like.

They'd all be full-grown adults now and would look considerably different, just as he did. He hoped that Caroline didn't get fat or anything and had thought of her often over the years. In many ways, it was the ultimate in foolishness. She was only nine when he had seen her last, and he knew that it was probably nothing more than a childish attachment. But he had promised to find her again in ten years if she couldn't make it, and he would.

Realistically, she was probably already married and living with her husband and probably had forgotten all about him. But he just couldn't let it go. Maybe if he hadn't seen those blue eyes filled with tears as she was being led away or perhaps if his last words to her weren't 'Trust me,' he wouldn't have latched onto the memory so strongly.

Joe was the most eligible bachelor in Lincoln, twenty-one years old, strong and handsome, with a gentle demeanor but with a deep strength underlying it. Many young women had set their caps for Joe, and there were quite a few times that Joe regretted his conviction to keep that promise to Caroline, especially when Abby Winters had made her intentions clear.

Joe could have easily seen himself spending his life with Abby. She was quite a girl, but he had demurred, causing a bit of a scene when he explained to Abby why he was waiting. He told her that he'd know what to do in May, but Abby wouldn't wait. She felt rejected, insulted, and hurt, and let him know …loudly and almost violently.

That was just three months ago. When he had seen her walk off, he was sure he had dodged a bullet. That was some kind of temper in Abby, and it was seemed to be easily triggered. He had learned a valuable lesson then. When folks were smitten, they weren't themselves anymore. They tried to be what the other person wanted, and he hoped Caroline wasn't like that.

Josephine would be either Josephine Schmidt, if she had been adopted, or Josephine Carlisle if she hadn't. He knew that fewer than half of the children on those trains were adopted, and even fewer had as good a set of circumstances as he had. He was now Joe Hennessey and had wonderful parents that meant the world to him. He wondered how the others had fared and hoped that they all had at least had a decent life, but knew that he'd find out in a couple of days.

He made his last rounds for the day and returned home for his traditional end-of-day cup of coffee before turning in.

———

The next morning, Joe ate his breakfast with his parents and left before his father. He would get to the office first, fire up the stove and put on more coffee. He and his father went through a lot of coffee. It was paid for by the town as a normal cost of operation, so they took advantage of it, coffee and ammunition just seemed to go together.

Joe had the coffee done and was having a cup when his father walked in. Joe was sitting on the side chair, letting his father have the larger, more comfortable desk chair as he deserved and needed with his aging joints.

"I'm gonna miss coming in here and finding the coffee already made, Joe," he said before he chuckled.

"I'll miss it myself. I've gotten kind of used to having coffee around all the time," he replied.

Joe finished his coffee and stood, adjusting his gunbelt before he said, "Well, I'll go and make the early morning rounds."

Joe waved as he left the office and his father waved back. For the daylight rounds, Joe only was armed with his Colt, but added the shotgun on his nighttime rounds. He'd soon wish he'd brought it with him on this one.

He walked along the boardwalk heading west. The stores and shops were open, so he didn't have to check doors or locks. He'd wave at the shop owners and customers as he passed, tossing in the occasional 'Howdy', or 'Good morning' as necessary. It took him almost twenty minutes at his morning rounds greeting pace to reach the edge of the town.

He was in the middle of the street crossing over to the other boardwalk to begin his return inspection when he glanced west and spotted two riders approaching. At this hour, that raised his interest a notch. They were strangers, and they were coming from the west. Sylvangrove was eighteen miles west of Lincoln, but it was a good three-hour ride. They would have had to leave really early to be getting here before eight o'clock. He continued walking until he reached the boardwalk, unhooked his Colt's hammer loop, sat on the bench in front of Willard Henderson's tonsorial parlor, then watched the two men as they entered Lincoln's outskirts. As they neared, he liked less of what he saw and decided he'd better stop them short of the town to see what they were about.

When they were about a hundred feet out, Joe stood, stepped down from the boardwalk and put up his hand, his badge displayed prominently.

Red Fletcher and Big Jim McAllister saw Joe step into the street, saw the badge and removed their hammer loops. Joe noticed the move.

"Morning, boys! What brings you to our town this bright morning?" he asked loudly, just short of shouting.

Red glanced over at Big Jim before turning his eyes back to Joe. It was a telling glance, and Joe noticed. They weren't close enough to see if Joe's badge was a deputy sheriff's badge, a sheriff's badge, or something else, nor were they sure if he was alone or had backup, but he seemed mighty young. It meant he probably wasn't that good with that hogleg at his waist.

"Just passin' through, Sheriff," Red replied.

Joe didn't clarify his title because there was no point as he asked, "Did you fellas stay in Sylvangrove last night?"

"Yup. Had has a few drinks and stayed at the hotel."

"Where are you headed?"

"Salina. We got a line on some work over there."

"What kind of work?"

Big Jim was getting nervous. He didn't like lawmen at all anyway, but this one was making him jumpy.

"You know, general labor kinda work."

"Well, if it's only that kind of work you're looking for, we've got plenty of that available right here in Lincoln. Why don't you both step down, and I'll tell you where to ask around."

Red was going to respond when Big Jim's anxiety erupted and made him suddenly reach for his pistol.

Joe was anticipating a move from the big man, whose large head had been twitching back and forth ever so slightly while shifting his eyes in both directions, looking for other guns or witnesses.

Joe reached for his Colt just after Big Jim had slapped his big hand on his Colt's handle.

Red's reaction was to utter a loud, "Damn!", as he was third to go for his pistol.

Big Jim may have been first to go for his weapon, but Joe was quicker to get his away from the leather and cocked. Joe's Colt was leveling at Big Jim while Red was still bringing his pistol out of the holster.

Joe fired as Big Jim's thumb had just finished cocking the hammer and his finger was on the trigger. Joe's shot hit him dead center in his sternum which was designed to protect his heart as a joint for the upper ribs, but it didn't matter. Even as large as he was, having a .45 caliber bullet rip into your chest from fifteen feet was not going to be recoverable. He jerked as the heavy round punched into him, his reflex causing his Colt to fire into the boardwalk to the right of Joe's shoulder.

Joe was already bringing his pistol to bear on Red when Red fired his first shot. At twelve feet, he shouldn't have missed, but his horse had been spooked by the sudden noise of Joe's first shot, so his shot went wide to Joe's right, hitting the sign in front of Barlow's Feed and Grain.

The same startled reaction by Red's horse made Joe's shot miss as well. Red didn't bother taking a second shot, but quickly whipped his gelding around, dropped over his horse's neck and shot away to the west.

Joe took two fast strides to Big Jim's horse, yanked the still breathing Big Jim from his saddle and let him hit the street. He'd die in less than thirty seconds.

Joe leapt into Big Jim's saddle and took off after Red. He knew that he should pace the horse, especially as it had spent some time carrying Big Jim's almost three hundred pounds around, but Red only had a hundred-yard lead as Joe got Big Jim's gelding moving. The horse, feeling almost a hundred pounds less load on its back responded quickly. After two years of having Big Jim up there, Joe felt like a jockey.

He began gaining on Red, who kept taking peeks at his pursuer. Joe took time to pull Big Jim's Winchester '73 out of the scabbard and lever a new round into the chamber. The chambered round flew out of the ejection chamber onto the passing dirt, leaving Joe with only fourteen rounds if it was carrying a full load, but he didn't think he'd need thirteen of them.

In his next glance backwards, Red saw Joe pull the Winchester, so he did the same. He twisted in the saddle and took a few shots at Joe, but knew it was futile before he pulled the trigger as the horse was bouncing and throwing his sights all over the place.

Joe simply ignored the incoming rounds because there was nothing he could do anyway. He had seen the muzzle of Red's Winchester dancing all over the place and knew it would take an incredibly lucky shot to hit him.

He closed the gap to thirty yards and was still gaining as Red began searching for any possible escape ahead and spotted possible redemption in a shallow gully to the southwest a quarter mile ahead. He left the roadway and kept charging, as his horse began losing his wind and slowing.

Joe wasn't slowing at all as the big gelding had a lot left and wasn't laboring even after a mile of pursuit.

Red was almost at the gully when he suddenly realized it wasn't as shallow as he had thought, but it was too late now and left the edge of the gully at speed. Joe knew the gully was there and had already pulled back on the reins of the big gelding to bring him to a sudden stop in a cloud of dust.

Red's horse left the edge of the gully and plummeted the eight feet to the bottom where his front hooves dug into the soft dirt at the bottom and Red flew over the horse's head, his Winchester flying off to his right as his Colt left his holster and followed him on his headlong dive into the southern edge of the gully. Red smashed into the wall of dirt and rocks face forward, snapping his neck backwards with a resounding crack. His fourth cervical vertebra was smashed into the fifth vertebra below it and both shattered, severing his spinal cord. His brain received no pain signals from below his neck, only the damage to his face, as the rest of his body plowed into the wall of the gully.

Joe had already stopped and dismounted as the huge cloud of dust stood suspended over the gully from the accident. He had the Winchester in his hand as he slid down the bank and stepped quickly across the twenty-foot wide gully. Red's horse stood nearby, breathing hard, but somehow escaping serious injury.

Joe knew that Red wasn't a danger any longer just by seeing his awkward position, then stepped up to him and rolled him over. As he flopped onto his back, Red slid another two feet down the wall toward the bottom of the gully. He was breathing but felt nothing and saw Joe looking at him.

"Shoot me, Sheriff. Please. I can't feel nothin' at all," he begged.

"I'd like to oblige, mister, but the law won't let me shoot you if you're still alive."

"Screw the law. Just kill me now."

"What did you two do? Why'd you run like that?"

"We done a lotta things. But Big Jim killed some whore in Sylvangrove last night in our room. I didn't even get to screw her. We took outta there right after figurin' they wouldn't even notice till late, and besides, she was a whore. Who cares about a whore?"

"My sheriff and I would care."

"How'd you get the word anyway? They send a telegram?"

"Nope. You two just looked bad."

"And you ain't gonna shoot me?"

"Sorry. What are your names, so I can put them on your markers?"

"I'm Red Fletcher and the one you shot was Big Jim McAllister. You can find our particulars on our wanted posters.

I'm wanted dead or alive, Sheriff. Nobody would ever know if you put a bullet through me."

"I'd know."

Red glared at him once and then, suddenly, managed to rotate his head quickly to the left. There was another crack and Red's head just flopped to his chest.

Joe just shook his head and picked up Red's weapons. He slid the Winchester into his horse's scabbard and his Colt back into Red's holster, flipping the hammer loop into place before removing the gunbelt and hanging it over his shoulder.

He lifted Red's body and carried it to the horse, apologized to the still winded animal for putting Red's body across the saddle, then tied the body down and slipped the gunbelt into his saddlebags. He then led the horse to a shallower part of the gully, up onto the flatlands and back to the big gelding who was biding his time munching on some prairie grass. Joe was impressed with Big Jim's mount. He was a good horse, and much better than the horse the town had issued to him four years ago. He'd ask his father if he could make the swap when he returned.

Back in Lincoln, Will had heard the gunfire and bolted from his office in time to see Joe ripping a big man from his horse and racing away after a second man, then jogged down the street where a crowd was gathering around the man on the ground.

He trotted up to the dead body and had everybody step away, then rolled the big man onto his back. When he first saw the size of the man, he suspected that he was Big Jim McAllister. If it was, then the man Joe was chasing was Red Fletcher. He trusted Joe's ability, but against a hardened outlaw like Red Fletcher, it was a dangerous chase.

The sheriff turned to one of the men and said, “Vince, could you go and get Clarence? Tell him we’ve got at least one customer for him and hopefully, Joe will be bringing back a second. If not, he’ll be hanged if Joe brings him back alive.”

Will didn’t even want to think about the third possibility of Joe’s encounter with Red Fletcher.

“I’ll do that, Sheriff,” answered Vince as he turned and began trotting to the other end of the town.

Will began going through his pockets looking for any signs of identification and found nothing but $83.45, which was a lot of money for a no-account like Big Jim McCallister to have on him. He stood, his knees cracking and shooting pain up his legs.

He waited five more minutes looking west when he spotted Joe leading a body on a horse about a half mile away. As he stared, the spectators looked west, and Will felt the pride of a father as he watched Joe riding toward them.

“What happened, Joe?” asked Will when Joe was within talking range.

“I saw these two riding in from the west and wondered why they would leave Sylvangrove so early. They both looked kind of mean, and I didn’t want them going into the town and risking anyone, so I stopped them before they got into town and began asking them routine questions.”

“The big man, that’s Big Jim McAllister by the way, was getting antsy, so he went for his Colt. I went for mine and that fella back there,” Joe said, jabbing his thumb backwards toward Red’s body, “drew his. I got my shot off slightly before Big Jim, I don’t know where I hit him, though. I didn’t have time to check. I was shifting to fire at Red Fletcher, but his horse got spooked by the gunfire and reared. His shot went wide and so did mine. He took off and I pulled Big Jim off his horse and took off after him.

"I almost caught him when he thought he could jump that horse over the gully about a mile west, south of the road. Maybe he didn't know how deep it was. Anyway, he was thrown from his horse and smacked into the far wall and must have broken his neck, because he couldn't move.

"He asked me to shoot him, but I couldn't. He told me why they had to leave Sylvangrove so quickly, too. He said that Big Jim had killed some prostitute in the town. He didn't seem to be upset that Big Jim killed the woman; he was just mad because he didn't get a chance with her. Anyway, his final act was to somehow twist his neck. That did it, too."

"Okay, Joe, let's get him down from there and lay him out next to his partner. Did you go through his pockets?"

"No, sir. I wanted to get him back here as quickly as possible."

They pulled Red from his horse and laid him out on the ground. Will found nothing but $63.40 in his pockets, which he stuffed in his own. Joe had pulled both saddlebags from the horses and found nothing inside but a couple of boxes of .44 cartridges and some dirty laundry...some very dirty laundry.

Joe replaced the saddlebags just as Clarence Bickerstaff drove up in his hearse, then he and the sheriff loaded the two bodies into the hearse and Clarence drove them off.

"Let's take these two horses back to the livery, son," Will said.

The crowd finally dispersed as Joe and Will led the two animals to the big barn at the other end of town where they left the horses and tack in the care of the liveryman, Ike Hampton, and returned to the office.

Once they were seated, Will pulled out his stack of wanted posters and found the two men that were riding in Clarence's hearse.

"Looks like you've got some money headed your way, Joe. Red had a three-hundred-dollar reward on him, and Big Jim had five hundred on his head."

"Could I see those posters, Papa? I should have identified them, but I didn't pick up who they were, and it bothers me."

Will slid them over to Joe, and when he examined Big Jim's, he saw the problem.

"No wonder I missed it. This says he's six feet six inches and over four hundred pounds. He was only about my height and three hundred, and he didn't have a beard."

"That's what happens with eye-witness accounts."

He looked at Red's, found almost a non-description, and the drawing wasn't even close, either.

"One of these days, we're going to have to get photographs of these outlaws to make our lives easier."

Will reached into his pocket and pulled out all the cash from the two dead men.

"Here you go, Joe. This should make your trip easier."

"Papa, you keep it. I've already got two hundred dollars."

"You never know, Joe. It may take you longer."

Joe sighed and took the cash.

"Papa, do you think they'd care if I swapped the horse that they issued to me when I got the job for Big Jim's gelding? That horse did a great job in running down Red."

"It's not their decision anyway. Go ahead and keep him. Same with the guns, too. You earned it, Joe. That was some mighty find law work."

"Thanks, Papa."

So, Joe would head out in the morning with over three hundred and fifty dollars in his pockets and another eight hundred going into his bank account, never believing that he'd ever have that much money.

———

The two outlaws were buried with simple markers identifying them to visitors. Will sent off three telegrams, one to the sheriff at Sylvangrove telling him of the deaths of both men and Red's admission to murder of a prostitute. He wondered as it was being sent if they even were going to bother searching for her murderer. Many lawmen considered whores being beaten or even murdered as just an occupational hazard. He sent off two more telegrams to those that offered the rewards, certifying their deaths.

Joe remained in the office, cleaning his Colt and had the other two pistols on the desk. He'd clean them both and take a look at their Winchesters, too, but he'd leave both rifles in the office. He might take an extra pistol with him, though. He'd already packed a box of the .45 caliber center fire cartridges for his '76 Winchester, another box of the .45 caliber Long Colts for his pistol, a box of #5 buckshot for the shotgun and two boxes of

.44 caliber rounds, recently donated by the deceased, for the new handguns.

After his Colt was cleaned, he examined the other two. One was Red's Colt Peacemaker, and the other was Big Jim's Remington New Army. He inspected the Remington more closely because he was unfamiliar with the model. It had been modified to accept the .44 cartridge, but Joe never cared for modified revolvers. He felt it depended too much on the person doing the modification as some were done well, and others not so well. He put it aside and cleaned Red's Colt, which he would keep along with the gunbelt. He set it next to his shotgun and Winchester '76. If he needed more firepower than what he had, he'd be in trouble. Besides, he was just going to Salina to meet his sister, Danny, and hopefully, Caroline. Every time he thought of Caroline, his mind would wander off into *I wonder-land*. He'd get the answers to all his imagination's questions in two days.

After lunch, he walked down to the livery and claimed the big gelding and spent a long time giving him a thorough inspection. He was a handsome horse, a chocolate brown with black mane and tail, four stockings and a star. He was only five or six years old and his joints and muscles showed no signs of injury, which he'd half-expected to find given the occupation of his previous owner.

He told Ike Hampton to put on some new shoes and get him some oats and paid for the work himself, sort of, as he used their cash. He didn't want the town to be able to lay claim to the horse, so he also mentioned to Ike that the horse he had been riding was now property of the town and they could do with him as they wished.

CHAPTER 2

Joe was up early, anxious to get going, but his mother was already in the kitchen and had breakfast waiting for him as he left his room while his father remained asleep.

She turned and smiled at him when she heard him enter.

"Mama, there was no reason for you to get up. I could have stopped at the café before I left."

"Nonsense. You just sit down and eat," she said in her official motherly tone.

She joined him at the table as he ate, and they talked about the anticipated changes in his sister and friends when he met them in Salina. After he finished, he rose, kissed his mother on the cheek and left the house, walked down the side street, then crossed the main thoroughfare, before heading toward the livery.

When he arrived, Ike was already up and had the horse saddled and ready to go.

"Figured I was going somewhere, Ike?" he asked with a grin.

"That's what the sheriff said," he replied as he smiled back.

"Thanks, Ike."

He led the big gelding out into the street and back to the sheriff's office, unlocked it and went inside.

"First things first," he thought as he fired up the heat stove to make the morning coffee.

Once it was going, he closed the firebox door and filled the coffeepot with water, then set it on the stove before picking up his saddlebags and putting the extra Colt inside along with the ammunition. He hung the heavy saddlebags over his shoulder and then picked up the shotgun and his Winchester before going back outside where he slid the long guns into their scabbards and set the saddlebags behind his saddle and tied them down, before returning to the office.

The water was bubbling five minutes after he returned, so he made the coffee for his father, closed and locked the door then mounted the gelding. He turned him east and set off toward Salina to meet his sister and Caroline, almost not thinking of Danny for some reason.

He kept a smooth, even pace knowing he only had thirty miles to cover today and as the big horse ate up the distance, found himself drifting as he anticipated seeing his sister and Caroline again, and every once and a while, even adding Danny to the mix.

There was such a huge change from a pre-adolescent to an adult, and he wondered if he would be able to recognize any of them or need to introduce himself. For the first time, he began to feel a bit awkward at the thought of meeting his long-missed sister and friends.

He arrived at Tescott in mid-afternoon, having been to the town a couple of times before when he had to transport prisoners to their jail, but didn't see any need to visit the sheriff today, so he rode to the livery and left his horse there. He put his saddlebags over his shoulder and walked to the hotel, and after getting a room, he headed for the local eatery for an early dinner, his stomach reminding him of the skipped lunch.

Tomorrow, he'd pick up the pace a bit and get lunch in Salina. Besides, he reasoned, he might find Josephine early, as she had been chosen in Salina and was in the town somewhere. His badge should be able to allow him to get her address from the local law.

—

In Salina, Josephine thought she would take the risk and ask one more time. She had to, so she approached Wallace carefully, with a weak smile on her face.

“Wally, are you sure I can't go to Salina the day after tomorrow? I promised my brother ten years ago that I'd meet him,” she begged.

Wallace Gunter slowly looked up from the lariat that he was making and snapped, “I've told you before, don't ever call me that again!”

“I'm sorry, but do you think I can go? It's only seven miles. I could ride down there, say hello to my brother and be back in time to fix you a nice dinner.”

Wallace slammed the unfinished lariat to the floor, jumped to his feet, then turned and took one step toward Josephine.

She saw the malice in his eyes and began to quiver as she stepped slowly back until she bumped against the wall.

“I've laid down the law on you before about that. You must be the stupidest female ever put on this whole damned earth to ask again.”

"I'm sorry! Really, I won't ask again!" Josephine said as she wished she could back away even more.

"It's too late, you cow! You screwed up my lariat and now you're going to pay for it! And don't you dare think it's gonna keep you from makin' my dinner!"

Josephine turned and began to run, but never got her second foot on the floor before Wallace grabbed her by the hair and yanked her back hard, then let go. Josephine crashed to the floor and slid four feet into the couch.

She knew that there was no chance of going to Salina and began to think she'd never see her brother again, or anyone else for that matter. Wallace was so very angry with her, and he hadn't even been drinking.

She curled up into her customary defensive ball and Wallace began to inflict his punishment after he picked up the unfinished lariat and began using it as a whip.

Joe was on the road at seven o'clock the next morning, having had a man-sized breakfast and anticipated being in Salina by noon or a little later. It had been a good ride so far. The weather had been spectacular, which wasn't unusual for May, there hadn't been any unexpected consequences which sometimes befell solitary travelers, either. He still tried to avoid woolgathering, though. He had his badge pinned to his shirt under his gray vest as there was no sense in making himself a target, but he scanned the landscape as he rode, just in case.

He was just about halfway out when he heard a rasping cry for help coming from the north, then quickly stopped the gelding, looked to his left, but still didn't see anything, and thought he must have imagined it. He was going to turn back toward Salina when he heard it again.

He stood in his stirrups looked more closely and spotted a patch of white hidden among the prairie grass about a hundred yards to the north. He trotted the horse toward the white and stepped down, grabbed his canteen, then jogged the last few feet and found a white-haired man, probably a farmer by the looks of him, lying on the ground, his head matted with blood.

Joe crouched down and poured some water on his head to cool him off and wash off the blood and found that it wasn't that bad. Joe was familiar with wounds caused by a pistol barrel, so he knew what had happened. He rolled him over onto his back and poured a little water on his forehead.

"Mister, can you tell me what happened?" he asked.

The man's eyes fluttered open, then he said hoarsely, "You gotta stop 'em, mister."

"Stop who? I didn't see anybody."

"About a mile north. The tracks. They're pullin' spikes."

Joe glanced north, but still didn't see anyone over the slight rise, so he said, "I've got to take you to the doctor or your house. Is it near here?"

"Leave me be right now. Leave me your canteen. I'll be all right. They're tryin' to derail the train."

Despite not seeing them, he understood that the lay of the land made it likely that the old man was telling the truth; that and the pistol barrel scar on his head.

"I'll go stop them and come back for you," Joe said as he stood, leaving his canteen on the ground nearby.

Joe took a few seconds to quickly remove his bedroll and stretch it out next to the man, then lifted him easily and set him on the bedroll and handed him the canteen.

"I'll be back as soon as I can."

"Go get 'em, son."

"I'll take care of it, sir," Joe said.

Joe trotted back to the gelding, mounted and set off across the prairie at a fast trot, hoping the horse didn't step in any gopher holes or other depressions. He had ridden for just a minute when the ground leveled, and he caught sight of them in the distance. They were using one of the six-foot long crow bars used to pull spikes out of crossties and wondered where they had gotten it, but it didn't matter right now. They had to be stopped and seemed so intent on doing the damage that they hadn't even spotted him yet.

Joe had no idea what time the train was expected, but he knew what their plan was. Yank out the spikes on one rail and then when the train hit the unsupported rail, it would be off the tracks. Whatever they wanted to steal they could get after the train plowed into the ground. It was an inexpensive method of train robbery that also would leave many dead in the process.

He grabbed his Winchester out of its scabbard and continued north but slowed the big gelding to give him a little more time to decide how to approach the two. If he rushed them, it would be their two rifles against his one, but he had a range advantage as it was unlikely that they'd have the more powerful '76 version of Mister Winchester's repeater. If he tried to take them quietly, the train may show up, so he decided to make a bull rush, hoping that the men would run once their plan was uncovered or that they were not accurate with their weapons.

He set the gelding into a faster trot again, estimating that he'd get to within a quarter mile before they heard the hoofbeats, but there would be no sense in shooting until he stopped, unless it was to keep them down.

He had the horse pick up his pace to a canter, so he was moving fast as he closed the gap.

Frank Pierce and Edgar Sorenson were so wrapped up in pulling the last of the spikes and were making a continuous series of grunts and other sounds of exertions that they didn't hear Joe's approach until he was about three hundred yards out. Frank heard it first and whipped his head in that direction.

"Crap! Get your rifle, Ed!" he exclaimed.

Ed turned, saw Joe, then dropped the large prybar across the rails, making a loud ringing clang as it hit the steel and bounced off. Each man ran the eight feet to his horse and yanked their Winchesters from their scabbards. They didn't wait for introductions, because any man who had seen them and come charging in their direction was an adversary. They began firing as Joe closed to within a hundred and fifty yards.

Joe knew the bullets could reach him, but their accuracy would be suspect, and the two men were snap firing almost in panic rather than taking their time to aim.

After a few more seconds, he pulled the gelding to a sudden stop and dropped quickly to the ground and assumed a prone shooting position, not wanting to waste ammunition as they had.

He let loose his first shot and somehow missed. He didn't know where it went, so he took more time before firing the second.

By then, both men had dropped to the ground themselves creating a standoff, or so the two men thought. But they also knew they were in a horrible position, and not because of the lawman. If the train from Salina was on time, the westbound locomotive would hit their loosened rail in about twenty minutes. When the train derailed, they'd be crushed under crashing rail cars. They had fifteen minutes to get rid of their intruder or at the very least, get to the other side of the tracks.

Joe was unaware of what time the train would pass, but knew they were in a bad location when it did, so he began to use the time when the westbound train arrived in Lincoln and run backwards. It was around nine-thirty now. The train arrived in Lincoln, fifty miles west, at eleven-twenty. If the train averages thirty miles an hour, including the stop at Tescott, it would leave Salina right about now, which meant he had less than half an hour to get them done and repair the track or warn the train.

There was no shooting at all for more than three minutes as the two men tried to come up with a way to kill Joe and Joe planned some method of getting them out of there.

They had one minor advantage, they were using Winchester '73s, so they could use the cartridges on their gunbelts and even scavenge the ones from their revolvers. Joe had thirteen rounds of the longer .45 caliber rounds in his rifle, but the rest were in his saddlebags. Joe's advantage was in the extra power of his '76 and his shooting skill, although it seemed to have left him with his first shot and was glad his father hadn't been there to witness the miss.

The two would-be train robbers decided to take advantage of their extra ammunition supply, so Frank Pierce turned to Edgar to tell him of his idea.

"Ed, let's try this. I need you to start firing in his direction. You probably ain't gonna hit him. I just want you to keep his head down while I crawl over to the east. Then while you're still firing, I'll pop up on his right side where he can't see me, spot him and finish him off."

"Good idea, Frank. Let me know when you're ready. I'm gonna fill my Winchester," Ed replied as he began pulling his spares from his gunbelt and replaced the Winchester's missing rounds.

"I'm almost ready, Ed. We gotta get this guy outta there quick."

As soon as he had filled his Winchester's magazine tube, Ed said, "Alright. I'm reloaded."

Ed began firing in a methodical, rhythmic cadence, shooting one round every ten seconds or so. That would give Frank two minutes to crawl into position.

When the shooting began, Joe didn't know why they were wasting ammunition. When he looked through the grass, he noticed that the gunsmoke clouds were only coming from one shooter. They both weren't wasting ammunition, only one of them was. He was shooting so regularly that Joe could predict the next shot, which only meant only one thing; he was trying to make him keep his head down while other man would circle around and shoot him from his flank.

That was simple to figure out, but the harder part would be to guess which flank he chose. Joe didn't have a lot of time to guess and didn't like the fifty-fifty chance. He needed better odds.

He finally went with human instinct. The flank-shooter would try to get away from the danger that the oncoming train posed. If he crawled to the west, the man would still be in the path of the derailing train, but if he went to the east, he had a better chance of escaping the falling cars. Joe gambled his life and began to wiggle his body to his right, into the still rising sun, but keeping the Winchester low so his partner wouldn't see it.

Frank crawled as quickly as he could. He wanted to kill that guy, but he wanted to get away from the train tracks, too.

Joe saw a small dust cloud rising from the grass a few seconds later, which confirmed his suspicion that the shooter would be there. This was now just a waiting game.

The other man continued to fire as Joe, without thinking about it, was counting the shots. He had already fired nine leaving him six more rounds, unless he was reloading between shots, but that would disturb the clock-like rhythm of his shots, and he hadn't detected any change yet.

That was the biggest advantage of the Winchester over its father, the Henry rifle. The loading gate on the Winchester allowed single .44s, or .45s in his case, to be loaded into the tube quickly rather than having to pull the tube out and reload all at once like the Henry, but it was unlikely that he had a Henry, which would have made his life easier at the moment.

The dust cloud kicked up by Frank's crawling was almost at Joe's three o'clock, or what would have been his three o'clock if he'd still been pointing his Winchester toward the first shooter, who had created an enormous cloud of gunsmoke over his position. Now, he was pointing his rifle toward the east and that tiny dust cloud.

Frank was crawling directly into Joe's line of sight without realizing the danger he was putting himself into. He finally reached where he wanted to be and shifted around just as Joe had a couple of minutes earlier, until he was pointing where he knew that lawman was lying on the ground. He figured he'd get two shots off before the intruder even noticed he was there.

He was smiling as he popped up, his Winchester angled slightly downward, looking for his target. His smile vanished when he saw the target's Winchester already aimed at his chest and as soon as that horrible sight registered in his mind, he began to drop to the ground again, but it was too late.

Joe fired and the more powerful .45 caliber round penetrated Frank's chest a small fraction of a second after Joe had pulled the trigger, the bullet drilling through the center of his upper chest, exploding blood vessels, ribs and finally his spine before Frank collapsed to the dirt, a thick pool of blood flooding the ground beneath him for a few seconds before he died.

Joe quickly swung his hips back to the north facing the tracks and the second shooter.

Ed had seen Frank pop up and anticipated seeing the smoke and flame belch from his Winchester. Instead, he heard a rifle fire that sounded similar to a Winchester, but different, saw Frank drop, and he began to panic. He considered Frank to be the brains of their two-man outfit, and now he was alone.

He fired three more quick shots in Joe's direction for a reason that not even he could explain.

Joe made a mental note. He'd fired twelve shots, leaving him three, unless he had reloaded single rounds and was gambling that he hadn't as he aimed in Ed's general direction and fired, quickly levering in a second cartridge.

Ed returned two hastily fired rounds, the gunsmoke above his position a thick cloud now, leaving him one cartridge in his Winchester…maybe. One more shot, and Joe would take the biggest gamble of his life and he'd rush the shooter.

Ed had lost track of the number of shots he had fired and hadn't even thought about shoving in another cartridge from his gunbelt because of the delay he'd have to face when he had to pull it free of the leather. He was so used to levering and firing, levering and firing, he hadn't given a second thought to the finite number of cartridges still available in his repeater. It was as if he thought that fresh cartridges were just magically appearing in the chamber. The panic had taken control of his mind, and all he could do was to keep shooting.

Joe fired two rounds in succession, bringing a fresh cartridge into position as his own gunsmoke filled the air above him acting as a screen just in case the other one had reloaded.

His second shot had barely left the muzzle when Ed fired his last shot and cycled the lever. The last empty brass spit out of the ejection port on the Winchester, so when he pulled the trigger, the hammer struck home on an empty chamber, and all he heard was the snap, then he finally realized his error, but it was too late.

Joe scrambled to his feet after that fifteenth shot, and rushed toward Ed, his Winchester held low in his right hand as he closed the gap.

Ed was fumbling with rounds from his gunbelt to ram into the feed port of the Winchester, when he looked up and froze.

"Drop the rifle, mister. I've got you under mine," Joe said in a calm, strong voice from just fifteen feet away.

Ed looked into the muzzle of his Winchester, dropped the cartridge from his fingers and thrust his hands into the air.

Joe growled, "Now, stand up fast. I've got to stop that train."

Ed stood, and Joe picked up his empty Winchester, tossed it across the other side of the tracks, then yanked Ed's Colt from his holster and hurled it away as well. He pulled some pigging strings that he always kept in his pocket for unexpected issues and tied Edgar's wrists behind him before tying his ankles.

"You stay here. You'd better hope that I stop this train in time."

Ed looked east and panicked as he exclaimed, "You gotta move me, mister! I don't wanna die!"

"You made this mess. If I can't stop that train, you'll get what you deserved."

Joe was going to ride to warn the engineer of the danger but realized that the engineer might not stop his train, so he turned, grabbed the loose, heavy rail and struggled to pull it off the ties and then swung one end across the rails, leaving the four-hundred-pound rail sitting parallel to the crossties. If the engineer couldn't see that, he figured, he shouldn't be an engineer.

With that done, he jogged over to his gelding which hadn't moved, despite all the shooting, climbed up and began trotting eastward along the rail bed. He hadn't gone a mile when he heard the sound of the spotted the black cloud from a locomotive's stack on the horizon. He picked up the pace a bit to give him as much time to deliver his warning as possible.

When he saw the train about three miles off, he quickly transferred his badge to his vest then rode another half mile and turned his horse to the north. As the locomotive came close, he began waving his Stetson to get the attention of the engineer.

The engineer saw the rider waving at him and waved back. Joe began wildly waving both arms over his head, with the hat in his right hand, and the engineer knew something was up, but didn't slow down. He thought Joe might be a train robber, and it wasn't until he was within a hundred yards that he saw the badge, so he pulled the throttle lever back but not all the way, still unsure of the rider's intent as badges weren't necessarily difficult to obtain.

Joe quickly swiveled his horse back west, yanked his hat back on, and shot him parallel to the locomotive. Even at its reduced speed, it was still moving faster than the horse could handle for very long.

Joe caught the eye of the engineer and mimicked spikes being pulled up and pointed ahead and showed two fingers. The engineer wasn't quite sure what the rider was trying to tell him, but it sure seemed like a warning. He leaned out of the cab and looked as far ahead as he could and saw the rail lying crossways across the track, then slammed the throttle into reverse and applied the air brakes.

Joe had veered quickly away when he saw the engineer suddenly yanking on levers and heard the steel wheels squeal as they fought to gain traction in reverse as sparks flew under the locomotives drive wheels. The train was shuddering as it tried to halt its rush to a derailing and passengers were thrown forward, one of them breaking his wrist.

The train began slowing rapidly as it approached the missing rail. The engineer had done all he could and with the new Westinghouse air brakes, he knew that they had a chance to avoid disaster. But he was now a spectator as he continued to lean out of the cab, watching the crosswise rail approach, knowing that this would be close. He saw the man sitting on the ground near the missing rail and at first thought he was stupid before realizing that he had been hogtied and began to understand why the rail was in that odd position and what the lawman was trying to tell him. He thought it would serve the bastard right if the train did derail.

The train finally halted about fifty yards from the missing track in a massive blow of released steam as the engineer closed the throttle and let the relief valves take care of the sudden pressure buildup. He and the fireman hopped down from the cab as Joe walked the gelding to the still-huffing steam engine.

Joe stepped down and approached the two men.

"What happened here, mister?" asked the a relieved engineer.

"I was heading to Salina and a hurt man told me these two jaspers were pulling spikes. I figured they were planning on derailing your train and making off with as much loot as they could before anyone knew what had happened. I rode fast at them and we had a Winchester party. I got one of them and got the second one to surrender. I'm going to take them into Salina with me, but first I've got to go and take care of the injured man."

"I reckon it was you who put the rail like that. Or am I wrong?" he asked as he pointed at the sideways rail.

"You're not wrong. I didn't know if you'd believe me, so I set it like that to warn you that it had been pulled out."

"Those things weigh four hundred pounds!"

"I didn't lift the whole thing, just the end. Then once it was on the tracks, I slid it a bit and then just rotated it."

"Well, it sure saved our bacon. What's your name, young feller?"

"Joe Hennessey. I'm the deputy sheriff at Lincoln. My father's the sheriff."

"Well, he should be a right proud papa when we tell him this."

"My father is always right proud, just like I'm always proud of him."

"Them are good words to hear, Deputy. We'll get this track fixed in a jiffy."

As they were speaking, the conductor appeared to see what had happened before the fireman trotted back to the caboose to get the tools they'd need for the repair.

Joe waited until they returned with a sledgehammer, then helped the three railroad men reposition the rail before they had to hunt for the pulled spikes. Once they'd been collected, the fireman and engineer began hammering the spikes into different locations on the crossties, so they'd have good purchase, rather than using the existing holes.

While they were quickly hammering in the spikes, the conductor left to explain to the anxious passengers what had happened and to check for injuries.

Joe walked to the spike puller, picked up the heavy piece of steel and carried it to the engineer and waited until they finished.

As the fireman quickly pounded in the last spike, the engineer turned to Joe and saw him with the spike puller.

"Where the hell did they get that?" he asked as he accepted it from Joe.

"You might want to ask somebody at the Atchison, Topeka and Santa Fe depot back at Salina."

"You're darned right I will," he replied before carrying the long steel tool back to his locomotive and tossing it on board with a loud clang.

He then walked back to Joe and said, "Well, I'm gonna go and get my girl ready to roll in a couple of minutes. Thanks again, Deputy."

"Just doing my job, sir," Joe said as he tipped his hat.

The engineer trotted back to his locomotive and was preparing to get underway as Joe walked back to his new horse, his noontime arrival delayed.

First, he needed to take care of the old man. He'd return for the trussed-up outlaw after he helped the farmer.

"You wait right there, as if you have a choice," Joe said to an unhappy Edgar Sorenson as he strode past.

He mounted the gelding, took the reins of one of their animals, then rode quickly to where he had left the white-haired man on his bedroll and found him sitting up and watching Joe ride towards him.

"Did you stop 'em, young feller?" he asked as Joe dismounted.

"Yes, sir. I had to kill one, though. They wanted to shoot it out with Winchesters. The other one surrendered and is sitting next to the rails. I'll take him into Salina after I get you home."

"My farmhouse is about a half mile northwest. I was out in the field when I saw those fellers pullin' the spikes. I didn't have a gun, but I started yellin' at 'em. Now that wasn't too bright, was it? Anyway, one of 'em run over and pointed his pistol at me and then conked me on the noggin. I woke up all woozy and started to walk to the house but musta headed in the wrong direction. I saw you ridin' by and started callin' but got too woozy again and fell down."

"Anybody at home to take care of you?"

"My son, his wife, and my two daughters. So, I'll be all right."

"Let's get you on this horse. Can you do that?"

"I think so."

Joe helped him up on the horse, and once on board, seemed steady enough to make the short ride.

"Just hold onto the saddle horn with both hands. I'll lead the horse to your house."

"Okay."

Joe mounted the gelding and took the reins of the other horse, then led the horse northwest and spotted the farmhouse and barn almost immediately once he was in the saddle, so he headed for the house. When he entered the yard, he walked the horses to the front of the house, stopped, dismounted and helped the old man down from the horse.

He assisted him up the steps and onto the porch where he said, "Just take me inside, son, if you don't mind."

"No, sir, not at all," Joe replied as he opened the door and guided him into the house.

Joe heard the sound of running feet as soon as the door closed.

"Papa! What happened?" a young woman of about twenty asked in concern when she saw her father's blood-stained head.

Joe lowered him onto the couch and replied, "Your father was knocked in the head with a pistol barrel by two men who tried to derail the train. I heard him, and he told me to go and stop them before helping him. After I did that, I brought him here."

The young woman was soon joined by two more young women and a young man. All of the ladies were in their early twenties and were pleasing to the eye. The young man was good-looking, too, but Joe didn't see any wedding rings, so he wasn't sure which one was the wife.

"Folks, I've got a prisoner to return to Salina. You take care of your father," Joe said before he turned to the white-haired gentleman.

"Sir, you saved a lot of lives today," Joe said.

"No, son. You saved 'em. I just got hit in the head, like the old fool I am."

Joe laughed, patted him on the shoulder, then said, "I wish more folks were your kind of fool then. It'd make my job a lot easier," then turned and headed out the door.

He was climbing up on the horse when the two unmarried daughters stepped outside and smiled. He waved as he took the other horse's reins, and they waved back as Joe turned and headed back to where he had left the outlaw.

All he could think about as he headed toward the tracks were of all the farmer's daughter jokes. Those two young ladies were far from jokes, though.

He reached the still sitting criminal and headed to the other horse, then, after reaching the animal, stepped down, untied him from the large bush that had served as a hitching post and led all three horses to the prisoner.

He looked down at the man on the ground and asked, "Which of these two is yours?"

He never looked up as he replied, "The bay."

Joe hitched the bay to a different bush and led the other horse over to the dead man. He ground hitched him and then picked up the dead man's Winchester and thrust it into the scabbard. He lifted the man and struggled to get him in an upright position and then lifted him over the saddle before tying him down to the stirrups.

He walked over to the prisoner and untied his ankles, expecting a quick kick for his kindness, but when it didn't happen, he guessed that the man's legs were too numb to do anything more than make him uncomfortable.

Joe stood his prisoner on his feet and helped him mount his horse, then walked to where he had tossed his weapons, returned the empty Winchester to the scabbard, then carried his pistol to his own horse and hung the gunbelt around his saddle horn.

He was going to ask the prisoner his name but realized he didn't really care. The man was going to try to kill a dozen or more people for maybe a couple of hundred dollars' worth of loot. He hoped they hanged him, but knew he'd probably only get ten years or so.

He mounted the gelding and took the trail rope, then headed southeast until he picked up the road to Salina. He figured he'd arrive by mid-afternoon and the paperwork would keep him busy for another hour. So much for lunch. Maybe he should have packed some jerky after all.

———

As Joe rode east, Josephine was hurting as she made Wallace his lunch. At least he hadn't broken any bones. His lariat had left welts on her arms and legs as she had covered her face for protection. They were all red and swollen, and she was happy that Joe wouldn't see her like this. She was so ashamed of what her life had become.

She hadn't gone with Wallace Gunter willingly, and she surely hadn't married him. Her guardians, just before she turned eighteen had sold her to Wallace for two hundred dollars. She was, by contract, supposed to get a hundred dollars from them, instead, she was taken to his poor excuse for a ranch, seven miles northwest of Salina. She had fought him off the first night as he demanded his husbandly privileges, even though he wasn't her husband. She was eventually taken, and since that night had lived in terror. She had cooked his food, done his laundry and kept the house clean, and when he wanted her, he took her to his bed, no matter if she fought or laid placidly, it didn't matter. When Wallace wanted her, he took her. Even more terrifying than the treatment she received was the fear that she might become pregnant. The very idea of her having a child by that monster was horrifying.

She hadn't been off the ranch since she was taken here, and she knew that in asking to go to Salina, she was risking a beating. Yet her desire to see her brother had make her take the risk twice. Now she didn't dare ask anymore as she knew she'd never see him again and didn't expect to survive much longer with Wallace's ferocious beatings.

Joe walked his prisoner and spare horse into Salina after three o'clock, had no idea where the county sheriff's office was, so he had to ask.

After getting directions from a passing freighter, he arrived at the sheriff's office, stepped down, tied off his horse and walked to the office, stepped inside and was greeted by a deputy at the desk.

"What can I help you with, Deputy?" the desk man asked as he looked up and spotted Joe's badge.

"I've got one live prisoner and one dead one outside. They were trying to cause a derailment about fifteen miles west of here. We had a shootout and I got one. The other gave up."

"What happened to the train?" he asked as he quickly stood.

"The engineer stopped it in time. They repaired the track and were off after a thirty-minute delay."

"Who are they?" he asked as he grabbed his hat from a peg.

"I never asked. I'm sure the prisoner can provide the information. Did you want me to bring him in?"

"No. I'll go and get him. We'll need you to write up a statement."

"Where do I go to write it?"

"Wait for me. I'll be right back."

The county deputy stepped outside and two minutes later returned with the scowling Edgar Sorenson.

He looked at Joe and said, "I know this one. He's Edgar Sorenson. The dead one is Frank Pierce. They're local bad boys," then looked at the prisoner and added, "Looks like you'll be heading for a hanging, Edgar."

Edgar stumbled, then let his bladder go with the deputy's announcement. Frank had told him there wasn't any chance of being hanged, even if the train derailed, but the sudden realization that he could soon be stepping onto those gallows steps was too much too bear.

The deputy didn't seem flustered at all as he led the ripe Edgar Sorenson to the back cells as Joe stepped around the puddle on the floor and stood on the other side of the desk.

The deputy returned and finally acknowledged the issue when he made a face and said, "I suppose I've got to clean that up before the boss comes back. Come on back and I'll show you where to write up the report."

Joe followed him to a small room where a stack of paper was sitting in the corner of a desk. There were three pencils nearby, so he took one, sat down and began to write. By the time he finished, he heard other voices in front, picked up his two-page report and headed back to the main office.

The deputy nodded toward Joe and said, "Sheriff, that's the man who brought them in."

Sheriff Isiah Nottingham saw his badge and asked, "Where do you work, son?"

"I'm the deputy sheriff at Lincoln."

"You're Will Hennessey's boy?"

"Yes, sir."

"You took down those two wanted men a couple of days ago."

"Yes, sir."

"I read about it in today's paper. Hell of job, Deputy."

"Thank you, sir."

"These two are just locals. Trying to derail a train in the middle of the day is one of the stupidest things I've ever heard of. But neither of these two has ever dazzled me with their intelligence."

"That was my impression."

"Well, we've got your statement. Great job on this one too, Deputy. Stopping that train saved a lot of lives."

"That's our job, Sheriff."

"It is. Lotsa folks seem to think it's just walking around being annoying."

"So, what do you need me to do?"

"We'll get a court date. Probably in a couple of days. Were you planning on sticking around?"

"I was planning on being in town for at least another day, maybe longer."

"What were you planning on doing in Salina?"

"I was going to have a sort of reunion with my sister and two friends. We all came to Kansas ten years ago on one of those kid trains."

"So, Will and Clara adopted you?"

"They did. Turned out to be the best thing that ever happened to me."

"Will seems to think it's the other way around."

"My sister is supposed to be in Salina. At least she was ten years ago."

"What's her name?"

"Her name is Josephine Carlisle. She was taken in by someone named Schmidt."

"That would be Paul Schmidt. He's the Bank of Salina's vice president. I think Josephine left about a year ago, but no one has seen her since."

"Well, maybe she'll be back tomorrow. We're all supposed to meet at the train station at noon."

The sheriff smiled and said, "Good luck. That should be some reunion. All of you were so young before and now you're all grown up."

"It's kind of scary, really."

"Well, I hope it works out. Where will you be staying?"

"Where's a decent place?"

"I suppose the Railway Hotel is the best for the money."

"I'll get a room there then, but I'll stop by sometime tomorrow to get the information about the trial."

"I appreciate it."

Joe left the sheriff's office and stepped up on the gelding. The advantage of staying at the Railway Hotel was that they were always near the station and had a livery next door. He headed to the station, found the hotel, then left the horse with the liveryman and took his saddlebags into the hotel, got a room and went upstairs to set his things inside. After he was settled, he returned to the hotel restaurant to have a late lunch/early dinner.

———

Josephine escaped further punishment by not saying a thing and making a big dinner for Wallace. She didn't dare bring up the almost bare pantry and larder and didn't know how much longer she could keep making his dinners, or even breakfasts without bringing up the topic. She thought that she might be able to get two more days' worth of meals and then she'd really be in for it.

"How ironic," she thought, "He won't let me get off the ranch, yet when there is no food, it would be my fault."

After cleaning the dishes and pans, she sat and just drifted, thinking of Joe and wondering if he was on his way to Salina or already here. She then escaped further into fantasy by imagining him coming to the door and taking her away from her nightmare. In her dreams, he was always tall and strong, and wore a badge because he was a good man, a brave man. She thought of him as the White Knight on the charger that he had told her would be waiting for her in the West. She almost laughed at her retreat from the reality that had found her.

———

Joe was up later than he anticipated. He had stayed up late wondering about today and how many would show and what they would look like. He dressed and had his breakfast in the hotel restaurant then headed out of the hotel a little before nine o'clock. It was too early for anyone to be there, even for his anxious mind, so he thought he'd kill a little time and headed to the Bank of Salina to speak to Mister Schmidt, hoping to get information about Jo's whereabouts in the hope that his sister was going to make it to the reunion.

He entered the very substantial building five minutes later and approached a clerk. It was a very profitable bank, by the looks of the building and the staff.

"Excuse me, I was wondering if I could see Mister Schmidt. It's a personal matter."

The clerk saw the badge, then replied, "Just a moment."

He then stood, turned and strolled to the back of the bank and knocked on a translucent glass-paned door that read: Vice President Paul Schmidt. He opened the door and said something, then returned.

"Mister Schmidt would like to know the subject of this personal business."

"Ten years ago, I arrived in Kansas with my sister, Josephine Carlisle. She was chosen by Mister Schmidt and his wife. We're supposed to meet today at noon, but the sheriff told me yesterday that no one has seen her for a year, and I'd like to find out where she is."

"I'll let him know," the clerk said before turning and heading back to the office and spoke to Mister Schmidt.

Schmidt's answer was loud and unequivocal before the clerk closed the door and walked back to his desk and sat down. He took out a pencil and wrote on the back of a blank back draft.

“Mister Schmidt will not see you. He said to not bother returning.”

“I heard his response. Thank you for your time,” Joe replied.

He was about to leave when the clerk suddenly thrust his hand out to Joe, and when Joe took his hand to shake it, he felt a folded piece of paper being pressed into his palm. The clerk looked at him with a tight jaw and just a mild nod.

Joe nodded in return, turned and left the bank and once out into the sunlight, looked at the palmed note.

Your sister is at the Slash G ranch 7 miles northwest.

Good luck.

He suddenly had a sinking feeling about Josephine. *What could be so bad as to cause this kind of ruse?*

He didn’t have time to hunt down his sister yet but went back to the hotel livery and went inside. The liveryman brought his horse around, and as accepted the reins, he asked the liveryman, “Do you know anything about the Slash G ranch?”

“Sure do, mister. I think it’s four sections. Only runs a few cows, though, maybe a hundred or so.”

“Who owns it?”

“It used to be owned by Peter Gunter, but when he died, his son took it over about three years ago. Gone to hell ever since.”

“What’s he like?”

“Big man. Real mean, too. He comes into town every now and then and gets into his drink.”

"I appreciate the information," Joe replied as his stomach churned.

He mounted the gelding and headed for the nearby train station, his mind racing with possibilities, and none of them were good.

He stepped down and hooked the horse's reins to the rail, then wandered over to the platform and took a seat on a bench by the rails and looked at the large tower clock near the ticket window. It was only 9:45. The train had just departed, so the platform was empty.

He didn't want to think too much about Jo yet because there was nothing he could do, but he did want to think about Caroline. *Would he finally see her in a little over two hours?* The clock dragged on as he had to stop thinking about what noon would bring.

He looked back at the gelding standing twenty feet away and figured he'd have to name the horse. He was brown with four stockings. *Boots?* Nah. Overdone. *What's brown?* The first thing that came to mind was totally unacceptable. Might as well throw out the whole color thing.

He couldn't think of many things that were brown that were pleasant. *How about a human name?* He turned his eyes back to look at the horse. Nope. He was too good to get a human name. Sooner or later, he'd run into some jerk with the same name and have to change it. Finally, he just caved and named him Duke. He felt he was taking the easy road, but it was short and easy to use, which were two major considerations.

After naming the horse, he looked at the station clock. It was only 10:20, and he still didn't see anyone even approaching the train station. He would have thought that they'd be as anxious as he was, and was disappointed that Caroline wasn't here yet, but he was more than anxious that Jo hadn't arrived. If she was only seven miles away, she should have been here first. Danny absence hadn't surprised him at all. Danny, even when they were on the train, seemed to resent Joe taking charge, and Joe had suspected that he had agreed just to end the conversation.

Time crawled by, but finally, the station clock's minute hand joined the hour hand pointing straight up and he found himself still alone on the platform. He'd wait fifteen minutes and then take the northwest road out of town.

As he waited those fifteen minutes, he wondered what he should do about Caroline. He had promised to find her ten years ago, and finally decided that after he found Jo, he'd have to go and find Caroline. But to find Caroline, he'd need to find Danny. His name wouldn't change if he married as Caroline's would, so he shouldn't be difficult to track down.

The clock said 12:15, and Joe quickly strode to Duke and mounted, turned from the station and trotted north, but once he left the town, he found the road heading northwest and soon left Salina behind him. Twenty minutes later, he had covered four of the seven miles.

—–

Wallace was in a foul mood. His breakfast had been two eggs and two strips of bacon and the coffee tasted weak, too. *Now, he was getting this crap for lunch?*

He picked up the plate with the slice of ham and some beans and threw it against the wall, then glared at Josephine, who was close to panic as she saw his reaction. She hadn't had much to eat at all the past week and didn't know what else she could do. He had just thrown away more than she had eaten all day yesterday.

As Wallace stood and clenched his fists, she began to back into the corner and cover her face with her arms, waiting for the blows to start falling.

———

Joe had set the big gelding to a fast trot after leaving Salina, so he began looking for access roads as he kept Duke moving quickly. The closer he got to the ranch, the more his anxiety grew, then he saw it. He had almost missed it as the sign was barely visible, and the access road was overgrown.

He slowed Duke, made the turn and accelerated down the access road, then slowed before reaching the house, pulled the gelding to a stop and didn't bother asking for permission to step down. The poorly maintained ranch house didn't seem to make it necessary. He threw Duke's reins over the rail and stepped onto to the porch then banged loudly on the door.

Wallace was reaching for Josephine's hair when the door was shaken by loud bangs. Wallace turned suddenly and glared at the closed door. *Who the hell was knocking at the door?* Nobody came here.

As Joe waited, he moved his badge back to his vest. He wanted some display in case it was necessary.

After Wallace left a shaking Josephine in the kitchen, she prayed for someone to come in and kill Wallace as she believed it was the only way she would ever be free of the man.

The hammering at the door continued and Wallace was getting really angry until he screamed, "Stop doing that!"

Joe stood back from the door about four feet, having no idea what to expect when the door opened.

Wallace almost ripped the door off the hinges when he finally reached it and glared at Joe as he snarled, “What the hell do you want, beating my door like that?”

Joe took one look at the enraged bully, sized him up immediately, and said, “I have a warrant for the arrest of Josephine Carlisle. Does she live here?”

Wallace saw the badge, but not reading it, and snapped, “What did that bitch do? She ain’t been outta here in a year.”

“She stole five hundred dollars from her employer when she left. He didn’t notice it until recently.”

“*She stole five hundred dollars from Paul?*” he exclaimed, then after he glanced back to the kitchen, said, “You can’t have her, Marshal. Not till she tells me where the money is.”

Joe noticed the use of the banker’s first name and replied, “Let’s go and ask her.”

“I’ll beat it outta her,” he growled.

“You can’t do that. She’ll never be convicted if the confession was coerced. I’m sure I can get her to talk.”

As much as he wanted to shoot the bastard standing in front of him, Joe knew his options were limited. How he had suddenly started this whole theft routine was beyond him. It just had popped into his mind and rolled out of his mouth.

Wallace had no idea what ‘coerced’ meant, but the man had a badge, so he said, “Alright. You can come in. But I get part of that money as a reward.”

“That’ll be up to Mister Schmidt. I’m sure you’ll be able to convince him to reward you handsomely.”

"He'd better."

Joe followed him inside, finding the house and furnishings clean but in a poor state of repair.

Wallace stopped and shouted, "Get in here, you bitch! You gotta answer some questions for this here marshal."

Joe wondered just how ignorant this man was as he stood calmly with his arms folded, waiting for his sister to appear from the hallway as his heart pounded in anticipation of not only seeing her but helping her. He heard quiet footsteps approaching and his heart almost stopped beating altogether when she stepped into the room.

Josephine saw the star on his chest and wanted to weep for joy but maintained her composure, knowing what would happen if she started crying. Wallace hated weepy women, and after the lawman left, he'd prove it to her. She began to think of ways to tell the young deputy sheriff of her predicament, but didn't know how she could without the bigger, more violent Wallace killing him.

Wallace then interrupted her thoughts when he said, "The marshal is here to arrest you for stealin' five hundred dollars from Paul Schmidt. Where'd you hide the money?"

Josephine was stunned. *What was he talking about?* She switched her gaze back to the tall, handsome lawman who was looking at her. Then she stared at him. It was his eyes; there was something about the eyes that spoke to her.

Joe looked at his sister, smiled, and said, "Hello, Jo. I'm not a marshal. I'm a deputy sheriff. My name is Hennessey. Joe Hennessey. We share the same name, kind of."

"Joe?" she asked, wondering about the coincidence.

"Yes, ma'am. It seems like you've been having a hard time of it."

"No, no, it's nothing."

Then Joe couldn't restrain his anger any longer as it burst out in a low, controlled growl.

"It is something. *What kind of sick bastard would beat my sister?*" he snarled as he turned on Wallace.

"What are you talkin' about? What about the money?" asked a confused Wallace Gunter.

Joe glared at him and continued to growl, "You dumb, pathetic son of a bitch! There isn't any money. I'm here to take my sister away from you. You don't deserve to live in the presence of a diseased sow, much less my sister. Jo, go out the front door while I have a chat with this poor excuse for a human being."

Jo was so stunned by the realization that this was her brother that she didn't move. *It was Joe! He'd come to take her away! It wasn't a fantasy. It was real!*

She finally nodded and started to move toward the door, but keeping her eyes focused on her brother.

Joe still stared at Wallace as he said, "And Jo, when you get out there, there's a loaded shotgun in my left scabbard. Take it out and cock the hammers. If this ignorant bastard somehow makes it out the door, let him have both barrels."

Jo finally realized that Joe was more than capable of handling the bully who had hurt her for so long and said, "Beat him, Joe. Beat him as badly as he beat me."

"Count on it, Jo. Now, go."

She turned and continued to head out of the house, crossed the porch, then stepped down beside his horse and slid the shotgun from its scabbard before she turned to witness what was happening behind the open doorway.

Wallace was seething, not really caring if she left or not. He just didn't like being threatened. He knew he was bigger than this lawman, and whether he was a marshal or a sheriff, didn't matter.

Joe undid his gunbelt and slid it to the door, watching Wallace grow angrier and knew he could use that anger.

Finally, he took off his vest and badge, and tossed them onto his gunbelt followed by his Stetson.

He kept his eyes focused on Wallace's livid face and said, "Okay, you, big coward. Let's see if you can beat a man as easily as you beat a defenseless woman. You're bigger than I am, so you probably have an advantage, but you're also one of the stupidest men I've ever met."

"I ain't stupid! You shut your mouth!"

Joe saw his temperature rising and wanted it higher as he replied, "The only thing smaller than your brain is probably your pecker."

That did it. Wallace charged, wanting to crush the smaller man, but Joe sidestepped slightly, caught him with his left foot and as Wallace began to fall, Joe clasped his hands together and crashed his right elbow into Wallace's ribs.

Wallace felt the pain and then added more when he crashed headfirst into the wall. It would have put most men on the ground, but not Wallace Gunter. He popped right back up and grunted loudly as he unleashed a huge right-hand crossing punch at Joe.

Joe couldn't step back far enough, so he ducked as Wallace's shot swooped over the top of Joe's head, but after Joe buried a left jab into Wallace's gut, the big man was bending over and suddenly wrapped Joe in a bearhug.

Aside from squeezing the life from his lungs, Joe was almost overwhelmed with the smells emanating from Wallace. He needed to act quickly as he was already graying out, so he lifted his right foot and slammed his heel down hard onto Wallace's left foot. Wallace screamed and let Joe go.

Joe staggered back, trying to regain his breath as the limping and injured, but still dangerous Wallace advanced more carefully this time. It was the one time that Joe was probably susceptible to the bull rush, but Wallace took his time, and that mistake would cost Wallace Gunter.

Joe wanted to hurt him, and he wanted it to be memorable, so he feigned stumbling backward.

Wallace saw him and changed his tactics again and rushed Joe. Joe waited until Wallace was almost on him and dropped into a tuck, rolling as he hit the floor right between Wallace's legs. Wallace stopped and tried to grab Joe's legs. but Joe was where he needed to be and slammed his fist as hard as he could straight upwards, catching Wallace flush in his crotch.

Wallace screamed again and grabbed himself as Joe rolled quickly onto his stomach and crawled away. Wallace had lost his steam and thought it was over, but Joe didn't.

He walked to Wallace's right side and stood facing him, then turned slightly, brought his foot back and snapped it out hard at

Wallace's right knee. Ligaments and tendons snapped liked rubber bands as Joe's boot exploded into the knee and Wallace screamed even louder as he dropped to the floor and began rolling in agony. Unlike the punch he had delivered to his privates, this was a permanent injury. Wallace would never walk again.

Joe looked down at the blubbering Wallace and said, "I'll notify the sheriff's office to come and visit you, Wallace, but I may not do it for a couple of days. I may have a hard time remembering what happened, so you just have a good day."

He turned and picked up his Colt, strapped it back on, pulled his hat on, then snatched his vest up as he left the room and when he was outside, Joe saw a satisfied Josephine standing facing the door with the shotgun still pointed at the door.

"Jo, could you put the shotgun down?" he asked.

"Oh," was her short reply as she lowered the shotgun.

She didn't have to ask if Wallace was dead as the howls were enough of an answer.

After Joe took the shotgun, he uncocked the hammers and slid it into its scabbard, then turned to his sister and opened his arms. She walked slowly toward him and then fell into his arms, clutching him tightly. Joe held her just as closely and just as tightly as they both released torrents of tears. Jo ignored the pain from Wallace's blows as she engulfed herself in her older brother's protection.

Josephine and Joe were reunited, ten years, two days, four hours and eleven minutes after they had been separated.

After two or three minutes of embracing, Joe finally stepped back and cleared his eyes.

"Jo, I'm going to take you away from here."

"But, Joe, where can I go now?" she asked as she wiped her eyes.

"I'm going to take you back to Lincoln, and you can stay with my parents. They're both wonderful people and you can start a new life, a good life, Jo. One you deserve."

"Joe, it's been so horrible since I left. The Schmidts treated me like hired help. I had to clean and even wear a maid outfit. They only let me go to school until the sixth grade and then they just kept me at their house working. I had to cook and clean and do the laundry. Mrs. Schmidt didn't do anything. I was nothing more than the hired help without getting paid."

"How did you get here?"

"When I turned eighteen, the contract said Mister Schmidt had to give me a hundred dollars, but he didn't. Instead, he had Wallace show up in the coach house and take me away to his ranch. Wallace always was complaining that the didn't get his two-hundred-dollars' worth. He kept me tied whenever he slept, beat me and blamed me for everything."

Joe was boiling inside. His precious sister treated like this because her parents didn't want them anymore.

He regained his composure as he said, "I know that this will sound like a ridiculous question, but is there anything you want to take with you?"

"No. Just get me away from here, Joe. Can Wallace chase after me?"

"Not unless he can fly. I shattered his right knee, Jo. He'll never walk again."

"Good. Take me away from here, Joe."

Joe stepped up on Duke and helped Josephine onto the back of his horse. They left the ranch behind and rode southeast and arrived in Salina before two o'clock.

"Where are we going, Joe?"

"First to the sheriff's office and then to the bank."

Jo was going to protest but decided that Joe knew what he was doing. He sure knew what he was doing to Wallace.

They arrived at the sheriff's office, and Joe let Josephine down before he dismounted. Her dress was very old and worn and Joe guessed correctly that it was the only one she had but would fix that after they made a trip to the bank.

But first, they stepped into the sheriff's office finding the same deputy at the desk. He took one look at Josephine with her bruises, then another at Joe's face and stood.

"I'll get the sheriff," he said without asking any questions.

Joe just nodded as he kept Jo's hand tightly in his.

The sheriff came around the corner, glanced at Joe and then looked longer at Josephine. He wasn't as angry as Joe had been, but Joe could tell that it was close.

"Come on into my office. Please," he said, gesturing toward his office in the back.

Joe took Josephine's arm and led her to the sheriff's office and let her sit in the only free chair as the deputy leaned against the door jamb.

"Deputy, what happened?" the sheriff asked.

“I went to the bank to ask Mister Schmidt where Josephine was. He wouldn’t see me, but a clerk slipped me a note letting me know that she was at the Slash G ranch northwest of the city. I rode out there and arrived just as he was about to beat Josephine again. You could hear him screaming at her from fifty feet outside the front door. I knocked, and he let me in, buying a nonsense story I gave him about her stealing money from Mister Schmidt. When I saw how he had beat Josephine, I kind of lost my temper. I put aside my badge and my gunbelt and we had a go.”

“Wallace must have you by forty pounds, Deputy.”

“It didn’t matter. He’s lying on the floor of his ranch. He’ll need a doctor, but he’ll never walk right again, if he walks at all.”

“I would have shot the son of a bitch,” he said before turning to Jo and saying, “Excuse my language, ma’am.”

“So, would I, Sheriff, if Joe hadn’t taken the shotgun away.”

“We’ll send the doctor out there when we think about it. Is he your husband, ma’am?”

It was a question Joe had never bothered to ask.

“No. After he paid Mister Schmidt for me, he just took me out to the ranch and used me.”

The sheriff was stunned as he asked slowly, “He paid Schmidt for you?”

“Yes, sir. Two hundred dollars.”

The sheriff shook his head as the deputy just stood with his mouth agape.

The sheriff said, “We can send him to jail for kidnapping and assault, Miss Carlisle.”

“No. I don’t ever want to see him again. I think Joe made that happen.”

“I understand. Where will you go now?”

“Joe is taking me back to Lincoln to live with his parents.”

“Two finer people you won’t find anywhere, Miss Carlisle.”

“That’s what he said,” she replied as she looked up and smiled at Joe.

Joe said, “Sheriff, before I take care of Jo, I’m going to walk her over to the bank and see Mister Schmidt. I won’t touch him, but what I aim to do might be misconstrued as blackmail. I will remind Mister Schmidt how he failed to meet the terms of the contract he signed ten years ago. He treated Jo like a servant, not a child, didn’t let her finish her schooling and didn’t give her the hundred dollars she was supposed to receive when she turned eighteen, then essentially sold her into slavery. Now, I don’t think Mister Schmidt would like that story to get out. Would you?”

The sheriff grinned and replied, “I like the way you think, Joe. Before I forget, the trial for Edgar Sorenson will be held tomorrow at ten o’clock. The prosecutor would like to talk to you at nine. Just meet him in his office in the county courthouse.”

“I’ll be there.”

Joe turned to Josephine and asked, “Shall we cross the street to the bank, my dear sister?”

"Thank you, brother dearest," she answered and felt a warm rush just saying it.

He offered her his arm and she rose, then put her hand tightly on his forearm, holding onto it like the life preserver that it was.

They left the office and crossed the cobbled street to the other side, then turned north and soon arrived at the Bank of Salina. He held the door for Josephine, and they walked inside.

Jo drew a few glances for her shabby appearance and her welts and bruises that were so easily seen, and it was also obvious that the young lawman with her was not the cause. Many eyes followed them as they stepped past a familiar, smirking clerk and Joe didn't bother knocking when he reached the office of the vice president. He just opened the door to Mister Schmidt's office and walked inside with Josephine, closing the door behind him, although part of him wanted to leave it wide open.

There was no, '*Who do you think you are?*' or, '*What do you mean coming in here like this?*'. The moment his eyes caught sight of a battered Josephine being escorted by a lawman, Paul Schmidt knew he was in deep trouble.

Joe sat Josephine down in one of the plush leather chairs and took the other himself.

Mister Schmidt jumped the conversation by simply asking, "How much do you want?"

Joe was startled by the question…for about half of a second.

He leveled his angry eyes into Paul Schmidt and said, "Now, Mister Schmidt, I left Wallace Gunter in his ranch house in a sorry state. I beat him to a pulp and he'll never walk again. It was a fair fight and I've already reported it to the sheriff."

That shook Mister Schmidt. *He already told the sheriff? How much had he told him?*

“What did you tell him?” he asked in almost a whisper.

Joe continued his glare as he spoke, saying, “Quite a lot. Our next stop after we leave your bank will be to the Salina newspaper. You sold my sister into slavery, *Mister Schmidt.* She was treated like an animal and abused physically and sexually for a year because of you, *Mister Schmidt.* She might have been dead if I hadn’t arrived to take her away from there, *Mister Schmidt.* If she had died, would you have even cared, *Mister Schmidt*? Or would you feel relieved that no one would be able to point the finger at you, *Mister Schmidt*?”

Each accusation ended with a sarcastic, emphasized, *Mister Schmidt* to let him know that he, even more than Wallace Gunter, was the cause of his sister’s abuse.

Paul Schmidt licked his upper lip, knowing that his life would be over if this hit the paper and might even go to jail if that idiot Gunter talked, and he was sure that he would.

“I repeat, how much do you want?”

“I don’t think you have enough money, *Mister Schmidt.* I can’t tell you how deep my anger is about how my dear sister was treated by you and your wife and then that sick bastard you sold her to. I think I’m done talking to you. I just wanted to let you know what was coming.”

He half-rose from his chair and exclaimed, “No! Wait! I know we hurt her, and it was a horrible thing to do, but my wife, you understand, she’s the one who made me do it. I really felt bad about it.”

Joe doubted that it was just his wife, but he could see how worried the banker was and the meeting was going as he had intended when he replied, "Not bad enough, *Mister Schmidt*. You should have had some balls, but obviously you gave them to your wife. Jo, let's get out of here."

Paul Schmidt suddenly said, "Twenty thousand dollars! I'll give you twenty thousand dollars!"

Joe looked over at Josephine and she gave the slightest of nods.

"I'll tell you what, *Mister Schmidt*. We'll go and open an account in Josephine's name. In case you've forgotten, it's Josephine Carlisle. I'll stop by tomorrow after the trial for the one of the two men I didn't kill yesterday to make sure the money is in there. If it is, then I'll let it go. If it's not. Let's just say there will be consequences."

"Alright. I understand," he replied as he slowly lowered himself to the chair, feeling an enormous sense of relief, yet pain at its cost.

Joe stood and offered Josephine his arm again, and she took his arm with a shaking hand, unable to believe what had happened in just one day.

He led her out of the office and to the desk of the clerk who had slipped him the note. Joe could tell how angry he was just looking at Josephine's welts and bruises.

Joe sat her down before the desk and read the nameplate.

"Mister Henderson, my sister needs to open an account today. She'll need some blank drafts as well."

Mister Henderson smiled as he wondered what would happen in Mister Schmidt's office.

"Of course, ma'am. I'll be right back," he replied before he stood, stepped away from his desk then returned a few minutes later with a ledger book and some forms. He had Josephine sign the forms and then added his signature.

Joe handed him fifty dollars to open the account, even though they only needed five. Joe figured she'd be good for it later. He handed Josephine the blank drafts then stood behind his desk. He was going to shake her hand but was worried it might hurt some of the bruises, so he just stood and smiled.

"Thank you for your business, Miss Carlisle."

"You're welcome, Mister Henderson," she replied as she smiled back.

She took her big brother's arm and they left the bank to the continued glances from the customers and staff.

One outside, Joe asked, "Where to now, Jo? Did you want to get something to eat? I'm hungry and you look like you're starving."

"I haven't had much to eat since I've been out there, Joe."

"We'll get your figure back soon, Jo. It's so wonderful to have you back with me again."

Jo was floating on air as she said, "You will never know what it was like to hear you say those words to Wallace about how he was treating your sister. It was my biggest fantasy, that you'd come walking in all big and strong and beat the daylights out of Wallace, and it all came true. Then to get that bastard Schmidt to cough up so much money. That's a fortune, Joe!"

He patted her arm and said, "You'll be able to do anything you want now, Jo."

They reached the diner and Jo drew more looks before Joe held her chair for her as she sat down. Josephine was in heaven as she took the seat, the smells of food were tantalizing her, and her big brother was sitting across from her.

"Life can't get any better," she thought.

Josephine wanted the chicken dinner for lunch as she hadn't had chicken in years, so Joe ordered the same. When the waitress brought coffee, Jo pampered herself by adding sugar and cream and Joe just smiled at his younger sister as she made big eyes sipping her coffee. His heart still ached when he even thought about what had happened to her since they had separated. The agency that arranged the child trains tried their best to make sure the children were well treated, but they couldn't come close to monitoring all the cases. They tried especially hard to watch the borderline parents, not a well-to-do banker. It was also a matter of distance, and they were at the end of the line.

As they waited for their order, they didn't talk much, but made almost young lover moony eyes at each other. Joe couldn't help but notice how thin she was and the almost uncountable bruises and welts that covered the skin he could see and was sure there were a lot more where he couldn't and never would be able to see.

Their chicken arrived, and Joe watched as Josephine took her first bite. She was almost crying as she chewed. The gravy and mashed potatoes and buttered biscuits all added to her deep appreciation of even the simple things, but she couldn't eat it all. It was simply too much for her stomach to tolerate so quickly.

After they finished, Joe paid the bill, then led his sister out of the restaurant, and down the street toward the hotel.

"Jo, before we get you a room, did you want to buy some more clothes and things?"

"Do you mind, Joe? I don't have any money, though."

"I have plenty with me, so let's go shopping. Don't buy too much today, though. We'll be traveling soon."

"Oh, that's right. Are we going to ride?"

"No, Jo. I think you'll take the train. It'll be like we just kind of picked up where we left ten years ago. I'll send a telegram to my parents letting them know you're coming."

"Why are you leaving?" she asked.

"I need to go and find Caroline and Danny."

"They didn't show up?"

"I'm not surprised that Danny didn't, but I was kind of disappointed that Caroline didn't."

"She really liked you, Joe, and I think she'd love you now. You've turned into quite a handsome gentleman, you know. Why aren't you married already? I'm sure some women have set their caps on you."

"They have, but I want to find Caroline before I do anything else. It's kind of silly, really."

"No, it's not. I think it's very romantic."

Jo was still in a state of bliss as they walked along the boardwalk to the clothing store, and after entering, Joe wasn't the least bit embarrassed to walk into the ladies' section with his sister. He wanted to make sure she bought what she needed.

Twenty minutes later, he was carrying two large bags along with a travel bag back to the hotel. He'd have to go and get Duke from the sheriff's office after Josephine was settled.

The arrived at the Railway Hotel and crossed to the desk.

"Yes, sir?" the desk clerk asked giving Josephine the onceover.

"Do you have a suite with a full bathroom available?"

"Yes, we do. It's fairly expensive, though. Five dollars a night."

"Fine. My sister would like the suite."

"Very well."

Jo signed the register while the clerk got the key.

Joe could care less what the clerk thought as he followed Josephine to her suite. The thought of a hot bath made her giddy, so she was practically skipping as she reached the room but couldn't get the key into the lock as her hand trembled.

Joe took the key and opened the door. It was a huge room and after Jo entered, she slowly spun around in wonder. Then she saw the bath and her eyes went wide as she looked at the collection of scented soaps and shampoos…and towels! Soft, luxurious towels!

She trotted back to her brother, hugged him again, and as her head was pressed against his chest, said softly, "Thank you so much for this, Joe."

Joe kissed the top of her head and replied, "I'll leave your bags here, but now I've got to go and get my horse put away and get cleaned up myself. My mother wouldn't be happy if she knew I skipped my bath."

Josephine tilted her head, and asked, "You really think of them as your parents, don't you?"

"They legally adopted me nine years ago, Jo, and I've never thought of them in any other way. When you've been with them for just a little while, they'll make you feel the same especially mama. You'll see."

"Now, I'm excited."

"You should be. Now go and take a nice, long, hot bath and I'll stop back up around six o'clock to take you to dinner downstairs."

"I'll be waiting, Joe," she said as she smiled broadly.

Joe smiled at his sister, kissed her on the cheek and closed the door behind him. He stood in the hallway, let out his breath and hoped he could keep Jo happy. He could feel her ribs when he hugged her this time and knew it would take time not only to get her weight back and heal her bruises, but to heal her soul from the damage that had been done to it for a decade. But he knew that he had the best help possible back in Lincoln, and that thought brought a smile to his face as he began to walk down the hallway.

He left the hotel and walked back to where Duke waited patiently in front of the sheriff's office, unhitched the horse, led him back to the livery and asked that Duke get extra oats. Before he returned to the hotel, he stopped at the nearby Western Union office and sent the following:

WILL AND CLARA HENNESSEY LINCOLN KANSAS

WILL BE SENDING SISTER TO YOU TOMORROW
SHE WAS IN BAD SITUATION AND WILL NEED YOU
SHE'LL TELL YOU THE STORY
LOVE

JOE HENNESSEY RAILWAY HOTEL SALINA KANSAS

After the telegram had been sent, he went to his room, cleaned up and changed as his clothes were a bit dirty from the excitement by the train tracks and had some of Wallace's blood stains, too.

Just around six o'clock, he knocked on Josephine's door, and it was opened quickly by a smiling Josephine. With freshly washed hair that had brushed until it shone and a nice, new dress and shoes, Joe noticed that his sister, although still thin and bruised, was a beautiful young lady.

She flashed a huge smile at him, and Joe said, "You are a beautiful woman, Josephine. I regret teasing you when you were seven and calling you a frog."

She laughed and the laugh itself made her happy as she hadn't laughed in such a long time.

"I'll forgive you, Joe."

"Shall we go and have dinner, dear sister?"

"I believe I could eat again, big brother," she replied as she took his arm.

Her new dress had sleeves that hid the welts and bruises and Joe wondered just how stunning she would be when she put on another twenty pounds. She'll turn a lot of young men's heads in Lincoln, he was sure.

They had the prime rib for dinner, and Josephine ate more slowly so it didn't fill her stomach so fast, but she still couldn't finish her meal. Joe was kind of stuffed himself, so they decided to sit in the lobby and just talk for a while.

While they were talking, Josephine noticed the Salina paper and thought she saw Joe's name on the front page.

"Joe, is your name in the newspaper?" she asked as she picked it up.

"Maybe."

She pulled the paper and read about Joe's prevention of the derailment and robbery. the story ended with a paragraph about how the same deputy had taken two wanted men out of circulation just two days earlier in Lincoln.

She set the paper down and looked at the young man sitting across from her. He looked so innocent, yet he had done all of this, then destroyed Wallace and humiliated Mister Schmidt to give her a lot of money. *How could anyone just twenty-one do so much in just a few days?* She was suddenly in awe of her older brother.

Joe noticed the look on her face and asked, "Is there something wrong, Jo?"

"Not at all, Joe. I'm just amazed that you could do so many things."

"It's all because of my father. He taught me a lot, Jo."

"He may have taught you, but you did it all, Joe. I'm so very proud of you."

"I'm just happy that I found you, Jo."

They talked for two hours, telling stories about their lives since they'd parted ten years earlier. Joe's were almost universally good while Josephine's were all bad, but Joe hoped she'd have nothing but good ones from here on.

They went to their rooms a little past eleven o'clock, agreeing to meet in the lobby for breakfast at seven. The train departed at 9:30, so that would give them time.

The next morning, Josephine was wearing her second new dress and had packed the remaining clothes in her travel bag. Joe had his saddlebags and had already checked out, so Josephine checked out and they walked arm-in-arm to the hotel restaurant for their breakfast.

Josephine had flapjacks smothered in butter and syrup, then looked at Joe and seriously said, "I hope I don't get fat."

Joe laughed lightly and just shook his head.

Forty-five minutes later, they walked over to the bank and Josephine checked her balance. It was $20,050. She withdrew a hundred dollars and handed half to Joe, who accepted the money without protest.

They returned to the train station, and Joe bought a ticket for Lincoln and handed it to Josephine.

"Aren't you coming?" she asked.

"No, Jo. Remember I told you that I had to go and find Caroline and Danny. Besides, I have to go and see the prosecutor in a few minutes over at the courthouse and then I have to be there for the trial. When you get to Lincoln, you'll probably be met by my mother. If not, go to the sheriff's office. Tell them after the trial, I'll be going on to find Danny and then Caroline."

"You found me and now I'll be losing you," she said softly.

"No, Jo, I'm only going to find them. I'll be back in a few days. Besides, this will give you more time with my parents. You'll feel more comfortable with them than you can imagine. Oh, and Jo, one more thing. Just to make sure Mister Schmidt doesn't try to welch on the deal and take the money back, open an account in Lincoln and have them transfer your money there where he can't touch it."

"Alright. But you hurry back."

"I will. I've got to run."

He gave her a hug and a kiss on the forehead, then whispered, "I love you, Jo."

She nodded, then barely whispered back, "I love you too, Joe. Thank you for saving me."

Joe nodded, then turned and jogged toward the courthouse.

Josephine watched him leave and sighed. It may be ten years later, but he was still her big brother and her protector. She hoped he could find Danny and especially Caroline and wondered, as he had, if she had already married. *If not, would he be bringing her back as his wife?* Whatever he did,

Josephine was now absolutely convinced that he could do whatever he set his mind to do. He was her big brother and her hero.

Joe reached the prosecutor's office just a couple of minutes early. The prosecutor, Arnold Baines, was impressed with his promptness. He quickly reviewed Joe's testimony and ensured it matched the report he had been given. It was a very detailed report. Sometimes, too much detail could be a problem because it invites the defense more opportunities to trip up the witness, but he was satisfied with Joe's responses, so they went directly to the courtroom.

Judge James Mercer was presiding, and the trial was almost a waste of Joe's time. There had been so much publicity surrounding the case that the defense attorney seemed to have thrown in the towel after he had asked Joe's name. The jury returned a guilty verdict in eight minutes and the judge sentenced Edgar to hang the next morning.

Edgar peed his pants again when the sentence was announced, and the judge was prepared to cite him for contempt of court, but quickly realized the folly of the order and simply dismissed the jury and scampered from the bench leaving the poor bailiff the chore of cleaning his courtroom.

Joe left the courthouse and immediately began thinking of how he'd approach trying to find Danny. Abilene was an easy one-day ride, and he'd rather ride the horse than take the train if it was less than a hundred miles. He decided he'd leave in the morning. If he left after lunch, which would arrive shortly, he'd get in around four o'clock, but he'd rather get in during the middle of the day, so he could hunt down Danny more quickly. He headed for the diner for his quick lunch and then he'd go back to the hotel and get a room again.

As Joe was walking out of the courtroom in Salina, his sister was stepping off the train in Lincoln, not knowing what to expect. She knew that Joe had told her how wonderful his adoptive parents were, yet she was still unsure, but it didn't last long for her to discover that he hadn't exaggerated.

As soon as she reached the platform, an older couple quickly stepped toward her wearing big smiles.

"You must be Josephine," said Clara, with extended arms.

Josephine couldn't help but return the warm smile as she replied, "Yes, I'm Joe's sister."

After she answered, she was enveloped in Clara's embrace.

"Welcome to Lincoln, Josephine. Come along and we'll get you settled. That ornery old man with the badge is Joe's father."

Will smiled at Josephine and replied, "Gotta keep up the image or the town would turn into a regular Sodom or Gomorrah."

Josephine laughed and took both of Joe's parents' offered arms. Will picked up her travel bag, and the trio walked to their home.

Once inside, Clara immediately showed her into the kitchen, promising to add some meat to her bones as any mother would. Will hung behind, pleased that his wife now had a resident female to keep her company.

CHAPTER 3

Joe was headed for Abilene a little after sunrise feeling good to be on the road again and feeling even better about Jo. He was totally happy with his work so far. His sister was at his parents' home, safe and secure, she had a lot of money in the bank and seemed to have withstood all those years of neglect and then punishment without damaging her character. When he returned, he expected Josephine to be close to the happy person he had always known her to be, even in the circumstances that they shared in Philadelphia and wondered how long she'd remain single.

He had Duke moving at a rapid pace and was sure he'd arrive in Abilene before noon easily, as long as he didn't run across any stupid outlaws again, or smart ones for that matter. He didn't, and he arrived in Abilene just a little past eleven and made his first stop at the sheriff's office to find out where Danny lived. He remembered that he had been taken by someone named Abernathy. So, he'd either be Danny Stevens or Danny Abernathy, if they had adopted him. He'd be twenty years old now, so he shifted his thoughts away from Caroline for a few minutes to wonder how Danny had turned out.

Danny had seemed to be almost on the periphery of the four of them when they were on the train, which he always found a bit odd back then because they were the boys. He would argue about some of Joe's ideas, but Joe had put it down to a bit of jealousy because both his sister and Caroline liked him better. Then he thought it might be because he resented Joe being bigger and a year older, but Joe had still regarded him as a friend and hoped he would be friendly enough to at least tell him where he could find Caroline.

He arrived at the sheriff's office and stepped down, tossed Duke's reins over the hitching rail without even looping them around. He knew Duke wouldn't go anywhere as he'd already developed a bond with the tall gelding, who was probably grateful for the lost hundred pounds. He stepped up onto the boardwalk and entered the sheriff's office.

"Morning. How can I help you?" asked the deputy behind the front desk.

"Howdy. I'm Deputy Sheriff Joe Hennessey from Lincoln. I'm looking for someone on a strictly personal basis and wondering if you could help me."

"You're that deputy that stopped the train wreck and caught those two criminals, ain't ya?" he asked with a grin.

"Afraid so. It seems to follow me around."

"Nothin' to be ashamed of. What do you need to know?"

"I'm looking for a man that I only knew for a couple of weeks when I was eleven. We came out here on one of those children trains."

"Yup. Seen 'em over the years. Who you lookin' for?"

"He's either Danny Stevens or Danny Abernathy."

"I wish I could help you, but nobody knows where he went."

"Went?"

"Danny Stevens is wanted for murder. He skedaddled out of Abilene two weeks ago."

Joe was stunned as he asked, "What happened?"

"He was working in his father's mill. He was made foreman there and some of the other workers resented it because they said he was too young. Anyway, he overheard a man named Mike Enberg make some comment that he didn't like, and they went at it. Danny hit him with a chair and knocked him right into the grinding wheel. It was a pretty ugly thing to have to see, I can tell ya'."

"And then he just ran off?"

"Kinda. He ran out of the mill and got on his horse but took enough time to get to his house, throw some food and clothes into his saddlebags and even stop at the bank and withdraw some cash before he left town. Left his wife and baby, too. By the time we found out about it, he was long gone. We notified the county and the U.S. Marshals, but they haven't caught up with him yet."

Joe shook his head. His only lead to Caroline was on the lam.

"Which way did he go?"

"He headed east, but his trail shifted north before we lost it."

"Where'd you lose it, do you remember?"

"Easy enough. If you go east about two miles, you'll come to this stream that crosses the road. His tracks turned north just after that creek. We lost him not half a mile from the road."

"We haven't had any rain in the past two weeks, so they may still be there. I think I'll try and track him down."

"You're gonna have to do it as a regular citizen, you know."

"I know. Does he have a wanted poster?"

"Sure. I'll get you one."

Joe was torn about his hasty decision. He should just ride to Junction City and start his hunt for Caroline on his own but had a sneaking suspicion that she wouldn't be anyplace he could find around Junction City because she hadn't shown up for the reunion.

The deputy returned with the poster and handed it to Joe. It had a full description and a drawing.

"How accurate is the drawing? Some of them are pretty bad."

"This one's darn near perfect. Blonde hair and blue eyes, too. They kinda stick out. Why you tryin' to find him so bad?"

"He's the only one who can tell me where his sister is."

"If he tells you, you gonna let him go?"

"Not on your life. He's coming back here."

"Appreciate it. Good luck."

Joe folded the poster and put it in his vest pocket, knowing it was time to get some food for the trail, and some food right now at the café. Then, he'd go after Danny.

After eating and picking up the supplies, he sent a telegram to his father.

SHERIFF WILL HENNESSEY LINCOLN KANSAS

ARRIVED ABILENE
DANNY STEVENS WANTED FOR MURDER
WILL CHASE THEN FIND CAROLINE

JOE HENNESSEY ABILENE KANSAS

He left the telegraph office thinking about how to find Caroline's brother, knowing it would be difficult trying to hunt down Danny. He had the wanted poster and the advantage that he stuck out with that blonde hair, but it was an old trail. He hoped he had learned as much from his father as he thought he did.

He found the stream after just fifteen minutes and stepped down on the eastern bank and saw the hoofprints clearly but assumed that they belonged to the posse. That would make the trail easier for the first half mile, or however far they followed. He assumed they weren't particularly anxious to go too far anyway, so once they lost the trail for some distance, they'd head home and send out their telegrams to those lawmen whose jurisdictions began where theirs ended.

Sure enough, the posse's tracks crossed over to the other side of the stream and returned after a few hundred yards. The stream was narrow enough that Joe simply walked Duke into the stream and followed north at a walk, scanning both sides of the stream as they moved. They went almost a full mile before he found where Danny had left the stream, and he shifted Duke to the northeast. He tried to picture a map of Kansas in his head and figured that Wakefield was about thirty miles ahead, but the much larger Clay Center was another ten miles, and more to the northeast. He thought if he was running, he'd head for the bigger town, but for now, he'd follow the tracks.

Danny Stevens wasn't in either of the locations that Joe thought he might be. He had reached Clay Center a few days after the killing and had stayed for a few more before he began to feel the scrutiny of the town marshal. Danny was close to panic, left his horse and took a train to Manhattan.

He was now in a boarding house and had to buy some more clothes and just lay low for a while, but his money was dwindling away. He hadn't closed his account in Abilene, but he had only left a little more than a hundred dollars for his wife to use, taking the remaining hundred and thirty with him. It had sounded like a lot of money at the time, but the train ticket, clothes and rent were eating into his wallet. He only had eight-two dollars left and was debating with himself about finding a job.

Joe had followed the trail another five miles and when it shifted more to the north, he decided to pick up the pace and head for Clay Center without bothering following the trail as the tracks were headed too far north for Wakefield. He set Duke to as fast a speed as he could safely move across the uneven turf knowing he had another two hours of daylight and estimated that he had another twenty miles to cover, so he decided to press on to Clay Center.

He arrived at Clay Center at just before nine o'clock and stopped at the livery first to take care of Duke. After Duke was in his stall and munching on a hefty portion of oats, Joe took his saddlebags and walked to the diner where he had his dinner before reaching the hotel before eleven o'clock, went to his room and was asleep by midnight.

At eight o'clock the next morning, Joe was walking into the city marshal's office, thinking that if Danny was in town, the city marshal would be more likely to know than the county sheriff.

"Mornin', what can I do for you?" asked the deputy marshal at the desk as Joe entered.

"My name is Joe Hennessey, I'm a deputy sheriff over at Lincoln and I'm looking for a man named Danny Stevens. I've got a wanted poster."

He pulled out Danny's poster and laid it across the deputy marshal's desk.

"I haven't seen him, but I think the marshal might have. He mentioned something about a blonde-haired guy that was looking really nervous."

"Can I talk to him?"

"Sure. Come on."

The deputy marshal led Joe back into the office and tapped on the door jamb of a large office.

"Marshal, this is Deputy Sheriff Joe Hennessey from Lincoln. He wants to know about that blonde-headed guy you were talking about."

"Send him in, Willy."

Willy nodded to Joe to enter the office then returned to his desk.

Joe stepped inside and the marshal stood to shake his hand.

"Have a seat, Deputy. What's your interest in this guy?"

"Would you believe it's to ask him where his sister is?"

The marshal had a good belly laugh and asked, "That's all?"

"That, and he's wanted for murder in Abilene."

"Now, that's a different story."

“I went to Abilene to ask about his sister and found he’d murdered a man and ran off. I tracked him to Clay Center.”

“You think he’s the blond guy that I noticed?”

“Could be. He’s on the run and probably got spooked when he saw your badge.”

“I haven’t seen him in a few days, though.”

“He’s either staying out of sight or took to the road again, but I’d imagine he’s gone. Are there any extra horses in the livery?”

“Never asked.”

“Well, I’ll go and find out. If he left his horse, he must have taken the train and maybe the ticket master remembers him. I’m going to act on the assumption that he’s quit Clay Center. If he shows up again, you know what you’ve got.”

“I appreciate the information. If you do catch up with him, include me on the list to notify. I’d like to know he’s gone.”

“I’ll do that.”

They shook hands again and Joe left the marshal’s office, crossed the outer office throwing a wave at the deputy marshal, then left the building and walked down to the livery.

‘Morning,” Joe shouted as he entered the large barn and spotted the liveryman at the back end of the barn.

He turned and asked, “Howdy. Come to get your horse?”

“Maybe. I’ve got a question, first. Did some blond-headed guy leave a horse here and didn’t come back for him yet?”

"You're darn right. That small roan out back in the corral. Paid for two days and it's been here over a week now."

"I don't think you'll be getting paid. I'm betting he took a train out of here. He's running from the law."

"Dang it! That horse ain't even worth that much."

"I'm going to mosey over to the train station and see if they remember him leaving."

"Old Bart might. He's real good when it comes to rememberin' faces and places," he said as he chuckled at his own poetic expertise.

"I'll probably be back in a little bit," Joe said before turning and leaving the livery.

He began walking to the train depot not far away, stepped up to the platform six minutes later and angled to the ticket window.

"Howdy, young feller. What'll you be needin'?" the ticket master asked.

"I'm not sure. Maybe you can help. I'm trying to run down a man about five feet and eight inches around twenty years old, blond headed. He should have come through here about a week ago."

Old Bart didn't take long at all to answer.

"I remember him. Real nervous feller. Bought a ticket to Manhattan. Do you need a ticket?"

"I think I'll ride. I get a lot more thinking done when I'm sitting on the horse."

"Tell the truth, I don't like riding trains much at all," he said as he grinned.

Joe smiled and said, "I appreciate the help," then turned and headed back to the livery.

Ten minutes later, he was leading Duke back toward the hotel. He checked out, slid his saddlebags across Duke's back and climbed aboard.

It was forty-two miles to Manhattan, and the road followed the tracks, so he figured he'd get there around four o'clock, if not sooner as he set Duke off at a medium trot.

He stopped for a break around noon, letting Duke water and graze while he munched on some jerky and apologized to his stomach and promised to make it up at dinnertime. He was back on the road after twenty minutes.

He reached Manhattan earlier than he had expected, getting in just after three o'clock, so maybe he was going faster than he had expected. He headed to the sheriff's office and stepped down.

Joe entered the office and approached the deputy at the desk who was reading a dime novel.

"Afternoon, Deputy. I just got in and I'm looking for a man who arrived here from Clay Center about a week ago."

The deputy put down his novel and looked at him and asked, "Are you law?"

"I'm a deputy sheriff out of Lincoln. I was looking for him for something else and found he'd killed a man in Abilene and took off. He's probably here somewhere."

"You got a wanted poster on him?"

Joe pulled the poster out of his pocket, unfolded it, and handed it to the deputy.

"I'm not sure, but I may have seen this feller. You might want to try over at Morrison's Boarding House on 2nd Avenue."

"I'm obliged. I hope things stay peaceful when I find him."

"Want someone to come along?"

"I might. I want to see how twitchy he is first, though."

"Good enough."

Joe left the office as his heart picked up its pace a bit. Danny was probably pretty close now. He stepped up on Duke and headed for 2nd Avenue which didn't take any special mathematic skills to find after he passed 1st Avenue. He saw Morrison's Boarding House easily as well, pulled up in front of the house and stepped down, tossed Duke's reins over the hitching rail and strode down the long walkway.

He had a real advantage over Danny because Danny had no idea who Joe was, yet the description he had was very accurate.

He walked to the door and went inside, not having to knock as it was a boarding house, removed his Stetson and looked around for the owner and didn't have to wait long.

"Hello. How can I help you?" asked a very attractive young woman.

She was obviously in charge somehow, but she wasn't even as old as Joe. The big blue eyes reminded him of Caroline, but the light brown hair negated that possibility.

"I just got into town and needed a place to stay for a couple of days."

"We have three rooms available and it'll cost three dollars a day."

"That's fine. I'll pay for two days," he said as he pulled the money out of his pocket and handed it to her.

She surely couldn't be the owner, so she must be a daughter of the owner.

"I'll show you to your room," she said as she smiled at him.

Joe followed her up the stairs, down the hallway before she stopped and opened the door to his room.

"Dinner will be at six o'clock. The dining room is on the right off the main hallway."

"Thank you, ma'am. I need to get my horse put up at the livery. I'll be back shortly."

She smiled and walked with Joe back down the stairs.

Joe glanced at her and asked, "You don't look old enough to be the owner, so can I guess you're the owner's daughter?"

"Sort of. They chose me from the children's train seven years ago."

Joe stopped walking and said, "I was selected ten years ago."

She halted as well, looked at him and asked, "Really?"

He smiled at her, and replied, “Yes, ma’am.”

“How was it for you?”

“I couldn’t have been luckier, and I was the last one chosen, too.”

She sighed and said, “I wish I could have been so lucky, but I’ll be eighteen next month and I’ll be able to get away from this.”

“If you don’t mind my asking, what’s your name?”

“Oh. I’m sorry. It’s Eva. Eva Porter.”

“I’m Joe Hennessey.”

“Pleased to meet you, Joe,” she said with a demure smile.

“Happy to meet you, Eva,” Joe said with his own, not-so-demure smile.

They continued to walk down the stairs and when they reached the floor, Eva said, “I’ve got to get back to start making dinner. I’ll see you later, Joe.”

“I’ll be looking forward to it, Eva.”

Joe watched her walk away, then she glanced back at him, smiled and blushed lightly, before he turned, stepped out of the boarding house and into the Kansas late afternoon sun.

For the first time, Joe had questions about his continued quest to find Caroline. He didn’t need to wonder why after talking to Eva, but it was a passing thought. He had promised Caroline and he never broke his promises.

He left Duke at the livery, slid his heavy saddlebags over his shoulder and walked back to the boarding house, opened the door and heard a heated argument taking place in the kitchen area. His curiosity drew him closer to be able to eavesdrop more successfully.

"...but you're supposed to give me a hundred dollars."

"What good would that do for you? You can't get any work around here. We'll pay you ten dollars a month, and you'd still have a room and food in your belly," said another woman's voice, but barely qualifying as a female voice.

"I want to leave. I'll be eighteen and I can, too."

"Well, you go right ahead, Eva. You go and leave. You'll be spreading your legs for a living if you do. There ain't no work out there for a decent woman. We ain't gonna put up with some ungrateful whelp that ain't even ours. We gave you a roof over your head for years, and this is how you repay us," the deep woman's voice continued.

"You've worked me to the bone since I've been here. I'll be leaving on the 5th of June as soon as I turn eighteen."

"You'll be back on the 6th of June when you find out what it's like out there," answered the woman with finality.

Joe turned and retreated to the main room and up the stairs. After reaching his room, he set his saddlebags on the bed and sat down. He needed to refocus on the task at hand. He needed to find Danny and then Caroline. What irritated him was that as much as he could wish that Eva would be able to strike out on her own, he knew the truth in what the woman was crudely telling her.

Single women had few options in what to do with their lives. Most just married and had children. A few became schoolmarms, but if they decided to marry, they'd have to leave the job. Waitress and store clerk and a few receptionist positions were pretty much all that was available to half the population.

The one job that many single women found themselves forced into was prostitution, and Joe actually felt a bit guilty. *How come he had so many options?* Then there was Jo's experience with a similar situation; guardians using her like hired help and refusing to pay her the money that they were obligated to give her at eighteen. He knew what had happened to Jo, and he hoped it didn't happen to Eva. He wished he could help Eva, but his promise came first. Maybe on the way back he could stop by and do what he could for her.

It was almost dinner time, so Joe prepared for the possible meeting with Danny, then blew out his breath and headed downstairs, leaving his gunbelt over the foot post of his bed. He found the dining room easily, walked in, and there, sitting on the opposite side of the table, his blond hair reflecting a shaft of late sunlight, was Danny Stevens.

He had grown up into quite a handsome young man. He was a little shorter than Joe, and a bit soft, which surprised Joe. He had been a millworker, which is not an easy job. Danny glanced at him but didn't pay him any attention as Joe took a seat opposite him. Danny's eyes were distracted by Eva, who was bringing dishes to the table. She noticed Joe and smiled at him.

"Hello, Eva," Joe said as he smiled.

"Hello, Joe. Is your horse taken care of?"

"Yep. Duke will be given some extra oats, too."

Danny removed his eyes from Eva and focused on Joe.

"You named your horse Duke?"

"Sure. If you saw him, you'd understand."

Danny stared at him more closely and asked, "Do I know you?"

"I don't think so. I'm not from around here."

"Just wondering."

As they ate, Danny kept sneaking looks at Joe. Joe just caught the glances out of his peripheral vision, but didn't think Danny recognized him, yet would be worried that Joe might be the law.

Finally, Danny spoke. "What's your name?"

Joe turned his head in his direction, "Mine?" acting as if it was directed to one of the other diners.

"Yeah, yours."

"Joe Hennessey. What's yours?"

"Harry. Harry Stevens."

Joe just nodded because there was no point in saying anything.

Eva brought another bowl of food and Joe smiled at her. She smiled back and had to return to the kitchen, having heard Danny's use of a fake name and wondered why. Danny had been paying a lot of attention to her since he arrived a week ago…too much attention. There was something about him that didn't seem right, but Joe was a whole different proposition. She had liked him the moment she saw his honest and quite handsome face.

Danny regained Joe's attention and asked, "Are you married?"

"Nope. You?"

"Why aren't you married?" Danny asked again, deflecting Joe's question.

"I had my chances. Just didn't find the right one."

"Picky, aren't you."

"I have to be. I'd hate to marry some girl and then find out a year later that I don't like her that much. People put on airs when they're looking to get hitched. They're not themselves. Then they get married and discover someone different in their beds. Suddenly, the romance is gone, and they're stuck with someone they don't like. Me? I want to marry my best friend."

The two married men at the table nodded their heads.

"Well, good luck with that," Danny replied.

They finished their dinner with little more conversation, but Joe did talk to the other diners. The subject of employment came up and Joe said he was just a ranch hand heading out to Junction City to work for his uncle.

Eva began collecting plates and dishes, had overheard Joe's comment about marriage and thought it was one of the wisest pieces of advice she'd ever heard. She vowed never to flirt or put on airs, failing to realize that she never had before as it wasn't in her nature. But she was more pleased with the question about whether or not he was married. *But an out of work cowhand?* It didn't matter. She liked Joe and liked him a lot. How much money he had wasn't important, especially as she had none.

Joe didn't want to let Danny out of his sight. He needed to get Danny arrested and in jail, so he could ask about Caroline. He guessed that Danny had a room near his, so he was the first up from the table, excused himself, smiled at Eva and walked down the hallway, quickly stepped up the stairway and into his room. He lifted the gunbelt from the bed and strapped it on, doing his quick verification of the loads in the weapon. It only takes a few seconds, but it was critical to make sure they were right.

He left his room door open and stood inside with his hammer loop off. He heard a single set of footsteps coming up the stairs, a man's step. He waited until the man passed his door, but it wasn't Danny. Several minutes went by, and there was still no sign of Danny. He began to wonder if Danny was going to make a break, maybe suspicious that the new boarder was a lawman.

He replaced his hammer loop and left his room, closing the door behind him, then walked down the stairs and out the front door before he scanned in both directions, but didn't see Danny. Joe knew he didn't have a horse, so he stepped off the porch then walked around the side of the house, looked in back and still found no evidence of Danny. *Where could he have gone?*

———

Danny was in the kitchen as Eva was cleaning the dishes and pots and pans, having another cup of coffee.

"Eva, it didn't mean anything. I was just nervous because he might be a lawman. I figured if I used my real name, he'd say I was wanted or something, just so he could get me out of the way. But if I said, Harry, and then if he said I was wanted, I'd be able to tell him it's not my real name. See?"

It rang hollow for Eva as she could see the lies in his pleading blue eyes.

"It doesn't matter, Danny. I'm not going to leave with you."

"Why not, Eva? We can go to Topeka or even Kansas City. Wouldn't you like that?"

"Danny, I've only known you for a few days. You could be married for all I know."

"Well, don't worry about it. I'm not married."

"Yes, you are, Danny," said the deep voice from behind him, "You left your wife and daughter in Abilene when you ran."

Danny whipped around as his eyes grew wide at the sight of Joe with a drawn and cocked Colt aimed at him, and he was wearing a badge.

A startled Danny exclaimed, "You're lying! I don't know what you made up, but it's all lies!"

"Danny, you were never a good liar. Even when you were ten."

Danny squinted his eyes, stared at Joe, then said, "You lied about your name. You're Joe Carlisle."

"No. I was Joe Carlisle until I was legally adopted nine years ago by my parents, Will and Clara Hennessey. Now, Danny, I'm going to have to arrest you for killing that man in Abilene. It sounds like it wasn't murder, so you won't hang. I'm guessing you'd only get twenty years for manslaughter. So, just come with me to the jail and face the music. It's better than a lifetime of running and trying to hide. Do your time and you'll still be a relatively young man and able to get on with your life."

Eva had been listening and was slowly backing away toward the door.

"Joe, you can't do this. We were friends on that train. You've got to let me go."

"No, Joe, I can't. It's because I'm your friend that I'm taking you in. The wanted poster said dead or alive. Danny, if you go out there with that blonde head of yours, it's only a matter of time before someone shoots you dead."

"You just want the reward, don't you?"

"No, I was planning on giving the reward to Eva. Don't you want to help Eva? I'd rather she gets the money and I leave with you still breathing. I don't want to have to kill you, Danny."

Danny licked his lip and then wiped it with the back of his hand. Joe could see his eyes searching furtively for an escape.

"Danny, don't do anything stupid. You can't run. The sheriff's office already knows you're here and they expect me to bring you in today. I'm telling you that the very worst that could happen is that you get twenty years. You get a good defense lawyer, and he could even get you off. He can say it was just a fight that got carried away. I've seen it happen. Danny, don't let your child to grow up without a father. Don't make him go through what we had to go through."

Danny sighed, knowing he had no chance, then said, "Alright, Joe. Let's go."

"That's smart, Danny. Things will work out."

Joe escorted Danny from the boarding house, uncocking and holstering his Colt as they walked.

"Joe, I'm sorry for all those things I said in the boarding house. I thought I could take Eva away and start a new life. I guess that was pretty stupid thinking."

"Yeah, it was. It wasn't you, Danny."

"Why did you come after me, Joe? Are you a deputy here?"

"No, I'm a deputy sheriff in Lincoln. My father is the sheriff. I came here because we were supposed to meet at the Salina station a few days ago and I was the only one to show."

"So, why didn't you just go home?"

"I had to find my sister and then I had a promise to keep that I made to your sister the last time I saw her."

"Joe, are you going to go and find Caroline?"

"That's the reason I even came this way."

"She was staying at a ranch outside of Chapman the last time I knew. It was the Crown D. I don't know much else. She only wrote me once. I think the folks that chose her ripped up her letters and mine. I think she had it bad, Joe."

"Remember my sister, Josephine? Her guardians made her a housemaid, cook and laundress. Then when she turned eighteen, they sold her to some mean bastard who owned this rundown ranch outside of Salina. He beat her something fierce. She didn't get much to eat and only had the one dress she wore when she was taken away."

"Did you get her out of there?"

"I did."

"Did you kill the bastard?"

"Nope. I did worse, Danny. He was a big son of a bitch, but I beat him up pretty bad and then I destroyed his right knee with a hard kick. I left him crying on the floor of his ranch, then told the sheriff about it, and he said they might forget to send the doctor out there for a few days."

"That was the right thing to do, I think," he said as he grinned.

"It gets better. After we visited the sheriff's office, I took Josephine to the bank where her guardian father worked as a vice president. We walked into his office and I basically blackmailed him, telling him it would all come out in the press. How he had violated the terms of the contract, sold Josephine to this man, and hoped he would kill her. He was close to peeing his pants and offered a financial settlement to Jo. She took it and I sent her to live with my parents."

"How much did you get out of him?"

"Twenty thousand dollars."

Danny stopped, looked wide-eyed at Joe and asked, *"Did you say $20,000?"*

"Yup. I probably could have pushed him for more, but Jo and I wanted to get away from the bastard. The sheriff knew what I was going to do and approved. He said that the rumors would start as soon as Jo had her money anyway."

Danny snickered and started walking again.

"What does Josephine look like, Joe?"

"She was thinner than she'll be the next time I see her, I think. But she was still a beautiful young woman. I don't know how she dealt with the problems without turning into a mean shrew or a frightened barn mouse, but she didn't. She was still the same Jo who I grew up with."

"That's good to hear. Joe. If I go to prison, can you, Josephine and Caroline come and visit? I'd like to see them both again."

"Did you want your wife and baby to visit, too?"

"I need to apologize to her, Joe. I should've taken my medicine then. She's a good woman. We have a little boy named David. And, Joe, don't tell her about what I tried to do with Eva."

"I won't tell her about Eva, but you tell her about the rest. If she's a good woman, she'll forgive you."

They reached the jail and Joe opened the door for Danny. The deputy at the desk was the same one he had talked to earlier.

"Evening, Deputy. I brought Danny Stevens in. He came voluntarily."

"That's good. I'll process him in a minute. There's a two-hundred-dollar reward on him, so if you leave me your information and I'll have it sent to you."

"Have it made out to Eva Porter at the boarding house. She's the one who cornered him. I just had him come along."

"I'll do that," he answered as he wrote down the information.

Joe looked at Danny and offered his hand. Danny shook his hand and then sat at the chair next to the desk.

Joe left out of the jail and walked back to the boarding house, opened the door and wasn't surprised to find Eva standing in the sitting room.

"Joe, can I talk to you for a minute?" she asked.

"Sure."

After they sat, Joe asked, "What would you like to talk about, Eva?"

"What just happened, Joe?"

"Danny and I were the last four on our train to get selected. We each had a sister. I was eleven, Danny was ten and my sister, Josephine, and his sister, Caroline were both nine. As we were rolling into Junction City, we made an agreement to meet at the Salina train station in ten years, but I was the only one to show up.

"I found my sister, and she was in a horrible situation. I got her out of it and sent her to my parents in Lincoln, but I needed to find Danny to know where Caroline was. It was important because I had promised her that I'd find her in ten years if she didn't make it to the reunion. I discovered in Abilene that Danny had run after killing a man. He had hit the man with a chair, and he fell to his death. I followed him here and you heard the rest."

"Why are you working so hard to find Caroline? She may not even remember you."

"That's true, but I made the promise, and like my father always says, fail to keep one promise and all the rest will be worthless."

"What will you do when you find her?"

"It depends on the situation she's in. If she's happily married or doing something she enjoys, I'll say hello and tell her what happened to Danny. Danny told me he wants to see her if he goes to prison."

"Does he want to see his wife and baby?"

"He does. He just told me that he has a son named David."

Eva then surprised him when she asked, "Are you going to marry Caroline when you find her?"

"That's an interesting question. You know, since I was eleven, I've always thought about Caroline. Over the years, she's become more than human, she's become an image. It's hard for any person to live up to an image, and then there's the change. People change a lot in ten years, especially early on.

"When I was that age, I was angry all the time for what had happened to me and my sister. Now, I rarely get angry. The exception was when I discovered what had happened to my sister and I beat that man so badly that he'll never walk again. I did it without any regret. It's the only thing that really makes me angry anymore, seeing innocent people hurt."

"How do you know who's truly innocent?"

"You can tell. My father taught me how to read people. I know, for instance, that you are an innocent. You're an honest person with a good heart. You'd probably give away your last bit of food to someone who had less. I find you very easy to read, Eva. And what I read is all good."

Eva blushed. She wasn't used to compliments, especially from someone like Joe.

"Why did you say you'd give me the reward?"

"It's only two hundred dollars, but you'll need it next month when you turn eighteen. If you want me to, I can convince the Morrisons to give you the hundred that's owed you as well."

"I think they'll probably give it to me, but the extra two hundred dollars will make it easier to get by for a while on my own. It doesn't answer the question. Why did you give it to me?"

"Because you're getting the short straw, Eva. You're a single woman without a family to support you. Your skills are limited to domestic chores, because that's how they used you. What Mrs. Morrison said to you earlier was cruel, but true. There aren't a lot of things women are allowed to do on their own. Speaking of the Morrisons, where are they? I've never even seen them. I've only heard the man-like voice of Mrs. Morrison."

"Oh. They stay in their small house behind the boarding house. They only come over here once or twice a day to check on me. Usually together."

"They don't do anything at all?" Joe asked incredulously.

"They keep the books. That's all."

Joe shook his head and said, "You have to take care of everything here without any help, so I'm afraid to ask. Do they pay you anything?"

Eva laughed and replied, "I'm surprised they don't keep a running tab for me and when I turn eighteen, they'll tell me that I owe them."

"Eva, what are you going to do? You'll be eighteen in, what, a week?"

"I don't know. I could be a housemaid, but there aren't a lot of wealthy people here. At least now, I'll have at least the two hundred dollars to get away."

"If you need anything, anything at all, send a letter to the sheriff's office in Lincoln, or a telegram if you're really in trouble. My father will know where I am. Just tell him that I wanted you to find me. Whatever you do, don't let yourself get depressed or hopeless. Okay?"

She smiled and replied, "I will, Joe. Thank you so much for the money and the advice."

"I didn't give you any advice."

"Yes, you did. When you were explaining to Danny why you never married. It's so true, isn't it? People put on their best faces while they're courting and it's hard to do for a long time. I'll never be that way, Joe."

"Eva, you impress me as someone who never could be that way in the first place."

Eva blushed lightly again, but asked softly, "So, does this all mean that you'll be leaving tomorrow?"

"I think so. I'll make a point of stopping back before I return to Lincoln, though. Hopefully, that will only be in a few days."

"I'd like that, Joe."

Joe's mind was churning. Eva was a delightful young woman, pretty, well-figured, and honest, and he was already powerfully drawn to her. He could talk to her, and now wanted to do that almost desperately.

"Eva, can you stay and talk for a while?"

"That would be enjoyable, Joe."

So, they talked. They talked for almost three hours as Joe told her about his parents in Lincoln, and she told him of how she had lived in Baltimore until her parents decided one of the children had to go and had chosen her because she was the youngest.

She asked about his adventures and gunfights, and he told her about Josephine. They spent those three hours learning more about each other than people who had spent years together. There were no facades nor embellishments meant to impress. It was a hundred and eighty minutes of honest conversation and, at the end, a joining of minds and hearts, although no words of affection were passed between them.

But Joe had to be leaving in the morning and it was getting late. Eva knew it as well.

"I'd love to spend more time with you, Eva, but I need to get going early tomorrow. I'll be heading up to my room now. You take care and remember how to get a hold of me. I'll see you in a few days."

"Aren't you going to have breakfast?"

"It depends on the time I get up. I've only got about twenty-five miles to get to Chapman tomorrow, but if I get there soon enough, I may be able to find Caroline and come back the next day."

"If I see you, I'll make something to take with you on your trip."

"Thank you, Eva," he said as he stood and smiled at her.

He felt himself weakening in his resolve as she gleamed a smile back at him with her blue eyes dancing.

They shared a few more seconds of eye conversation before Joe regretfully knew he had to turn away.

Joe smiled once more at Eva, and after she smiled back, he turned, then climbed the stairs, returned to his room, removed his gunbelt and then his boots. He walked down to the washroom and cleaned up, brushed his teeth and went back to his room. He stripped down and slid under the quilt, even though it was barely nine o'clock. He was just plain tired.

When he slept, he dreamt of finding Caroline, but in his dream, Caroline looked like Eva. It was a very pleasant dream.

Eva had no other faces to fill her fantasies other than Joe's as she lay on her bed and secretly hoped that Caroline was married and had six children already.

When Joe woke early the next morning, there was the barest hint of sunlight creeping through the window. He remembered the dream and wished he could go back to sleep and let it continue, but he knew it didn't work that way. If he closed his eyes and drifted off again, he'd probably have some nightmare involving snakes. He hated snakes.

So, Joe stood, stretched and dressed, belted on his Colt and put on his Stetson. After a quick visit to the washroom, he walked as quietly as he could down the stairs and was just going to go out the front door when he heard Eva whisper loudly, "Joe?"

He turned and saw her in the hallway wearing the same dress she had worn when he had arrived. Joe walked on his toes toward her.

“I thought you were going to stop in the kitchen to see me?”

“I figured you’d still be asleep, Eva.”

She smiled and said, “I get up at five o’clock every day, Joe.”

“Have you ever had a day off, Eva?”

“Not in the last seven years. Come to the kitchen.”

She turned, and Joe followed. His eyes naturally followed her movements as she walked before him and recalled his dream and the reality of Eva compared favorably.

They reached the kitchen and Eva made him sit down. She had already sliced some ham and had the frypan ready as she poured him a cup of coffee and turned to cook his eggs and ham.

Joe stood and took one step to the shelf and took a second cup and plate and put them on the table, then placed the silverware beside the plate. She hadn’t noticed as she made his breakfast.

When she had cooked his food, she turned and saw the extra place setting.

“I’m not eating alone, Eva. Now, you sit down, and I’ll serve you.”

“But this is my job, Joe.”

“Not right now. Sit down.”

She sat as Joe poured coffee into her cup and added more ham to the frypan. After flipping it, he cracked open three eggs, then took her plate, slid the ham onto it and then quickly fried the eggs. After they were added to the plate, he placed it in front of her.

"Now, Miss Porter, we can eat breakfast properly."

"Thank you, Joe. This is really a nice way to begin a day."

"Eva, if you've worked every day since you arrived, didn't they ever let you go to school?"

"No. I reached the fifth grade when I left Baltimore, but that's as far as I went."

Joe didn't have an answer for that as they both ate their ham and eggs. When they had finished, they sat and sipped their coffee, looking at each other.

"When you get the reward, Eva. You should hide it from the Morrisons."

"I had every intention of doing that. It would be gone in a flash if they knew about it."

"If they do anything like that, I'll take care of it when I return. Alright?"

"I know you will, Joe. Take this with you. I made it, so you could have lunch," she said handed him a paper bag.

"Thank you, Eva. That was very thoughtful."

Joe and Eva stood as Joe prepared to leave. Joe really wanted to kiss her but thought it would be presumptuous.

Eva really wanted him to kiss her but was concerned he'd think she was being too forward.

So, he just smiled at her which she returned. Joe really had to fight the urge to give her a hug, so he pivoted and walked normally down the hallway, his boot heels making loud thumps as he walked away.

Eva had a sinking feeling that he'd never return. *Why should he?* Chapman was twenty-five miles to the west. *Why should he come back in this direction when his home was in the other?* But he said he'd be back. She remembered how they had talked and how their eyes had met.

But then there was Caroline. His first girlfriend. She was probably prettier, and she was already nineteen. She probably had a better figure, too. Eva went from being sure of Joe's return to being not quite so sure, to being convinced he'd go off with Caroline as she began to set the table for the guests.

Joe made it outside successfully, fighting the temptation to return. He took a few minutes to walk the three blocks to the livery.

When he arrived, he found, as with most liverymen, he was up early.

"Gettin' ready to head out?" he asked.

"Yup. Heading west to Chapman."

"I grew up there. Made the move to the big city four years ago. Where you headed?"

“I need to see someone at the Crown D ranch. Ever hear of it?”

“Yup. Just south of town, maybe four miles. Good-sized spread, nine sections. Run over a thousand head of cattle. Last I knew, they had four full time hands and seasonal hands when they needed ‘em.”

“What do you know about the Drapers?”

“Husband and wife. Never had no kids. They must be around forty-five or so now. Seemed decent enough, but never knew ‘em all that well. Stuck to themselves mostly.”

“I appreciate the information.”

He saddled Duke and put his saddlebags in place and lashed them down. He climbed into the saddle and headed west.

CHAPTER 4

He set Duke at a reasonable fast pace, hoping to make Chapman and the Crown D by noon. His thoughts drifted between Eva and Caroline, with an occasional thought of Danny. Every once and a while, he'd think of Josephine and wondered how she was making out with his parents.

He tried to keep his attention on the road and his surroundings but kept drifting. It was never a good idea to drift on the open road.

He was almost halfway to Chapman when his woolgathering almost cost him his life. The morning sun was at his back, making his dark gray vest heat up like a cook stove, so he had to take it off or roast alive. He stopped Duke suddenly to remove the vest when the unmistakable sound of a Winchester rolled across the prairie. Joe heard the bullet buzz past in front of him and didn't think as he and Duke shot off quickly. Joe was looking to his left for the source of the shot and found it easily from the cloud of smoke rising from a gully about fifty yards to his left. No one was in sight, though. He must've ducked down after taking the shot. His next concern was numbers. It was unlikely there was only one highwayman. These guys usually operated in pairs.

Sure enough, a second rifle blasted from his right a few seconds later. But Joe was hunkered down, and Duke was flying. The second bullet struck his lower back, but it didn't hit skin. It had glanced off his spare .44 cartridges on his gunbelt. Even with the heat on his back, his spine chilled at the thought of the cartridges going off.

He rode another quarter of a mile and slowed Duke, then turned him left and stepped the tall gelding into the same gully that the first bushwhacker had used. He dismounted, dropped his Stetson to the ground and grabbed both the Winchester and the shotgun.

Joe scrambled to the top edge of the gully and looked back to the east, hoping they had given up on their prey, but they hadn't. He watched as the first shooter scrambled out of the same gully he was in, leading his horse while the second shooter trotted his horse to the roadway. They stayed motionless and must have been talking as one or the other would occasionally point in his direction.

Joe knew that they had seen him go into the gully but wasn't sure what their plan was. He let go of the shotgun and let it slide along the face of the gully and cocked the Winchester.

The two men spread out about thirty feet apart, dismounted and dropped their horses' reins and advanced quickly, their Winchesters ready. Joe watched and just waited, still trying to understand their strategy, if they had one.

This didn't make any sense to him as he watched them jog straight at him, keeping the same thirty-foot spread, and he began to think that there might be a third man still in the gully that would soon flank him, so he began tossing an occasional glance down the gully between watching the two oncoming outlaws.

When they got about a hundred and twenty yards out, just past the effective range of their Winchesters, they opened fire. Joe was stunned when the rounds impacted with a lot of power just a few feet to his left and right. *Where did they get the extra range?* They were using Winchester '73s, so they must be using hot loads, which is why they probably felt safe standing out there.

He knew that if he stuck his body out to take a shot, he'd be hit, so he needed an edge. They were walking closer and continuing to fire to keep him down, the edge of the gully being chopped away by the repeated rifle fire.

Suddenly, when the ground just in front of him exploded in dust and debris, Joe threw up his arms and the Winchester flew from his hands as he slid down the embankment.

The two men broke into a sprint toward the gully, their Winchesters still at the ready, but their firing stopped.

Joe had slipped to the bottom of the gully and quickly grabbed and cocked the shotgun. This was going to be close and could be a serious mistake. He lay flat on the bottom of the gully, hoping that the spread on the two barrels would be wide enough. If they were still thirty feet apart, he could only take one and then he'd have to use his Colt on the other man armed with his Winchester, which would put him in a bad situation.

He waited and heard them coming closer.

The two men had angled closer, coming to the point where they had seen Joe fall back. It was a fatal error.

The two men's heads popped over the edge of the gully expecting to see a wounded victim as Joe pulled the trigger. Both men were thrown back by the blast of dozens of #5 buckshot pellets at only twenty feet, and Joe scrambled to his feet, dropped the shotgun, grabbed his pistol and clawed up the side of the gully.

When he reached the top, he found one man obviously dead, his face having caught a healthy amount of the pellets. The second was groaning on the ground and rolling back and forth on his back with his hands over his face as blood poured between his fingers. Joe walked up to him and pulled his

Winchester away from his side then unbuckled his gunbelt and tossed it near his rifle.

Joe walked up to the man. In addition to his hand-covered face wounds, and it looked like two of the pellets had penetrated his left upper chest and Joe knew he wouldn't last long.

"What's your name, mister? I'll see that you get a decent burial."

All the man uttered was a weak, "Mama…", then he died.

Joe pulled the gunbelt from the other man and put all four weapons in a pile. He went through their pockets and found $27.16 between the two, but no identifying material. He pulled off their hats and looked at the inside of the rim. One had written Jim Anderson and the other had scrawled what looked like a drawing of a snake. After holstering his pistol, he walked back to the gully, slid down the bank, picked up the shotgun and Winchester, then walked back to his horse, stuck both of his long guns in their scabbards, then mounted Duke. He had to ride down another quarter mile to find a shallow enough point to allow Duke to climb out.

Joe returned to the two dead men's horses and stepped down. He went through their saddlebags, finding not much useful except two boxes of .44 cartridges. Both had XX marked across the box, so they must be the hot loads they were using. Using hot loads would reduce the life span of those Winchesters, and it sure reduced their life spans today.

He trail-roped the two horses and led them to the bodies. Joe got both men on the horses and slid the Winchesters into the scabbards and put the gunbelts into their saddlebags, then returned to the road and didn't get to Chapman until after noon, irritated by the delay.

He led the horses and bodies through the main street of Chapman, drawing more than a passing interest from the townsfolk, pulled up to the sheriff's office and stepped down. He didn't even bother tossing Duke's reins over the hitching post. He'd stay.

Joe walked inside finding the sheriff at the desk and guessed that he didn't have a deputy. The town fathers must be tight with the purse strings.

"Sheriff? I've got a couple of bodies outside. They tried to bushwhack me about ten miles out of town. I took off and hid in a gully and they tried to come at me, but I got them both with a shotgun."

The sheriff sighed and followed Joe outside.

"You know who these men are?" he asked looking at the bodies.

"The only thing I found was the one on the left had Jim Anderson written on the inside of his hat and the other one had a drawing of what looked like a snake."

The sheriff's head snapped up before he said, "Jim Anderson and Snake Jones. I'll be damned. Never would have believed they'd make it this far east."

"Who are they? I never saw them in any of the wanted posters. I never even heard their names."

"You a lawman?"

Joe showed his badge and said, "Joe Hennessey, deputy sheriff in Lincoln."

"You're Will Hennessey's boy?"

"Yes, sir. And proud of it."

"Damned straight you oughta be. He's one of the best men I know. If this pans out that you're right, you've got a hefty reward headed your way, I reckon. I have no idea how much. These two operated in Colorado for years. Pretty much doing what almost happened to you. Sometimes they'd take on a small bank or something. Killed about ten men last time I knew. I'll send a few telegrams and find out. I'll have any rewards sent to you in Lincoln. You headed back that way?"

"No, sir. I need to ride down to the Crown D and find an old friend named Caroline Stevens. The Drapers claimed her off the same train that took me to find my father and mother in Lincoln."

"Well, son, I'd say you got the better deal. Henry and Nancy Draper don't cotton too much to company. They send a hand in once a month for supplies. Didn't always used to be that way. Just the last couple of years."

"I aim to grab some lunch and ride down there and see if I can talk to her. We were supposed to meet in Salina a few days ago, but she didn't show. I promised her ten years ago that I'd find her."

"Well, Deputy Hennessey, I'll take care of these two. About time I got off my butt anyway. Things have been quiet around here lately."

"Then I'd better head out soon. Trouble seems to be following me around this trip."

They shook hands, and Joe walked Duke down to the café. He'd need to check on his Winchester in more detail when he got the chance. Tossing a rifle to the dirt like he had done in the gully wasn't a kind thing to do to a weapon.

Forty minutes later, his stomach filled, he was heading south to the Crown D ranch.

He spotted the outfit and decided that the liveryman was right. It looked like a pretty good-sized spread. He turned onto the access road, walked Duke toward the ranch house and had his badge displayed this time. It didn't mean much as far as jurisdiction, but it might help to loosen a few tongues if Caroline wasn't there.

He stopped short of the ranch house and sat before shouting, "Hello the house!"

About a minute later the door opened and a middle-aged woman, her hair already showing streaks of gray stood at the door. A cute blonde little girl that Joe guessed was about two years old was standing behind her skirt, peeking out at him and he couldn't help but smile. Joe assumed it was a granddaughter.

"What do you want, Deputy?" she asked.

"Good afternoon, ma'am. Are you Mrs. Draper?"

"I am. What can I do for you?"

"I'm here looking for Caroline Stevens. You and your husband chose her ten years ago from the child train."

Joe saw her face register a mix of shock and anger, before she snapped, "She doesn't live here anymore. Took off with one of our seasonal hands a year and a half ago."

"Do you know where they went?"

"No. It isn't any use going to find her, either. She's probably dead by now. The man she run off with was a no-account. We were glad to get rid of him."

"Do you remember his name?"

"Can't say that I do."

"Mind if I ask your foreman?"

Nancy Draper had to think about it for a second. He would probably go and talk to him anyway.

"Go ahead if you can find him out there."

"Thank you, Mrs. Draper."

Joe turned Duke's head to the right and set out across the pastures. He'd talk to any cowhand he could find, but the woman's sudden shift in demeanor after he'd mentioned Caroline's name had created suspicions in his mind and doubts about her story of Caroline riding off with a cowhand whose name she couldn't even remember.

Back at the ranch house, Nancy Draper went looking for her husband. This could be trouble.

It took Joe almost twenty minutes to find the herd and some hands. There were five of them working one group of cows.

They saw Joe coming and one pulled back out of the group and rode toward him. Joe slowed as he approached.

"Howdy, what can I do for you, Deputy?"

"Afternoon. The name's Joe Hennessey. I'm a deputy sheriff in Lincoln. I just talked to the missus and she said I should ask you about the cowpoke that Caroline Stevens ran off with."

Jason Arbuckle pushed his Stetson back on his head before replying, "Jason Arbuckle, Joe. To be honest, I'm not sure ran off would be the right way to put it. More like taken away, if you ask me. And it wasn't a cowhand."

"I need you to understand that I'm not doing any real law work here. I came out here on the same children's train as Caroline, her brother and my sister. I promised her that I'd come back and find her in ten years if she didn't make it to the rendezvous we agreed to back then, so I'm trying to locate her."

The foreman looked around at the other men, ensuring that they were all far enough away.

"Now, this is all just rumor, understand? I can't prove a thing. Caroline was brought in as a helper to Mrs. Draper. That was before I got here. She was a real nice gal, about fourteen when I arrived. She stayed mostly in the house anyway, but we didn't see her for a while. Then, Mrs. Draper had her baby. But she and her husband had been married for eighteen years and didn't have any kids. The rumor was it was Caroline's baby.

"She must have had a frolic with one of the hands or someone, but nobody confessed to it, although, to be honest, not one of us would mind. She was one handsome filly. Now, after the baby was about six months old, this unsavory gent shows up and takes her off. His name was Phil Hostetler. From what I heard, from other ranches, he took her to Alta Vista. That's all I can tell you."

"That's good enough. I really appreciate your honesty."

"We all felt really bad by not being able to help her. We were all sent to the far end of the ranch to repair some fence when it happened."

"I'll see if I can make it right, Jason."

"Good luck, Joe."

Joe wheeled Duke and started across the pastures back toward the access road. Alta Vista was only about fifteen miles southeast of Chapman, and he was already five miles or so in that direction, so he thought that he may as well head that way.

He felt skittish as he went past the ranch house. He should have spotted it right away. The blonde head and blue eyes on that little girl almost screamed, "Caroline!"

The instant he heard the foreman repeat what he considered to be a rumor he knew it was true. He had seen Caroline's little girl.

He trotted Duke up to the trough and let him drink. He had been cropping grass while he and the foreman had been talking, so he'd be all right for another couple of hours. While Duke was drinking, he transferred his badge to his shirt. Duke finished drinking and Joe headed him down the access road, reached the road and turned left toward Alta Vista.

It was a little past three o'clock when he arrived at the town. Alta Vista was about the same size as Chapman, just not as prosperous. He looked for the sheriff's office and couldn't find it, figuring that they must not have any lawmen at all. It was borderline needing two, but he couldn't find a jail, so he headed for the dry goods store, stepped down and walked inside and caught the eye of the proprietor.

He smiled at Joe and asked, "Howdy there, young feller. What can I do for you?"

Joe smiled back and asked, "You wouldn't know a man by the name of Phil Hostetler, would you?"

The proprietor's friendly demeanor faded quickly as he asked, "You a friend of his?"

"Hardly," Joe said as he flashed his badge.

The proprietor's attitude shifted again as he asked, "What did that no account do now?"

"I'm not sure. I'm looking for a blonde young woman that he brought here named Caroline."

"You must mean Carol. She's one of his working girls down at the Happy House Saloon."

Joe's stomach dropped as he said, "I was afraid of that. Does he own the place?"

"No, it's owned by another plague on humanity named Russ Edwards. Phil acts as his recruiter and his enforcer. He keeps the girls in line and finds new ones when they die off."

"You don't have any law in town?"

"Nope. Every time we try to hire one, the bar owners vote it down."

"How many saloons to you have?"

"Three. The Happy House is the biggest and the only one running working girls."

"I guess I'll be paying a visit to the Happy House."

"Watch out for the barkeeper. He keeps a sawed-off shotgun beneath the bar. Known to use it on occasion, too."

"Anything else that can give me trouble?"

"Deputy, everything in this town can give you trouble on that side of the street."

"What do you have in firearms that could help?"

"A shotgun isn't going to do you any good. They'd see it coming. How about a Webley Bulldog?"

"If you have a shoulder holster for it, you've got an interested buyer."

The proprietor pulled out a boxed Webley and slid it across the counter, then walked to the back of the shop and brought back a shoulder holster for the pistol.

Joe slid off his vest and put on the shoulder holster and adjusted it to his chest size, pulled out the Bulldog from the box and felt the hammer and trigger action. It was a bit stiff, but that would change with use. He added a box of .44 cartridges and paid for the order. He loaded the Webley, filling all five cylinders, then placed it into the shoulder holster and put his vest back on.

"Can you see anything that looks like I'm armed?" Joe asked turning.

"Nope. Can't see a thing."

"I hope it doesn't come to gunplay, but I'm not holding my breath, either."

He left the store, mounted Duke then walked him to the livery on the same side of the street, which was seemingly some form of unintended urban design in Alta Vista; saloons on one side and normal businesses on the other. He stepped down and walked Duke inside. He paid for extra oats and let the liveryman handle stripping him down and brushing him.

For the first time in a long time, Joe felt like he was in over his head. Everything was unknown, and he had no one to cover his back. He wasn't even sure of the Bulldog's accuracy. The short barrel probably meant he couldn't count on it past thirty feet. Coincidentally, it was the size of most bars, and wondered if that was intentional, but its double action might come in handy, too.

He walked across the street to the bad side, stepped up to the boardwalk and headed for the Happy House. It was after four now, so some working girls might be out. He stepped through the batwing doors and found that some girls were working the uncrowded room. There were two of them, and one was a blonde, but her back was to him. She had a nice shape, though, but he had no idea how old she was, but after listening to the storekeeper, none lasted too long.

He stepped up to the bar and glanced at the man in front of the line of bottles. He looked plain ornery, and unlike most men of his profession he wasn't fat. He was tall and thin with a hawkish face and long thin nose and his eyes were like a bird of prey, black and watching.

"Beer," Joe said, tossing a nickel on the bar. The bartender looked him over once, then filled a glass, slid it to Joe and took the nickel.

Joe walked to the side of the room that the blonde was working, sat down and waited. He took a sip of the beer finding it not as bad as he expected. He could see the blonde approaching him out of the corner of his eye.

"Well, hello," she said in a sultry voice.

Joe looked up at her smiling face and knew that if she wasn't Caroline, he couldn't imagine who else she'd look like.

"Howdy, ma'am. Won't you have a seat?" he said in his best cowhand voice.

"Why, thank you," she said as she smiled and sat down.

"What'll you have, ma'am?"

"I'll have a whiskey, if that's all right."

Joe held up a finger and the bartender arrived with the glass of tea and Joe handed him a quarter.

"I'm Carol. What's your name?" she asked as she smiled softly.

"Joe," he answered.

Carol didn't have a big reaction, just a slight twitch.

"Well, Joe, are you in town very long?"

"I don't reckon so."

"I can make your time memorable, if you'd like."

"And how much will this memorable time cost me?"

"Two dollars. You look like a man who could afford that."

"I'm sure you're worth every penny, Carol."

"Just leave the two dollars on the table and follow me."

Joe pulled out the money and left it next to his almost full beer.

Carol took his hand and led him up the stairs. As she did, Joe was looking for other ways out. When they reached the hallway, he was disappointed to see that there was no door at the end, so there were outside stairs leaving only way out was through the bar.

She reached her room and opened the door. Joe stepped inside, and she closed the door behind her and stepped up to him and kissed him passionately, curling her toes, which shocked her because it had never happened before.

When they separated, she smiled at him and began to run her hands across him.

That stopped when Joe said quietly, “Caroline.”

Caroline stepped back, a look of disbelief on her face.

“What did you call me?”

“Caroline. I promised you ten years ago that I would come and find you and now I have.”

“Joe?” she asked wide-eyed.

“Yes, Caroline. Your boyfriend when you were nine.”

She suddenly rushed Joe and clutched onto him, her tears running down her face in torrents. Joe held her and let the tears flow. *How could the sweet girl he knew be forced into a life like this?* This made Eva’s situation look like heaven on earth but had to admit that Josephine’s was probably worse.

He continued to hold her as she sobbed and was ashamed to admit that having so much female skin against him was having an impact. This wasn’t the time.

“Caroline, I want to get you out of here. How can we get out?”

Caroline held on but whispered, "I can't get out, Joe. I just can't. They'll never let me go. Jack is downstairs with his shotgun, and Phil will be in the bar in a little while and Russ will be in his office. It's impossible. Just go and leave me."

"I'll never do that, Caroline. I promised you I'd find you. Now, what kind of a boyfriend would do that to his sweetheart?"

She sniffed loudly then laughed quietly before asking, "You're serious, aren't you?"

"About this I am. How much time before they expect you back downstairs?"

"About twenty minutes or so. They'll come and pound on the door in a half an hour."

"Alright. Here's what I'm going to do. I'm going to go downstairs in ten minutes. You'd probably take a few minutes to get dressed anyway, so after five more minutes, you come downstairs. Now, I'll be gone, but I'm going to go down to the livery and saddle my horse really quickly.

"When you come down, act like you're working the room and drift toward the doors. I'll ride close to the front of the bar. I'll pull my Winchester and put a few rounds through the ceiling. They'll all duck. The moment they hit the floor, you run out the door and I'll scoop you up and we'll ride out of here as fast as we can. All we need is a couple of miles. Will that work?"

"I think so. I don't know if they'll send anyone after me."

"If they do, I'll be ready."

"I pray that this works, Joe. Just like I've prayed every night that you'd remember your promise."

“How could I not, Caroline. You were my girlfriend.”

She smiled then they sat down on her bed.

“Joe, what do you do now?” she asked as she tried to fix her makeup.

Joe flashed his badge.

“You’re a sheriff?”

“No, a deputy sheriff in Lincoln. It’s where you’ll be going when we’re out of here.”

She looked down and said, “Joe, there’s so much you don’t know about me. That might not be for the best. I can go and stay with Danny, if he’ll let me.”

“On my way here, I had to arrest Danny for killing a man in a fight. It wasn’t murder, so I don’t know how it will turn out. He’ll probably go to trial soon, though.”

“You arrested him?”

“I had to. He had a ‘dead or alive’ wanted poster on him. I wanted to make sure he came out of it alive. He came along peacefully.”

“But there are other things, Joe.”

“You mean your little girl, Caroline?”

Caroline’s head snapped up as she asked, “You saw her?”

“I did. She one of the cutest little girls I’ve ever seen. Probably because she looks just like you.”

"I'll tell you about her when we get out of here, Joe. It'll take a while. I think it's time."

"Alright. Be strong, Caroline. This will take some nerve."

"I've got that, Joe."

Joe gently ran his fingers across her cheek, walked out the door, closing it behind him, then trotted down the stairs, smiling at the bartender as he did. He walked quickly, but not too quickly across the saloon and out the doors. Once outside, he picked up the pace as he trotted down to the livery to get Duke ready to go. The liveryman was surprised to see him but helped him get Duke saddled.

Caroline was nervous, but after waiting for five minutes, she left her room after checking herself in the mirror, then took her time going down the stairs as she usually did, smiling as she was accustomed to doing after a customer left.

The bartender watched her come down the stairs and returned to polishing glassware. As her foot hit the barroom floor, she noticed that Phil Hostetler had arrived and was sitting in his dedicated table near the short hallway leading to Russ Edwards' office.

There were four more new arrivals in the saloon, which should make her movement seem more natural, so she walked slowly toward two men seated at the table one away from the batwing doors. One was a regular customer and he smiled when he saw Caroline approach.

Joe was up on Duke and took the precaution of taking ten more .45 cartridges for the Winchester from the box and putting them in his vest pockets. You never have too many rounds. He started Duke at a walk toward the Happy House and cocked the hammer on the Winchester. He was counting on Duke's proven steadiness as he reached the saloon and glanced at his surroundings. There were people in the street, and two of them looking like potential saloon customers as they headed for the doors.

Joe suddenly whipped the Winchester toward the saloon and fired. The powerful .45 caliber round ripping through the upper part of the casing of the big window out front. He levered in another round and fired again. The men in the street hit the dirt.

Caroline watched everyone in the barroom drop to the floor, the immediately lifted her voluminous skirts and ran, smashed through the batwing doors and saw Joe sitting on a big horse, his right arm out to help her mount. She flew across the boardwalk and grabbed his arm. *Propriety be damned!*

She lifted her left leg and flopped across Duke's hind quarters, and had barely wrapped her arms around Joe before Duke shot away from the saloon, raising a cloud of dust behind him.

The men in the street heard the hooves coming and covered their heads, as if it would stop an iron clad hoof from crushing through their hands.

It must have been an odd sight for the few who witnessed it. Riding off into the sunset, as it were, a man and a whore with her dress flying above the horse's tail.

They left Alta Vista in just thirty seconds as Caroline kept glancing behind her. She had told Joe that they wouldn't chase after her but was no longer sure that was the case. She may be a whore, but she was their best money-maker.

Back at the Happy House, Phil Hostetler and Russ Edwards were not happy at all. It wasn't just the abduction of their whore that riled them, it was the sheer arrogance of the man who took her and had shot up his bar, and Russ took it personally.

"Get the horses and rifles. Let's get this bastard!"

Phil was out the back door in a flash. Both horses were already saddled in the small corral behind the saloon, so he just had to grab the two Winchesters and put them into the scabbards and was back out front less than two minutes later.

"You want me to come, boss?" asked the bartender.

"No, Ben, you stay here and make sure no more of those whores tries to make a break. We should be able to take care of one lovesick cowboy."

Phil stuck his head into the saloon and shouted, "Ready to go, boss!"

Russ trotted over to Phil, then they quickly mounted their horses and raced out of town just minutes after Joe had absconded with Caroline.

Joe had slowed Duke to a trot to conserve his strength. Luckily, he had been fed and watered, but he'd be tired after the long ride, and now he was carrying a double load. Caroline wasn't very heavy, so he guessed that even with the two of them, they didn't equal Big Jim.

Caroline kept looking back to check to see if anyone was coming. She was beginning to relax when she saw a dust cloud in the distance.

"Joe! Someone is coming fast!" she shouted.

Joe had been expecting it, despite her assurances that it wasn't likely, and been searching for any kind of defensive location and wasn't finding any, so he picked up Duke's pace. He knew they had probably spotted them easily enough as Caroline's bright red and white dress was hard to hide.

He kept the big gelding moving as quickly as he dared when he finally found what he would consider the absolute minimum of protection, a dry creek bed that didn't even qualify as a gully, but it was all that was available. He turned Duke to the northeast and reached the creek bed, slowed and walked Duke into the bed.

"This is the best I can find, Caroline," he said before holding his arm out to let her down.

After she was on the ground, Joe stepped down, removed his shotgun and Winchester from their scabbards, then pulled his saddlebag with its cache of ammunition. Then he pulled his gray slicker from inside the bedroll.

"Caroline, put this on. It'll hide you somewhat," he said as he held the slicker out to her.

She nodded and slipped it over her head. Her petticoats were still visible, but it was a lot better.

"Caroline, I need you to lay down against the front edge of the creek bed. Just snuggle in there. I'm going to give you a pistol in case something bad happens."

"I've never shot a gun before."

He slipped the Bulldog from his shoulder holster and handed it to her.

"All you need to do is point the gun at the target and pull the trigger."

"Alright, but only if it's really necessary," she replied as she took the revolver.

Caroline then walked to the edge of the creek bed, laid down tight against the edge and pulled the slicker over her blonde hair knowing how visible it was.

Joe walked Duke about fifty yards down the creek bed and just dropped his reins to keep the attackers from shooting him accidentally.

He trotted back and looked down the road, only seeing two of them. It could be worse. He set the shotgun against the creek bed. This time it was different because he was ready for them and was almost certain he had a range advantage, so instead of taking a prone position, he stood before the dried-up stream bed and just waited, but took the time to refill his Winchester's magazine tube. If they chose to return to Alta Vista, which would be the smart thing to do, he'd just let them go.

Phil and Russ had watched Joe leave the road two miles ahead. It was getting late and there was only about an hour of decent daylight left and they knew they had to get him fast.

"What do we do about Carol?" Phil asked.

"Shoot her."

Phil was surprised, but let it go. He's the boss.

By the time they were close enough to see Joe, Joe had his badge on his vest, and his Winchester '76 butt on his hip. For anyone other than Russ and Phil, it would have been an impressive sight.

They got within a quarter mile when Phil noticed the badge.

"He's a lawman, boss. Do we keep going?"

"I don't care if he's Jesus Christ. He's gonna die."

Phil shrugged. He's the boss.

———

Joe kept his eyes on the two men and said, "Here they come, Caroline. Just stay right there. Are either of these guys any good with those Winchesters?"

"I've never seen them practice," came the muffled response from under the slicker.

"I think it's going to get noisy in a minute, I was wondering if seeing my badge would make them smart enough to head back to Alta Vista, but they aren't as smart as I thought they were."

"But they're really mean, Joe. Be careful."

"I will."

———

Russ and Phil had gotten within two hundred yards before dismounting and leaving their horses standing as they approached just four feet apart, their Winchesters cocked. Joe didn't believe what he was watching. This was even worse than those drygulchers and he was wondering if all of the outlaws in Kansas were taking stupid pills.

Russ and Phil had started out thinking they were chasing a smitten cowboy, but even after seeing Joe's badge, they didn't change their tactics, or lack thereof. Having almost no interaction with lawmen over the years, they had never developed a sense of respect for their abilities, especially when it came to the use of firearms. To them it was simple, there were two of them and one of him.

Joe spoke to the hidden Caroline, saying, “These guys are incredibly stupid. I had to shoot two highwaymen earlier today that were a lot better at this then they are. They’re coming right at me with their rifles and they’re almost shoulder to shoulder.”

“You killed two men today?” Caroline asked from under the slicker.

“They tried to drygulch me. They chased after me and into a gully. I pretended to be hit and got them with one shotgun blast. Turns out they were Colorado bad boys. No more talk, Caroline. Here comes the noise.”

At a hundred and twenty yards, Russ and Phil opened fire, but Joe didn’t. He knew the bullets could hit him, but he wanted them a little closer. He didn’t want to have to run anyone down.

At a hundred yards, Joe took his first shot, when he pulled up his Winchester, aimed at the man on the right, and missed a little low, wondering how he could have missed so badly, but he quickly raised his muzzle as one of their rounds exploded the ground to his right about two feet short, then squeezed his trigger.

Russ felt the .45 caliber slug slam into his right thigh. The powerful round smashed into his upper femur and ricocheted, severing his femoral artery, and he didn’t realize that he’d be dead in less than a minute as the blood spurted from the open wound. He just fell to his knees as he screamed out in pain, then yelled at Phil, “Go kill that bastard!”

He was the boss, so Phil started walking quickly, firing as he stepped forward. Joe was readying his third shot when he felt the heat of a round ride the length of his left forearm. It threw his shot off, but he levered in a new round quickly as Phil continued to fire.

Phil had Joe dead in his sights and squeezed the trigger. His ears gave him the bad news when they reported a loud click as his Winchester's hammer fell onto an empty chamber. His panicking attempt to reload never materialized as Joe's fourth shot hit him flush in the lower right side of his chest. The bigger, more powerful round disintegrated two ribs and ripped his lung to shreds before exiting his chest. He dropped his rifle, clutched his chest and fell face forward into the dirt, still breathing but shaking badly as his life's blood pooled onto the dry Kansas ground. He continued to shudder for another ten seconds before he closed his eyes, and blood drooled from his mouth as he stopped breathing.

Joe quickly raced toward the two fallen men, reached Phil first, quickly diagnosed his lack of life and then trotted over to Russ' body. The amount of blood on the ground told the tale. He quickly went through his pockets, finding an impressive $335.50, put it in his pocket and took his gunbelt from him. He picked up the Winchester and made a pile like he had done earlier. He returned to Phil and went through his pockets. He didn't have that much, but another $90.25 was an impressive amount to have tucked away, then he made another weapons pile and walked back to Caroline.

"Caroline, you can come out now. They're both dead."

Caroline threw back the slicker and stood up, taking a deep breath. *She was really free!*

"Let's go and get Duke. They left their horses here, so you won't have to ride double."

"I don't mind," she said as she grinned.

“Duke might. He may have been used to carrying Big Jim McAllister’s three hundred plus pounds around, but he’s probably gotten used to my one-eighty.”

“That’s his horse?”

“It was. It’s mine now. He tried to shoot it out back in Lincoln a few days ago.”

As Joe walked to retrieve Duke, Caroline finally got to see what a man Joe had turned into. He had just gone through a life-or-death gunfight with two men and didn’t seem to be affected at all.

Joe returned with Duke and said, “I’ll go and get their horses. I’ll drag the bodies into the creek bed. Normally, I’d take them in, but these two can rot for all I care. What they did to you was unforgiveable.”

Caroline just nodded. Joe seemed so hard, which surprised her because she remembered him as the soft, sweet boy of eleven. *What had happened to him?*

Joe went to the two horses that had stayed pretty close, went through their saddlebags but not even finding any spare ammunition. They would have been down to pistols in another minute.

He led the two horses to the bodies and used the attached rope and looped it around their chests and then wrapped the other end around the horse’s saddle horn. He led the two horses to the dry creek bed and let the bodies slide down the edge. He untied the rope from the saddle horn and just tossed it onto the bodies before leading the two horses back out of the creek bed to where Carol stood.

"Caroline, this one seems like a good horse. The stirrups might be too low, but it should be all right for the short ride to Chapman."

Caroline was going to agree when she saw his left forearm and exclaimed, "Joe! You've been shot!"

Joe bent his left arm at the elbow and saw some blood, but not much. He unrolled his shirt and found a burn mark like a dark line right along the skin. There were two spots where the skin had been broken which accounted for the blood.

"It's all right. The bullet must have just ridden right along the skin. I've never seen anything like that before," he said as he examined the wound.

"Joe, what's the matter with you? Why aren't you upset that you just killed two men or that you've been shot?"

Joe looked into those amazing blue eyes and said, "There's nothing wrong with me at all, Caroline. My father taught me years ago that tears and sadness were wasted on the evil men who harm good people. He said to save them for the innocent people that deserve them. You wouldn't think there was anything wrong with me when you saw me with Josephine a few days ago."

Caroline's eyes widened as she asked, "You saw Josephine? How is she?"

"Believe it or not, she was in a worse situation than you were. Let's get mounted up and start back. You'll need to get a hotel room, and tomorrow, I'll buy you some more subdued clothes."

She looked down at her dress and laughed softly, "This is pretty bad, isn't it?"

"It announces your job pretty well."

"Joe, do you have anything to eat? I'm kind of hungry."

Joe was going to say he didn't when he remembered Eva's bag of food.

"Hold on. A girl at the boarding house where I stayed gave me some food for the trip."

For some not-so-inexplicable reason, Caroline felt a flare of jealousy as she asked, "Is she pretty?"

"Very. She was like us, Caroline. She was brought over on a children's train. Her name is Eva and she'll be eighteen shortly. She's doing all the work in the boarding house and the owners don't do a thing to help."

He found the bag, opened it, and was taking out a sandwich when he noticed a note. He took out the note and handed the sandwich and his canteen to Caroline, who quickly took a bite.

"What's that?" she asked.

"Looks like a note from Eva," he replied before reading:

Dear Joe,

I know you probably won't be coming back to see me. You're going to find your girlfriend from long ago and then return to Lincoln. I just want you to know that in the short time you were here, you made my life better. You will always be in my heart.

With all my affection,

Eva

Joe folded the note and put it in his vest pocket with the .45 caliber cartridges.

“Was she sad that you left?”

“She was.”

“Are you going to go back?”

“I have to, Caroline. For the same reason that I had to come back and find you. I promised.”

“You did, didn’t you?” she said as she smiled.

Joe smiled back and said, “Yes, ma’am.”

He helped her into the saddle, adjusting her dress as well as he could, and she grinned as he maneuvered her petticoats into different locations.

Joe took the two Winchesters and put them into the scabbards and put the two Colts in the nearest empty saddlebags.

It was after seven o’clock when they set out for Chapman.

“Joe, what happened to Josephine?”

“Her situation was worse than yours. She probably would have been dead if I hadn’t shown up. Now, she’s safe with my parents and considerably richer.”

He told Caroline the full story, then came the question he had anticipated.

“Did Danny make the reunion?”

"No. He was on the run after killing a man in Abilene. I arrested him in the same boarding house where I was staying."

"You arrested him? I thought you were his friend."

"I am his friend. He was on the run, Caroline. There was a wanted poster out for him…dead or alive. I talked him into giving up rather than have some bounty hunter shoot him. He hadn't murdered the man. It was a fight. I think the worst that could happen to Danny is a twenty-year sentence, and I don't think that will happen. He may even walk away if he has a good lawyer. He'll go back to his wife and son without having to worry about who was chasing him."

"*He has a son?*"

"Yes, ma'am. You're an aunt."

"I can't wait to see him. Joe, about my daughter. I hate to ask you this."

"You want me to try to get her back for you."

"Could you do that? I know it's asking a terribly dangerous thing for you to do."

"I'll do it for you, Caroline. Do you know who the father is?"

"Yes," she answered so quietly that Joe barely heard her over the horses, "It was Henry Draper."

Joe was stunned into silence before he asked, "What happened, Caroline?"

"I found out that when the train arrived, they were looking for an older girl. I was only nine, but they chose me because, well, I was only one of the two girls on the train. For the first few years,

I was treated okay and worked in the house and the kitchen. But I felt odd, like I was being examined by Mister Draper. I didn't know anything about sex, so I just thought he was different. Even Mrs. Draper began watching me differently. Then, when she helped me undress for the bath, she would feel me. Not sexually, almost medically. I was a bit immature in my development, so that's all it was for a while.

"It stayed that way until I reached fifteen, and then I began to blossom, as they say. Then things changed quickly after that. Mister Draper would come to my bed and talk to me. He'd act all fatherly at first, then he began to fondle me. I felt odd but didn't understand what was happening. I thought he was just doing what Mrs. Draper used to do. When I was sixteen, he began showing up without any clothes on and taking my nightdress off. He said he wanted to show me what to expect when I left the ranch in two years.

"He first took me when I had just turned seventeen. It wasn't violent or anything. He just told me it was to show me how it felt. I had to admit I enjoyed it, Joe. I just didn't know how wrong it was. Then, when my monthlies stopped, they were both happy, but I didn't know why. Mrs. Draper got mad at him when she found he was still visiting with me. Then my belly began to grow and so did my breasts. I thought I had a disease and was going to die, and that's when Mrs. Draper told me I was going to have their baby. I was terrified because I didn't know how this could happen. I didn't even relate what Mister Draper did to me with my having a baby, that's how ignorant I was.

"I went into labor and had my little girl. She was so beautiful, Joe, and they kept me there to feed her. I was so close to her, Joe. She was mine. She came from me. I named her Joanne, Joe. After you. They named her Edith, but they didn't even let anyone know she was mine. They pretended that Nancy Draper had given birth to her. Then they needed to get me out of the picture, so they arranged to have Phil come down and take me away to his whore house. That's what I've been doing for over a year now, Joe. I'm just another whore. But I want my baby! She belongs to me, not those two, evil people!"

"I'll get her back for you, Caroline. But where will you go when I do?"

"I haven't thought of that."

"Maybe Danny will let you stay with his wife. She'd be lonely if he goes to jail. If he doesn't, then he'd probably love to have you there. He asked about you and said if he went to jail, he'd like to see you."

"He did?"

"Danny isn't a bad sort. I don't know what happened in the mill, but he didn't seem like any of the bad men I've seen."

They passed the Crown D and Joe thought about going in to take Caroline's daughter back, but he wanted to go and talk to the sheriff first as he wasn't even sure who's jurisdiction it was.

They arrived at Chapman before nine o'clock, stopped at the hotel and Joe helped Caroline down from the horse. It was too late to go and see the sheriff, so he led Caroline into the hotel. The desk clerk looked up and tried to hide his distaste but failed.

"Yes, sir?"

"I'm Deputy Sheriff Joe Hennessey from Lincoln. I just rescued Miss Stevens who had been kidnapped and sold into prostitution. She'll need a room for the night. I'll need one myself. Is the sheriff available? It's kind of late."

The clerk's attitude shifted remarkably.

“Yes, of course, Deputy. If you’ll sign the register, I’ll get your keys. The sheriff is usually at home by this time. He’s already made his evening rounds.”

“It’s not an emergency. I’ll talk to him in the morning. We need to buy Miss Stevens more appropriate clothing as well.”

The clerk smiled and said, “Very good, sir.”

Joe led Caroline to her room and opened the door.

“I’ll go see the sheriff first thing in the morning and we’ll get you properly attired. Then we’ll go whichever way we need to go depending on what the sheriff finds out.”

“Thank you, Joe. Thank you from the bottom of my heart,” she said softly, her eyes beginning to tear.

“I’ll knock after I go and see the sheriff. We’ll have a late breakfast. Now, you go and get some sleep, Caroline.”

She smiled and wiped her face as she stepped backward and closed the door.

Joe sighed. Getting her daughter added a whole new wrinkle to the problem. He left the hotel and led the three horses down to the livery. The liveryman was in his attached quarters and heard Joe enter, so he helped Joe unsaddle the three horses and took over after that. Joe paid his fee and returned to the hotel.

He passed Caroline’s room, glanced at the door, then walked to his room two doors down, went inside, closed the door and put his saddlebag on the floor near the bed. He hung his gunbelt and is shoulder holster over the bed post as he thought about the problem. *Where would Caroline go? How would he get her daughter away from the Drapers? Was the father legally entitled to the child?* He took off his boots with a lot more questions than answers.

But surprisingly, there was one question he did have answered. Caroline was as pretty as he'd expected with an exceptional figure, but he didn't feel close to her as a person. When he kissed her, it was almost as if he was kissing Jo. There was a young lady in Manhattan that was just as pretty and well-figured, but had touched every part of his mind, heart and soul.

He took out her note again, read it and smiled. He wanted to get this whole issue behind him so he could return to Manhattan and surprise Eva, who obviously didn't expect him to return.

He folded the note and put it away, then closed his eyes and eventually drifted off to sleep still dressed, his creased gunshot wound untreated.

———

Joe woke up with a start with the sun pouring in his eastern facing window. He was late, so he quickly donned his boots and his Stetson, jogged down to the washroom and cleaned up before hurriedly returning to this room, strapped on his Webley shoulder holster and his vest, put on his gunbelt, then trotted outside and crossed the street to the sheriff's office. He guessed it was close to eight o'clock.

He opened the door and was greeted by the sheriff, who was writing a report.

"Welcome back, Deputy. I found out about those two you brought in yesterday. I already wired the ones who posted the rewards. You've got a hefty thousand dollars headed to you in Lincoln. Probably a lot of folks will sleep easier with those two out of the way."

"Sheriff, I have some things I need to talk to you about."

"Well, have a seat and call me Hank, will you?"

Joe smiled and replied, "I'll do that if you'll call me Joe."

"Okay, Joe, now that we have the name calling figured out, what can I help you with?"

"Remember I told you I was going down to find my friend Caroline down at the Crown D?"

"Yup. How did it go?"

"Bad, Hank, really bad. First, I got to the ranch and they said she ran off with some cowhand. Then, the foreman told me that she had been abducted by a man named Phil Hostetler and was taken to Alta Vista."

The sheriff snarled, "That bastard. He actually came into my jurisdiction trying to snatch women. I scared him off more than once."

"Well, I got to Alta Vista and found out she was in the Happy House Saloon working as a prostitute. After I went in and found her, I concocted a plan to get her out. It worked, too. I just had her drift to the front of the saloon, and I took a couple of shots at the top of the façade, figuring they'd all hit the floor.

"When they did, Caroline came running out, I scooped her up and got her on the back of my horse. We took off without a problem until Phil Hostetler and the saloon owner, Russ Edwards, came after us with their Winchesters ready. I found a shallow creek bed and had Caroline hide against the bank. I had my badge displayed and my Winchester on my hip watching them approach.

"I was hoping that they'd just leave, which would have been the smart thing to do, but would you believe that those two stupid bastards came on anyway? The end result was that both of them died and I left them in the creek bed."

Hank leaned back and asked, "You get hit?"

"Just this," he showed him his creased forearm.

"Damn! That was as close as you can get. I'll notify the county about it. They'll probably send you a letter of thanks. Those two have been a pain in the county's ass for years now."

"There's more, and this gets a bit touchy and some vague legalities are involved. When I went to the Crown D, I met Mrs. Draper at the door. She had a toddler, a little girl with blonde hair and blue eyes that I guessed to be around two or so, behind her skirt looking at me. I found out from Caroline that when they chose her, they were looking for an older girl, but she and Josephine were the only two girls left, so they chose her. Hank, they raised her just so Henry Draper could use her to father a child for his wife."

The sheriff's eyes and mouth popped open as Joe continued.

"She was only nine when they brought her there and she knew nothing about how babies were made. The Drapers took advantage of that and over the years, kept checking her to see if she was ready to have a baby. Finally, he took her many times and she was so innocent, Hank, she thought it was normal. She didn't even know what was happening when she became pregnant. She thought she was sick. Then she had the baby and they kept her around long enough until the baby was weaned. Then they had Phil Hostetler come and get her."

The sheriff, who thought he had heard everything sat there with his mouth open.

"Joe, that's one of the worst stories I've ever heard. To spend years to do that and not develop any feelings of affection for the child and then to treat her like we treat cows in the pasture. I'm just stunned."

"Now comes the last, most difficult part. She wants her daughter back. She's asked me to go and get her and I told her I would."

"I'm not going to stop you. If you can do it without killing those bastards…on second thought, I don't care about that, either. I'd rather you got her out of there clean, though."

"I think I can do it, Hank. By the way, I have Hostetler and Edwards' horses down the livery. You need them?"

"Nope. In fact, you have two more you need to take with you. The other two are in Jeremiah's corral behind the livery. One of them is a pretty little mare."

"I'll go see Jeremiah in a bit. Right now, I've got to go and buy a conservative dress for Caroline. You wouldn't know anything about women's dresses, would you?"

"Not a thing. You're on your own on that front. But Joe, if you have a chance, can you bring the little girl by? I'd like to see her and her mom both. Not for any legal reason, just curiosity."

"Count on it, Hank. You're a credit to the law enforcement community."

"You're better than I am already, Joe, and you're just a pup."

They shook hands and Joe left the office feeling better. He did have a plan for getting Caroline's daughter away from the Drapers as he walked quickly to the mercantile.

He stepped inside and approached the counter.

"Can I help you, sir?" the proprietor asked.

"I have a difficult situation. Last night, I rescued a woman who had been kidnapped and sold into prostitution. She's over at the hotel right now and I need to buy her a nice dress to replace the rather provocative one that she was wearing. She's about average height and weight. Can you help me find something she could wear? I have no idea about such things."

"My wife can help you."

He called his wife from the back room and ten minutes later Joe was walking back to the hotel with a large bag. He waved at the desk clerk as he passed and reached Caroline's room, tapped on the door and she opened it quickly. She must have been waiting.

"Good morning, Joe," she said with a big smile. She looked so much nicer without the makeup.

"Good morning, Caroline. I have no idea if this is right. The storekeeper's wife picked it out. I'll wait for you in the lobby and then we can go have breakfast."

"How did your conversation go with the sheriff?"

"Fine. I'll tell you the details when we're in the café."

"Be right out."

Joe walked to his room and put his saddlebags over his shoulder, then checked to make sure he hadn't forgotten anything, then closed the door and walked to the lobby to wait for Caroline.

Caroline bounced out of her room and into the lobby five minutes later, transformed and looked as innocent as a schoolgirl. She was positively beaming as she stepped closer to Joe.

"Good morning again, Miss Stevens. May I escort you to breakfast?" he asked.

"Thank you, Mister… What's your new name now?"

"Hennessey."

"That's right. Well, then I'd be honored, Mister Hennessey."

She took his arm, and Joe noticed that the bag with her other clothing was gone. She probably left in her room and it wasn't a great loss. He realized she'd have to buy a riding outfit before they left.

He escorted Caroline to the diner and as they entered, many heads turned at the handsome couple, and Joe could tell that Caroline seemed to enjoy the attention.

Caroline reveled in the wonderful breakfast of bacon, eggs and biscuits as her breakfast for the past year and a half had been leftovers.

As they ate, Joe filled her in on what the sheriff has told him, and her smile grew wider the more he told her. She had been worried that Joe might go to jail for shooting them or she might have to go back for some reason. There would be no courtroom embarrassment for Caroline.

"Caroline, you can stay in the hotel while I head down to the Crown D. You need to think of where you'll be staying after I return. If you'd like, we can go back to Manhattan and you and Joanne can stay at Morrison's Boarding House until we find out what happened to Danny, or I can take you and Joanne to Abilene where I can set you up in a hotel. You can see Danny, too."

"Can you take us to Abilene?" she asked expectantly.

"I can do that. Did you want to take the train or make the two-hour ride?"

"I'd rather ride, if that's alright."

"It is. But you'll need to get a riding outfit and probably one of those saddle cribs for Joanne."

He reached in his pocket and pulled out fifty dollar and gave it to her.

"That should be plenty. Hopefully, I'll be back in time for lunch."

"That would be wonderful, Joe."

Joe paid for their breakfasts and escorted her to the dry goods store, and before she entered, said, "I'm off, Caroline. Hopefully, I'll be back in a few hours with your daughter."

"Thank you so much again, Joe."

Joe smiled at her and turned toward the livery. It was time to go and get a baby.

Joe saddled Duke and was soon headed south toward the Crown D. He had two plans in his head, but he didn't know which would be better, a lot depended on the reaction of Mrs. Draper. He had thought after hearing Caroline tell the story that she would be the biggest obstacle. Even though she had no part in the conception or labor, she probably viewed the baby as hers. *How much of a problem would her husband be?*

He decided on Plan B and would bypass the Drapers altogether.

He reached the ranch and rode past the entrance road for another half mile and then turned east onto Crown D land. He could see the house in the distance to the north and hoped they wouldn't see him. He continued east until he was in the pastures and could hear the lowing of cattle in the distance. He hoped the hands were working the cows and not repairing fences or some other task away from the herd. As he crossed a gentle rise, he saw the herd and then the cow hands. There were five again, and one was Jason Arbuckle. When he was close enough, he waved. The foreman waved back. So far so good.

As he approached, the foreman rode out quickly to meet him, obviously not want to have the others hear what he needed to say.

"What can I do for you today, Joe?" he asked when he was within six feet.

"I rode to Alta Vista and found Caroline. Hostetler had her in the Happy House Saloon. She was a prostitute, Jason."

Joe saw the foreman cringe, then said, "I got her out of there and Hostetler and the owner of the place, a man named Russ Edwards came after us. We had a shootout and I got them both and left them in a creek bed. I told the sheriff about it and he said good riddance. I left Caroline at the hotel. She's all cleaned up and looks like a schoolgirl, but now comes the real problem."

"The baby," he said without prompting.

"The baby. She wants her daughter back. You wouldn't believe the story she told me. It seems that in selecting this nine-year-old girl ten years ago, their plan from the start was to use her as a vessel so Mister Draper could give his wife the baby she'd always wanted. They actually began to feel her and see when she was ready to produce the baby when she was as young as eleven.

"When she was old enough, Draper convinced her that what he was doing was just preparing her for the real world. Even after she was pregnant, he still kept going to her bed. Mrs. Draper found out about it and that ended that. She didn't even know what was happening to her when she was pregnant. She thought she was sick. Then, after the baby was born, they only kept her around long enough to wean the baby. Then they called Hostetler."

The foreman was rocked. He had an inkling, but nothing like this.

"I always thought she just had a fling with some cowpoke."

"It was much worse than that."

"How can we help?"

"I need to get the little girl. I think Nancy Draper will be the biggest problem. Mister Draper probably just enjoyed the sex part of it. It was rape, no matter how he described it. Any ideas how we can do it?"

"We'll be going to the house for lunch in a little while. The little girl has a room to herself. It's the first room on the left after the main room. She's usually in her day bed around lunch having a nap."

"I don't want to get any of you fired."

"To be honest, we probably won't want to stay around after this anyway. If we can, we'll grab them both. Give us five minutes after we're inside. I'll go and talk to the boys right now. I'll be right back."

He turned his horse and rode to the other side of the pasture where the hands were sitting on their horses wondering what was going on. The foreman reached the group and began talking.

Joe could see the looks of disgust and disbelief on their faces, but he could also see the revelations appear as it all made more sense than the rumors they had been hearing over the years.

The foreman broke away from the group and headed back.

"They're all on board. Most of 'em wanted to shoot Henry Draper."

"I appreciate the help. In fact, why don't you all follow me into Chapman and meet Caroline after we have her daughter. You'll get to see the reunion of mother and daughter."

That suggestion put a smile on his face before he wheeled his cow pony back to the hands and told them of Joe's suggestion and Joe could see them all break into grins, making Joe feel better about his fellow man.

They all kind of milled around when the lunch bell finally rang, and Joe stayed put as the men set their horses to a trot and headed for the house. He took a minute to retrieve his bedroll, let in unravel, then folded it over twice and put it over his saddle horn in preparation for his small passenger

After a couple of minutes, he had Duke slow trotting toward the house, but didn't know what to expect as he slowed down when he was close to the house. Suddenly, he heard shouting and an ear-piercing scream. Even fifty feet outside the house, it sent chills down his back.

Then the foreman appeared from the back of the house carrying little Joanne. She wasn't even crying, which surprised Joe.

"Well, here she is," said the foreman with a grin.

He passed Joanne to Joe who he sat her down on his makeshift saddle chair.

"What happened to the Drapers?" he asked.

"We just gave them a little love tap and left 'em."

"Well, let's go, boys. We have an anxious mama waiting," he said loudly.

The men quickly exited the house, climbed aboard their horses, then they left the Crown D and formed an honor guard around little Joann, who seemed to be enjoying the ride. She was laughing and making words that sounded like, well, toddler words.

The group of men plus a little girl arrived in Chapman around noon and headed for the hotel. Joe thought he'd try to surprise Caroline, but she didn't give him a chance. She had been pacing outside the hotel for almost two hours with a bag in her hand.

When she saw Joe and the hands ride down the street with a golden-haired little girl sitting happily on Joe's horse, she dropped the bag, ran down the steps and raced down the street toward the men. Townsfolk all stopped to watch the display and wondered what was happening.

The men were all grins as Caroline finally reached them and Joe picked up little Joanne then lowered her into the waiting arms of her mother. Caroline held her as the tears flowed with her face almost blinding in the bright Kansas sun. Her blue eyes, despite the tears, were filled with a radiant joy.

Joe looked at the cowhands and saw some looking away, trying to mask their emotions. Two were pretending the sun was making their eyes water, but Jason just smiled.

Caroline finally looked up at Joe.

"Joe, thank you so very much! My baby. I have my baby!"

"Thank Jason and the boys, Caroline. They're the ones who did it, even though it cost them their jobs."

She looked at the men and thanked them one at a time.

"Folks, it looks like we're blocking traffic. Why don't we all head to the diner. I'll buy lunch. It's the least I can do," Joe said.

They all agreed, so they parked their horses at the hotel hitching post and walked down the street to the diner. Jason walked on the other side of Caroline and Joanne.

Joe looked at him closely. He may have been the foreman, but he couldn't be much older than twenty-five or so and saw him watching Caroline, with a look of much more than concern. Jason was smitten, as were probably all of the ranch hands.

Joe knew how he had felt. As soon as he had seen her, he knew immediately and without a second thought that he had found the woman he wanted to marry, but he had found her in Manhattan.

He was sure that it was Eva, and it wasn't because Caroline had been a prostitute or had a baby. It was that Caroline didn't reach him like Eva had done so effortlessly. Eva made him think.

One of his hidden worries on the trip to find Caroline after leaving Manhattan was that he might find her and that ancient puppy love would re-emerge, but it hadn't. He had Eva now, or at least he had her firmly in his heart and hoped she would feel the same way when he returned, because he was reasonably certain that Caroline felt the same toward him as he now felt toward him, more as siblings than anything else.

They reached the diner and walked inside where the staff had to push two tables together. Caroline was new to the feeding of a toddler, so the waitress suggested a bowl of oatmeal as the adults ordered fried chicken.

"So, Jason, where will you be going?" Joe asked.

"I've been offered a lot of jobs at other ranches before, but I'm thinking of starting my own spread if I can find one cheap enough."

"I know where you can probably get one for not much money. It'll take some fixing up, though. It's four sections about seven miles northwest of Salina and owned by a character named Gunter. He's out of commission, so I bet he'll sell cheap."

"You think so?"

"If he doesn't, tell him I'll come and visit him again."

Jason grinned and said, "Why do I think that there's a story in there somewhere?"

“I’ll tell you later. We’re going to be heading out to Abilene in the morning and you’re welcome to come along. Then it’s only a short ride to Salina.”

“That sounds like a plan to me. You boys want to come along? If this ranch works out, you’ll all have jobs.”

“How are you on money, Jason?” Joe asked.

“I can handle it, Joe. Been saving most of my money and I had a nice account from my parents when I left home.”

“Good. How about the rest of you boys?”

Joe could tell that they didn’t want to say they were broke.

“Well, I’ll give you each fifty dollars for your help with Caroline’s daughter.”

“No, sir. We couldn’t take your money,” said one of the men.

“It’s not my money. I took it off the body of the man who grabbed Caroline in the first place. He’ll be paying for what he did.”

“In that case…” he replied with a grin.

Joe doled out fifty dollars to each of them, including Jason, who had most of his money in the bank.

The waitress arrived and brought lunch to a very happy group. After lunch, they all left the diner and headed toward the hotel.

“Gentlemen,” announced Joe, “I have one more promise to keep. Caroline, we need to go and see the sheriff.”

Caroline's smile vanished as she thought something was amiss and asked, "What's wrong, Joe?"

"Nothing, I promised him that he'd get to meet you both."

"Oh," she said as she released her breath.

The entire group made their way to the sheriff's office, and Joe held the door for Caroline and Joanne. As she entered, he caught the sight of a grinning sheriff rising from behind his desk.

"Hank, I'd like you to meet Caroline Stevens and her daughter, Joanne."

"Miss Stevens, you and your daughter are a sight to behold."

As Hank and Caroline exchanged compliments, Jason caught Joe's eyes and motioned to the outside for a moment.

They stepped just outside the office and Jason leaned over.

He spoke softly, "Joe, um…I don't know how to ask this, but…well, would you mind…you know, I mean…."

"Hank, don't worry. I'm pretty sure that Caroline sees me as a big brother now. There's a young lady in Manhattan who I'll be going to see when we get this all settled down."

Hank's subdued manner disappeared, and he asked, "Really? Do you think it would be okay?"

"It's not up to me, Jason. But to be honest, let me get a better read on Caroline so you don't have to worry."

"You'd do that for me?"

"You're a good man, Jason."

Jason grabbed his hand and almost shook free of his wrist before giving him a hard pound on the back.

They returned to the jailhouse and Caroline was just beginning to wonder where Joe had gone when she saw him and Jason return.

"Hank, we're going to let Caroline and her daughter get better acquainted before we head over to Abilene."

"Don't forget those horses, Joe."

"I'll pick them up right now."

The crowd left the sheriff's office and walked along the boardwalk.

"Caroline, did you find your riding outfit and something for Joanne to ride in on the way to Abilene?"

"Oh. I dropped my bag," she replied as she scanned the opposite side of the street and saw the bag, "I'll get the bag and then get changed in a minute, but she seemed to like your bedroll throne, so I didn't buy anything for her to ride in."

"That's fine. I need to run down to the livery and pick up some horses. Guys, could I talk to Caroline for a minute? We'll be ready to head to Abilene in a few minutes."

They all acknowledged in one form or another and crossed the street, heading for the hotel.

"What's wrong, Joe?" asked Caroline after the men were gone.

"Not a thing, Caroline. But can I ask you something that might sound awkward?"

"You can ask me anything, Joe."

"How do you feel about me after all these years? Now, I need an honest answer."

She looked at him, unsure of how to tell him, but she knew he deserved the honest reply.

"I love you very much, Joe. But I feel like you are another older brother. The bravest, most thoughtful older brother a girl could have."

Joe smiled and said, "Good. I'm asking because Jason asked me if he could ask to call on you."

A broad smile began growing on her face as she asked, "He did?"

"It was a very difficult thing for him to ask me. He's a good man, Caroline."

"He is. Thank you, Joe. This means a lot to me."

"Well, I'm going to go and get the horses. They should be ready to go."

"I'll go and talk to Jason," she said, still wearing the big smile as she turned.

Joe caught Jason's anxious eyes and nodded before Jason popped a grin and Joe jogged down to the livery.

He and the liveryman got all three horses saddled in ten minutes before he mounted a solid black gelding that seemed sturdy and led the other two out of the livery, heading toward the hotel.

He barely made it a block when he saw a buggy come trotting down the street toward the hotel, and recognized Henry Draper driving and Nancy Draper beside him with a Winchester in her arms.

Joe didn't have time to think. He let go of the trail rope and turned the black horse to his left and raced between two buildings he hadn't even identified. When he reached the back alley, he yanked the horse sharply to his right. The horse was quick on his feet and must have been a cow pony at one time. The horse shot past two buildings and Joe turned him one more time back toward the street, spotting the buggy stopped in front of them about a hundred feet away.

He could hear Mrs. Draper yelling, but only caught the last two words, "…my baby!"

Joe couldn't risk firing a gun, so he used the big weapon under the saddle and urged the horse forward at a gallop. The horse obeyed without hesitation and shot out between the buildings.

Caroline had been talking to the men, waiting on Joe as they were mounting their horses, and by the time anyone noticed the passengers in the buggy, she was the only one on her feet. They only became aware of the problem when Nancy Draper first screeched her threats and pointed the Winchester.

Jason awoke from his trance and jerked his head toward the buggy. They were all caught unaware and had their Colts still strapped down and now Caroline was under the muzzle of a cocked Winchester. Jason was debating about jumping from his horse when he first noticed the sudden echo of pounding hoofbeats from the buildings across the street.

They all turned at the sound, even the Drapers. Nancy Draper quickly shifted the Winchester to the threatening sound, but in the three seconds from the start of Joe's charge until the collision, everything seemed to happen in slow motion.

Caroline was shielding Joanne by turning her body to take Nancy Draper's shot, the five men all were open-mouthed at the sight of the charging animal and Nancy Draper began to turn to shoot the new threat, but it wouldn't have mattered even if she had managed to get off a shot. Henry Draper's eyes were wide and white as the exploding sight of a large animal appeared before him and Joe gritted his teeth in anticipation of the massive collision.

The horse plowed into the buggy causing the Winchester to fire as Joe flew over the top of the buggy toward the boardwalk and the front of the hotel. The Drapers were tossed into the air, hitting the buggy's roof as the vehicle shattered and overturned.

Joe knew it was going to hurt when he landed, and it did. He smashed once into the boardwalk, slid six feet and crunched into the façade of the hotel. The black horse, miraculously, just bounced back up from the crash, shook itself and trotted over to the ranch hands. The Drapers were inside the wreckage that was once the buggy and the five ex-ranch hands dismounted rapidly with their pistols drawn.

The sheriff had heard Nancy Draper's ranting and was just stepping out of the office, his pistol coming out of his holster when he saw her with the cocked Winchester and heard the roar of hooves. He turned slightly and saw Joe driving the horse into the buggy. It was one of those images that stays in your mind.

He ran to the scene as other citizens started trotting toward the what they all thought was a horrible accident. Stupid cowboy couldn't even control his horse.

Joe was hurting, but not as badly as he expected to be. He gingerly rolled away from the hotel and crawled to his feet. His back and side were sore, but nothing seemed broken as he probed with his fingers, figuring he must have landed right. He walked toward the buggy, drawing his Webley which somehow managed to stay put in its holster.

The boys were all jogging to the buggy except for Jason who remained with Caroline and Joanne.

Joe and the sheriff arrived at the buggy first, and the sheriff peered over the top and looked down. Mister Draper was dead. The buggy had turned over onto the edge of the boardwalk, and it looked like his neck had been broken when his head had hit the end of the boards. Nancy Draper wasn't in very good shape, either. Her left arm was snapped in half above the elbow, and she probably had several broken ribs when the left side of her chest had been rammed violently into the same edge of boardwalk that had killed her husband.

Joe holstered his Webley at the same time that Hank returned his Colt to his holster.

"Mrs. Draper, we're going to get you out of there," the sheriff said.

"My baby. Where's my baby?" was all she said before gasping once and dying as her lungs fill with blood.

Less than a minute later, the cowhands pulled the remains of the buggy upright.

Hank looked over at Joe and said, "Joe, I didn't know how I could take her out before she fired that Winchester at Miss Stevens. That was a brilliant thing to do."

"Tell that to my back. Are they both dead?"

"Yup. Good riddance, too."

Jason and Caroline approached the buggy as Joe looked at the sheriff.

"Hank, correct me if I'm wrong, but isn't Joanne the legal heir to the Crown D now?"

The light went on and Hank grinned and said, "You're damned right, Joe. She is."

Caroline suddenly realized what they were saying. She and Joanne now had a home.

The sheriff said, "I'll get Judge Abernathy to take care of the estate transfer. He'll need affidavits from Miss Stevens and probably the ranch hands, but I don't see any problems, especially after I tell him the whole story."

Joe looked over at the cowhands and said, "Unless I'm wrong, you've all got your jobs back under new management. Caroline, can you live in that house again?"

"It wasn't the house or the ranch's fault, Joe. I just won't sleep in the same bedroom."

"Jason, can you and the boys take care of the ranch? Caroline and Joanne need to go to Abilene to see her brother. We'll be back in three days or so."

Jason grinned, and replied, "We'll be happy to. We'll head back now, Caroline. I'll look forward to seeing you again soon."

"I'll be back as soon as I can, Jason," she said as she smiled back at him.

"Jason, could you take three of the horses with you back to the ranch? That black gelding did a mighty fine job. He seems to be okay, but check him out, will you? We've got to get going if we're to get into Abilene."

"We'll take care of the horses, but you're going to have to tell me how you got four of them."

"We'll have time when we get back," he said before walking over to Duke and mounting.

Jason and Caroline exchanged one more, long look before Joe arrived on Duke and lifted Joanne from her arms.

"Caroline, you need to get inside and get changed."

"Oh! I forgot. I need to change. I'll be right back."

She snatched the bag from the street, lifted her skirts, and trotted back into the hotel and into her room to change.

Jason mounted his horse while the men retrieved Joe's horses and added the black gelding to the string.

"Joe, I've got to tell you, that was the most impressive thing I've ever seen in my life," Jason said as he sat next to Joe.

"After Caroline."

Jason smiled and said, "Well, yeah, after Caroline."

The hands arrived with the three horses and Jason held off departing until Caroline returned from the hotel. She looked incredible in the simple riding skirt and white blouse. She was prettier than Eva, Joe thought, but it didn't matter. He only thought of Eva because she was simply the one.

He looked at the horses and spotted the gray mare that he'd noticed before and marked her as Eva's horse.

He had Joanne sitting cheerfully on the bedroll as Caroline mounted her horse before they all set off to the west. Jason and the boys then turned south toward the Crown D and Jason glanced back for one last glimpse of Caroline as the two parties parted.

"Where did you get four horses, Joe?" Caroline asked.

"The one you're riding and one of the others we got from Russ and Phil. The other two were from two bushwhackers named Jim Anderson and Snake Jones. They did that for a living. They tried to get me on my way to Chapman, but I wound up getting them instead. You know, I just realized that I have all this reward money coming. I hadn't given it much thought before. It'll make life a little easier."

"You're going back to Manhattan after this is over, aren't you?"

"I have to, Caroline. I made a promise."

"To Eva?"

"No, to myself."

Caroline smiled, happy for Joe and even happier to have Joanne back. Jason was just the topper.

The ride to Abilene took longer than Joe had expected because they took it slow for Joanne. They also had to make a stop when the two inexperienced young people were introduced into the world of diapers. They didn't have any diapers, but Joe sacrificed his only towel, leaving the used diaper by the side of the road.

They arrived in Abilene after five o'clock with a sleeping Joanne as they headed for the hotel. Caroline stepped down first and Joe lowered the still sleeping Joanne into her arms. He dismounted and escorted them into the hotel, signed for two rooms and escorted Caroline and Joanne to their room.

After opening the door, he said, "I'll be back in a few minutes. We'll go to the café for dinner and stop at the store for some more diapers and other things she may need."

"Thank you again, Joe. It seems like that's all I do these days."

"You just need to relax. I'll be back in a few minutes."

Joe went to his room, left the saddlebags on his bed before leaving and heading out the door to the sheriff's office.

He walked inside and noticed empty cells first, so Danny wasn't there. Either he was exonerated or on his way to prison.

"Evening, Deputy. Did Danny Stevens have his trial already?"

"Yes, sir. Yesterday morning and the jury found him not guilty. There shouldn't even have been a trial in the first place, if you ask me. It turned out it wasn't as bad as it sounded the first time. The guy he hit with the chair had drawn a knife. Once that came out, the case kinda fell apart. He's at home now."

"Why didn't he just say that in the beginning?"

"I think he was just scared. He saw the man fall into the wheel stone, panicked and ran. It never must have occurred to him that he acted in self-defense."

"Where's his house?"

"I'm not sure. I think it's over on 4th Street. I know what it looks like, though. It's a brown house with red shutters."

"Thanks."

Joe left the jailhouse in an ebullient mood. Danny was free, Caroline was free, and Josephine was free, and soon, he'd free Eva. It didn't get any better than that.

He returned to the hotel, jogged across the lobby and tapped on Caroline's door when he reached her room.

He heard, "Come in, Joe," from the other side of the door and opened the door.

"What happened to Danny, Joe?" she asked, a now awake Joanne on her lap.

"He was found not guilty, Caroline. He's at home right now."

She lit up and exclaimed, *"He's free?"*

"Yup. The man he hit had a knife, but Danny never mentioned it to me. If he had, I would have told him he'd be set free as soon as he returned. But it went to trial, and I don't know why. The deputy I talked to didn't either. Do you want to get some dinner first and then go see him or go visit him first?"

"Could we see him first?"

"Of course, let's go."

She settled Joanne on her hip and they left the room, walked out to the horses and Joe stepped up. Caroline handed him her daughter and mounted her horse. They turned and rode north along the main street until Joe found a sign for 4th Street and turned east. It didn't take long to spot the brown house with red shutters.

They pulled up and Caroline stepped down to accept Joanne, and he could see the excitement of anticipation in her face. Soon, she'd see a brother that she hadn't seen in ten years, and each one with a child now.

He dismounted, then they walked down the bricked walkway and took the three steps onto the porch. Joe knocked on the door and they waited. Less than a minute later, the door swung wide and a pleasant-looking young woman looked at them questioningly.

"May I help you?" she asked.

"Yes, ma'am, I'm Joe Hennessey and this is Caroline Stevens and her daughter, Joanne. Is her brother in?"

Her hand went to her mouth, then she smiled and said, "Yes, he is. Come in, please."

Joe held the door for Caroline and Joanne and closed it behind him as they walked into the main room.

"Have a seat and I'll get Danny. We were just getting ready to sit down for dinner."

They sat, and Joe could hear her tell Danny that he had visitors but didn't say who they were, obviously wanting to watch the look on his face, so did Joe.

Danny walked into the room, probably expecting newspapermen again, then stopped when he saw Joe and then his eyes shifted to the right to the two blonde heads. One belonging so obviously to his sister.

"Caroline?" he squeaked out.

She stood and left Joanne to Joe's care before she approached her brother.

She was beginning to cry as she whispered, "Hello, Danny. It's been a long time."

Soon they were embracing with faces awash in tears. So was Danny's wife, but Joe managed to hold his emotions in check as he was now more accustomed to them.

It took some time for the emotional reunion to subside to conversation, but it finally did. They invited them to stay for dinner, but Joe figured there wasn't enough for all of them, so he begged off saying he needed to send a telegram.

Danny's wife, Elizabeth, asked Caroline to stay with them for a day or two, and she agreed as Danny brought their son, David, in and introduced him to his cousin.

"Caroline, I'm going to send a telegram and then head to the hotel. Did you want me to run your clothes over later?"

Elizabeth interrupted, saying, "She'll be fine tonight. She can borrow one of my nightdresses."

Joe smiled and said, "That's a relief. I didn't want to be seen carrying petticoats again anyway."

Danny hugged Joe before he left, thanking him profusely for getting him out of that situation that he was in.

Joe finally shook his hand and left the house. It was time to get his own life sorted out.

He stopped at the diner and had his dinner before leaving for the Western Union office. He sent two telegrams.

WILL AND CLARA HENNESSEY LINCOLN KANSAS

DANNY AND CAROLINE OKAY
WILL RETURN TO MANHATTAN IN THREE DAYS
THEN RETURN HOME
MISS YOU
LOVE TO BOTH AND JOSEPHINE

JOE HENNESSEY ABILENE KANSAS

Then he sent the second, even more important message.

EVA PORTER MORRISONS BDNG HOUSE MANHATTAN KANSAS

WOULD LIKE TO RESERVE A ROOM
ARRIVING IN THREE DAYS
WILL STAY UNTIL YOUR EIGHTEENTH
JOIN ME THE NEXT DAY
FOREVER

JOE HENNESSEY ABILENE KANSAS

The operator didn't even make a comment beyond, "That'll be ninety cents."

Joe paid the man, left the office then walked Duke to the livery before returning to the hotel.

———

Forty-five minutes late, a messenger was knocking on the door of the Hennessey home in Lincoln. Josephine opened the door, and had to rummage for a nickel, but found one and handed it to the young boy.

"Papa, you have a telegram," she said as she walked back into the kitchen.

She handed Will the telegram and sat back down to finish her dinner.

He read the telegram and said, "It's from Joe. He said that both Danny and Caroline are okay and that he's going to Manhattan in three days before coming home. He also sends his love to all of us including Josephine."

He handed the telegram to Clara who read it quickly before giving it to Josephine.

"What do you think, Jo?" asked Will.

"I'm not sure. I know he was going to find Danny first and then Caroline. But he says that they're okay, which implies that they hadn't been before. I wonder why he's going to Manhattan."

"I have no idea. You don't think it has anything to do with Caroline, do you?"

"To do what, Will?" asked Clara.

"I know what you're thinking, Clara. I think if he was going to get married, he'd say something. It seems like he's been getting into trouble ever since he left. First there was the train situation and then these reward vouchers showed up. Clara, these are for five hundred dollars each. Do you know how few men have that high a price on their heads? Only the really bad ones, and he got two of them. Plus, the other ones for Red Fletcher and Big Jim McAllister. I just hope he comes home in one piece."

Jo said, "Papa, I watched Joe work. I've never seen anyone like him. He's only two years older than I am and he seems like it's ten sometimes. He's so calm and assured even when it gets dangerous, especially when it gets dangerous. I'm so proud of my big brother."

"We're just as proud of our son as any parents could be, Jo. We just want him home safely," Clara said.

In Manhattan, another messenger was knocking on the door of Morrison's Boarding House. It took a minute for Eva to leave her dirty pots and pans and walk to the door. When she saw the messenger, she had a problem as she didn't have a tip.

"I have a telegram for Eva Porter," he said as he held out the yellow sheet.

She was surprised it was for her, but said, "That's me. I'm sorry, I simply don't have any money with me."

The young man smiled at the pretty young woman as he replied, "It's all right, ma'am. Some folks just slam the door in my face," then handed her the message.

"That's terrible. I wish I had some change, though."

He just smiled at her and left.

Eva wondered who would send her a telegram. The Western Union voucher for the reward was given to her two days ago by a deputy, so it wasn't that. She had it in her pocket because she didn't trust the Morrisons to not go rummaging through her room while she was upstairs. They'd done it before.

She stepped inside but before she took one step, she realized that only one person would be sending her a telegram, and her pace quickened as she jogged back to the kitchen where she took a seat at the kitchen table.

She hesitated for a few seconds, almost fearing that Joe might be telling her that he wasn't coming back because he'd found Caroline.

But her pessimism was quickly pushed aside as she opened the sheet and read:

EVA PORTER MORRISONS BDNG HOUSE MANHATTAN KANSAS

WOULD LIKE TO RESERVE A ROOM
ARRIVING IN THREE DAYS
WILL STAY UNTIL YOUR EIGHTEENTH
JOIN ME THE NEXT DAY
FOREVER

JOE HENNESSEY ABILENE KANSAS

She dropped the sheet on the table and sat in stunned disbelief as her heart threatened to pound its way out of her chest. The man she thought she'd lost forever just proposed to her in a telegram, but maybe she misread it. It wasn't possible because good things just didn't happen to her.

She read it again slowly, word for word. There was that one word that meant so much...forever.

She closed her eyes and clutched the telegram to her chest. Joe was coming back to her and taking her away from this place.

It was a bad moment for Mrs. Morrison to enter the kitchen.

CHAPTER 5

Joe was eating breakfast at the café. He had counted his remaining cash and found that he still had over three hundred dollars, or to be exact, there was $327.45.

After all the tumult of the past week, he finally was able to concentrate on the one person he needed to think about, Eva. After he had sent the telegram, he began to wonder about money. He knew he had more than enough money to set up a home for Eva, but was his deputy salary enough to support a wife and children?

He almost laughed at himself as he forked some eggs into his mouth. He had known Eva for such a short time, yet he was already so convinced that she was the one and wanted to be just as sure he could take care of her.

He was being paid thirty dollars a month, but living with his parents, so his expenses were low. If he bought a house, he'd still have over fifteen hundred dollars in the bank. If he got below five hundred, he'd start looking for another job. He knew only one thing he was sure of was that he'd never look for another wife. It could only be Eva. The more he thought of her, the more he seemed to understand her.

He wasn't smitten in the traditional fashion, like Jason was with Caroline. He had liked Eva immediately. She was pretty and had a wonderful figure, but it was much more than that. He wanted to talk with her, to listen to what she said. He wanted her for a friend, a best friend, and he wanted her as a man wanted a woman. It didn't get any better than that.

He paid for his breakfast and left the diner, boarding Duke and heading for 4th Street, arriving at the brown house two minutes later and trotted up the walkway and hopped up to the porch.

He rapped on the door and waited. It was only a few seconds this time before Elizabeth Stevens opened the door.

"Good morning, Joe. Come on in," she said as she smiled.

"Thank you, Elizabeth," he answered before he walked inside, and found the entire group in the sitting area.

"Come and have a seat, Joe. We were just talking about you," said Danny.

"That's bad. So, what's the plan for today?"

He replied, "We were wondering about that. Can Caroline and Joanne stay here another day?"

"It's up to her and you. I need to get back to Manhattan, and I'll need to stop by the ranch on the way to pick up some horses. Maybe just one horse."

"Then can you stay another day and then you can take Caroline and Joanne back to the ranch?"

"I can do that. In the meantime, I need to get over to the dry goods store and buy myself some more clothes. This shirt isn't very good."

"What happened to your sleeve, Joe?" asked Danny.

"Had a .44 slide through. Oddest thing I've seen in a while, and that's going some. The very edge of the bullet must have slid across my forearm and only broke the skin in a couple of places. You know, a couple of days ago, when I was bushwhacked, one of their bullets ricocheted off my cartridges in my gunbelt. I'd totally forgotten about that."

"You've been in two unrelated gunfights in two days?" he asked with wide eyes.

"Three, if you include those two guys trying to derail the train and four if you go back a few more days. So, four in about a week. I really don't want to see a fifth."

Joe had to spend another hour explaining the gunfights. Then, after Danny asked where Josephine was, he had to explain that situation.

Finally, Joe begged off to go to the store to buy some more clothes, leaving them to spend some time together as family.

Joe and Duke made the short ride to the mercantile and Joe found a surprisingly good selection. He bought a new vest, three new shirts, two pairs of denim pants, some new underwear, and, finally, he bought the pocket watch he'd been trying to remember to buy. He went across the street to the tonsorial parlor and paid for the works: a haircut, shave and a bath. He then changed into his new clothes and felt immensely better. He wanted a to make a good impression when he went back to Manhattan.

In Manhattan, Eva was sitting in a dark room that was now her prison. She wasn't weeping, she was furious. That large woman, Gertrude Morrison, had ripped the telegram from her and read it before ripping it into pieces then grabbing Eva by the hair and walking her back to the small house. She had thrown her into the room without a word then slammed and locked the door. A little while later, she had tossed a chamber pot into the room and relocked the door behind her.

Eva, despite her furor, began plotting her escape. It was just two days before her eighteenth birthday. She didn't expect a party, nor did she think she'd get her hundred dollars, but she didn't care. She had the two-hundred-dollar voucher in her pocket and just needed to get out because Joe would be coming for her soon and would be joining her…forever.

———

Joe was already getting restless, and he had another day and a half to spend in Abilene. He had dropped Duke off at the livery again where he could rest up after all the hard riding the past few days. Joe had decided to take two of the horses with him, the black gelding that had slammed into the buggy and the gray mare and let Eva choose which one she liked.

He really wanted to see Eva and tell her all that had happened since he had left Manhattan and smiled with the realization that he had just made Eva his best friend, someone to share experiences and someone to share his life.

But he was in Abilene and she was in Manhattan, fifty miles away. He would get to Manhattan on the third day and regretted agreeing to wait the extra day. He felt somewhat selfish for feeling that regret knowing that Danny and Caroline had so much to talk about, including their children. Yet he had only spent a few hours with his sister, so he could find Caroline. He knew there was no purpose in wallowing in emotions, but he did need to find something to occupy his time.

———

Back at the Stevens' home, things were working in Joe's favor. After the initial rush of reunion, Caroline found herself wishing she were back at the Crown D getting to know Jason better. Danny and his wife were nice people, but she found that she had little in common with them other than those uncomfortable childhood memories she had already shared with Danny, and there were soon longer and longer periods of silence with nothing to say. She wished Joe would come back, so she could ask him to come up with an excuse to leave early.

She wasn't aware that Danny and Elizabeth felt exactly the same way. Danny had only been back for a day when Caroline and Joanne arrived and they hadn't had time to resume their spousal relationship, and both felt awkward having Caroline, with her past, in the house when they did. But none of them admitted to their secret desire to end the reunion sooner rather than later.

———

Joe finally had lunch at the café, but it was only a little after noontime when he finished, and he hadn't found anything worth doing. He didn't have any place to go and practice his shooting, which was the only pastime he could come up with.

He may as well go back to the house and see what everyone was doing, so rather than go back and get Duke, he walked to 4th Street, then up the walkway to the brown house with red shutters and knocked on the door. It was opened four seconds later by a grinning Elizabeth who seemed almost ecstatic at his unexpected appearance.

"Joe! We're glad to see you back!" she exclaimed.

"I got bored, so I hope I'm not intruding."

"No, no, not at all. Come on in," she said as she grabbed hold of his arm and almost yanked him inside.

Joe noticed that everyone seemed genuinely happy to see him and wondered what was going on.

"Have you had lunch, Joe?" asked Elizabeth.

"Yes, ma'am. I'm fine."

"Joe," asked Caroline, "were you going to go to Manhattan to see Eva?"

"That was my intention."

Caroline turned to Elizabeth and said, "Elizabeth, I really would hate to be the cause of Joe's delay in seeing Eva again. I know how much she means to him, and he's done so much for all of us, so I think we can sacrifice one day so he can see her sooner. Don't you think?"

Elizabeth was immensely relieved and replied, "You're right, Caroline. We all owe it to Joe to start thinking about him for a change."

Joe caught on quickly that it wasn't concern for him that had inspired the shorter duration of the visit. The old saw about fish and relatives outliving their welcome must have proven true already.

"Well, I really appreciate it. To tell the truth, I was getting a bit anxious to see her again."

Caroline beamed and said, "Then, it's settled. Tomorrow morning, Joe will escort me and Joanne back to the Crown D. I do apologize, Danny and Elizabeth, but we can't think of ourselves so much."

"I couldn't agree more, Caroline," Elizabeth said, her smile never leaving her lips.

Danny was also relieved, but thought Caroline was just being considerate.

Eva's plan to escape was simplicity itself. She'd use the chamber pot to smack the head of Mister Morrison when he brought her lunch. It wouldn't work with Mrs. Morrison as she was not only bigger and stronger, she was highly suspicious by nature. She wouldn't turn her back on Eva for a second.

One quick smack with the heavy pot and she'd be off. She'd run through the back alley, go to the bank and cash the voucher. Then she'd go to the store and buy a new dress and a travel bag, board the train to Lincoln, then find Joe's father. He'd know how to find Joe. Maybe Joe would already be there, but he said he'd come back, so he could almost be here already. Either way, she knew she had to get away before she turned eighteen. Somehow, she felt that Mrs. Morrison was planning something once she was legally an adult.

Joe had dinner with the Stevens and kept the conversation from dragging with more stories. Danny had been surprised with the revelation about Eva, but didn't dare ask Joe about it, especially not with Elizabeth sitting next to him. Besides, his wife hadn't even asked where he'd stayed in Manhattan, and Joe hadn't specified.

After the coffee, they all adjourned to the sitting area, the two toddlers hemmed in by the adults to restrict their curious wanderings.

Even with Joe present, the conversation dragged a bit, but Joe had the advantage of being able to say he needed to leave so he could prepare for tomorrow's departure and told Caroline that he'd be back at eight o'clock for her and Joanne. He left the house, happy to be getting back to Eva a day sooner, regardless of the reason.

He really did have preparations to make as he left the house and pulled out his new watch. It was 7:20, so he headed down to the livery and asked that the two horses be ready to go at seven-thirty tomorrow morning. He knew he didn't have enough room for all his new clothes in his saddlebags, so he pulled the second set from the horse Caroline would be riding and returned to his room to pack. He needed some room for the two diapers they'd be taking along, just in case. It was only a fifteen-mile, two-and-a-half-hour ride, but accidents do happen.

Joe was satisfied all was ready and went to sleep early in anticipation of seeing Eva in two days. He pulled out her note and read it again.

"Soon, Eva," he thought, "Soon."

———

Eva had been thwarted in her lunchtime plan for escape. Gertrude Morrison had brought her lunch and now dinner. She began to think that the evil woman was a witch who could read her mind.

She was getting more exhausted the longer she stayed locked in the room, as she had to sleep on the floor and was unable to sleep well. She felt dirty too, and yearned for a nice, hot bath. She thought about four things: Joe, freedom, a hot bath, and real food, in that order.

But her mind was set. The next time that mousy husband arrived, she'd put him down.

———

Joe was up earlier than he needed to be, 5:40 by his new watch. But he washed, shaved, dressed and put both saddlebags over his shoulders before leaving the room by half past six. He checked out of the hotel and wandered to the café for a big breakfast, then took his time and stretched his coffee until it was time to go.

He was at the livery five minutes early, but both horses were saddled and were ready to ride. Joe tossed the saddlebags in place, tied them down, then led them outside, mounted Duke and trailed the other horse down the street, feeling good about moving again and with the knowledge he'd be heading back to Manhattan and Eva a day early.

He walked the horses to 4th Street and then to the brown house, stepped down and loose;y tied Duke to the hitching post. He removed his bedroll and fashioned Joanne's riding seat before walking down the entrance to the house and checked his watch. He was fifteen minutes early, but they should be ready.

Caroline was more than ready. She was already getting antsy, even though it wasn't even eight o'clock yet. Joanne had just been changed, so they'd probably be good for the short ride.

When Joe knocked on the door, Caroline popped up and trotted the six steps to open it.

"Joe! Come on in. We're ready anytime you are," she said with a big grin.

"Good morning, everyone. Sorry I'm a little early. I'm just kind of anxious to get going."

"We understand completely," said Danny, feeling a bit anxious himself as he glanced over at Elizabeth.

There were farewell kisses from the women and a manly handshake between Joe and Danny. Promises of future reunions were passed between the Stevens, and after five minutes, Joe, Caroline and Joanne were out the door. Danny and Elizabeth stood on the porch waving as they got underway.

Joe and Caroline waved as they left. After their final wave, Danny and Elizabeth went inside, closed the door, and scurried past little David to the bedroom.

Joe and Caroline left Abilene at eight o'clock exactly.

As they trotted along, Caroline said, "Joe, I have a confession to make. I really just wanted to go and see Jason. It was already getting boring. We ran out of things to say after a few hours. Does that sound horrible?"

"No, it doesn't. Elizabeth felt the same way."

"She did? How'd you know?"

"You could read it in her eyes. It was the same with you. Danny was buying the fake reason at first, but when he realized that he and Elizabeth could spend some private time together, he joined in wholeheartedly."

"How do you know that?"

"My father showed me how to read people. He spent more time with that than anything else. It's what makes a good lawman better. You can be a great shot with a pistol, and lightning fast, but if you don't know who is likely to shoot you in the back during a barroom fight, you're dead. If you can spot those men first, you can avoid a lot of pain. It all comes from that. Listening to how things are said as much as what is said and always watching the eyes. It's easy to see what's a lie and what's not. Most people, when they lie, won't look you in the eyes. There are exceptions and some lie so well, it's believable. But there are other ways to spot the untruths."

"Is that why you like Eva so much and so quickly?"

"One of the many reasons. We talked for three hours a few nights ago and could have gone another ten or twelve. There was no empty conversation at all. Everything she told me was meaningful and showed me more about her than if I'd known her since childhood. She's just eighteen and she's much more mature than that. In many ways, she's more mature than I am. But that aside, she's got a wonderful sense of humor, not the giggly little girl humor, but a wit that I imagine, if turned loose, could emasculate any man she chose. But her nature would prevent that. She's such a good, considerate person."

"Wow, Joe! You really are smitten," she smiled.

"It's well beyond that, Caroline. I wouldn't even dare categorize it as smitten because it almost cheapens what I feel for her. Eva, in just a short time, has captured my heart and soul. I already see her as my best friend and haven't a doubt in my mind or heart that she's the one woman for me."

"I'm happy for you, Joe, and for Eva, too. I'm even a little jealous, if you must know. You're going to make her a very happy woman."

"I hope so, Caroline. I just need to get her out of there."

They continued chatting affably during the remaining hour and a half, and Caroline began to look at Joe differently and began to be a bit jealous of Eva, knowing what she and Joe shared.

Joanne slept most of the ride and was still wearing the same diaper when they arrived at Chapman a little past ten as Joe was able to pick up the pace quite a bit.

"Caroline, let's stop at the sheriff's office and see if he found out about getting the deed for the ranch transferred to Joanne."

"I'm glad you remembered that, Joe," she replied.

They pulled up before the sheriff's office. Joe lowered Joanne, who had been getting fidgety after an hour, to Caroline, then stepped down and they went inside.

As soon as they entered, the sheriff stood and smiled.

"Morning, folks. How'd the visit go?"

"Wonderful," answered Caroline.

"Hank, what did Judge Abernathy say about the Crown D?"

Hank's smile expanded into a wider grin as he replied, "Just a minute."

He pulled out his desk drawer and pulled out several sheets of paper.

"When I told the judge the story, he was furious, pulled out a sheet of paper and began writing."

He slid the papers across the desk.

"The first one is an order appointing Caroline the legal guardian of Joanne. Because her birth was never recorded, you can get that done any time you wish, Caroline. Second, this is the court order awarding ownership of the Crown D to Joanne as the sole surviving heir. That also means she gets the balance of their bank account, $2478.55, but because she's a toddler, Caroline has total control of the money."

Caroline was speechless. Now, she had more than a home. She had everything she could ever ask for and knew that Jason was back on the ranch waiting for her.

She took the precious pages and folded them.

The sheriff said, "Just take the one to the bank, so they'll put your name on the account. Then take it to the land office to change the deed, and you'll be all set."

Caroline handed Joanne to Joe, walked around the desk and planted a big kiss on Hank's cheek.

"Thank you so much, Sheriff."

"You're welcome, Miss Stevens."

"Call me Caroline, please."

"And call me Hank. If anyone gives you trouble you come and see me. I'll be a lot closer than Joe."

She thanked him again then they left the office, went back to the horses, and Caroline asked if it would be okay to get the bank and land office visits done while they were there. Joe told her it would be fine, as he wouldn't be leaving for Manhattan until the morning anyway.

Both visits went smoothly, and they even took time to have lunch at the café before heading south to the Crown D. Caroline was getting more excited with each step the horses took in anticipation of what she expected would be a far less boring reunion.

———

Eva's breakfast had been delivered by Gertrude Morrison, and Eva was beginning to get frustrated. She regretted not making her escape the first day when Nate Morrison had brought her lunch and hoped it would be today.

Ten minutes later, she heard the lock turn and hadn't heard Mrs. Morrison's decisive, hard-heeled steps. *It must be Nate!*

She grabbed the chamber pot and waited for the door to open as she stood against the door frame, away from the door opening. The door swung away, and Nate's small, balding head peered inside with the tray.

She swung hard, the pot smashing into his scalp, and he dropped like a rock. She took a second to make sure he was still breathing and then ran quickly through the door, turned to her left, and moved hurriedly down the alley feeling exhilarated. She was free. She had just turned eighteen, but this was the best gift of all, and she had given it to herself.

Eva finally slowed down when she neared the main street. She had to go to the bank first. *Would they even cash the voucher? She knew she looked shabby, but they had to, didn't they?*

She tried to look as dignified as possible as she walked into the lobby of the First Kansas State Bank and stepped up to the cashier's window and slid the voucher across the shelf.

"I need to cash this, please."

The cashier looked at the voucher and flipped it over.

"I'm sorry, miss. I can't cash this."

Eva was devastated. Her chance for escape had just vanished.

Then he said, “You haven’t endorsed it yet.”

Eva recovered quickly, smiled and said, “Oh, I’m sorry,” as she took the offered pen.

She signed the back and returned it to the cashier who counted out the cash.

“Thank you,” she said, still smiling as she slipped the cash into her dress pocket.

“You’re welcome, miss,” he replied with his unsmiling business face.

Eva strode from the bank feeling more confident and then walked to the clothing store, bought a new dress, camisole, stockings, shoes and a travel bag. She was even able to buy a hairbrush there. She paid for the order and then walked quickly to the Railroad Hotel and rented a room, took the room key and went to her room. She left the clothes and travel bag on the bed, then left the room and trotted down the hallway to the bathroom.

She took her hot bath but had to abandon the soothing water sooner than she wished. Time was critical, she believed, expecting the witch woman to be searching for her. She returned to her room and quickly changed into her new clothes and brushed her hair. She felt like a real woman for the first time in her life and wished Joe could see her now.

“Soon, Joe,” she thought, “Soon.”

She checked out of the hotel and walked to the ticket agent’s booth at the adjoining train station. She knew that Joe said he’d be coming, but she couldn’t risk being discovered by Mrs.

Morrison, who would probably have her arrested for assaulting her husband.

"Excuse me, could you tell me when the next train to Lincoln departs?"

He looked at his board.

"It'll be arriving in twenty minutes, Miss."

She smiled at her good fortune and said, "I'll take a ticket, please."

"That'll be $32.15."

Eva took out her bills and paid for the ticket. She put the $7.85 cents in the small pocket on the dress and put the other bills in her travel bag.

Eva didn't realize it, but she had committed the cardinal sin of new travelers; never show anyone how much money you have. As it happened, there was another woman on the platform with her waiting for the train, and she noticed Eva put the bills into her travel bag.

Fifteen minutes later, the train for Lincoln arrived. Eva was excited beyond her imagination. In just a few hours, she'd be in Lincoln and maybe Joe would already be there. But if he hadn't returned, she'd find his parents and sister, Josephine, and they'd know where to find him.

She boarded the train, found a seat near a window then the train pulled out of the station just minutes later and Eva, who had been almost sleepless the last few nights, promptly fell asleep as the train turned north.

———

After the train had gone, a furious Gertrude Morrison found her pathetic, whining husband still sitting on the floor at the room's entrance. She was angry at the girl for escaping, angry at her stupid husband for letting her escape, and mostly, she was angry because now, she'd have to start taking care of the whole damned boarding house by herself. Her husband was useless.

"But, Gertie," he tried his most mollifying voice, "at least we didn't have to give her the hundred dollars."

Gertie reached back and slapped him across the side of his already damaged head, knocking him back to the floor.

She was mumbling, "weak bastard" as she left.

As Eva's train was travelling away from Manhattan, Joe and Caroline were getting Joanne settled in her accustomed bedroom. Jason had been delighted by their premature arrival.

After Joanne was down and napping, Joe said he needed to go and check out the horses and left Jason and Caroline alone to get better acquainted.

He walked out to the corral to check on his four horses, climbed the fence and headed for the black gelding, the buggy gelding. Joe knew he had to take him along. He also had to wear that moniker forever – Buggy. Buggy was a handsome horse, but smaller than average. He did seem to have fire in his eyes though and Joe wondered if it was because he was small and had something to prove.

Then he checked out the gray mare. She wasn't very old, unlike the popular tune of the day. Joe stepped up to her and rubbed her neck. She was very responsive. He walked her around the corral, checking her gait and found it very smooth. She earned her name with that walk, Silk. So, Buggy and Silk would be coming with him to bring Eva to Lincoln. He was pleased with both horses as he left the corral and walked to the barn, stepped inside and found the saddles and firearms he had liberated from the miscreants.

He began examining the Winchesters. Just looking down the barrels, he could tell which two had been used with the hot loads. He chose the other two. He may as well add one of the Colts while he was at it. All seemed in good condition, but he selected the best of the bunch. Then he took off his own gunbelt and was going to exchange it with one of the others because of the damage done to the cartridge loops by the .44, but he decided against it. They still worked except for the one that had been hit and lost its cartridge, and he wanted to show his father the close call, but surely wouldn't show mother as it would be akin to committing suicide.

Finally, he checked out the saddles and found two he liked. He took a few minutes to adjust the stirrups of the one he would give to Eva, already sure of her height and probably could guess her weight within a pound or two as well. He set aside the two saddles, Winchesters, and the Colt and added two ropes as well. He wouldn't be needing them, but you never knew. The last thing he wanted to find was the nicest bedroll, and two were almost new. He guessed they had belonged to the Alta Vista duo who probably never spent a day without a roof over their heads. A rig just didn't look right without a bedroll, so they must have added them for show.

He had two sets of saddlebags already, so he grabbed a third and two more canteens to finish the ensemble.

He left the barn and was going to return to the house but didn't want to interrupt anything, so he stopped and returned to brush Duke and then Silk and Buggy.

While Eva's train hurried along the tracks, she continued to sleep. Unknown to her, she had a bench mate during the long trip. The woman on the platform who had watched her shove her stack of paperbacks into her travel bag was sitting next to her watching the boring Great Plains landscape roll past. The car only had four other occupants, all of them in front of their bench.

The woman reached down into Eva's travel bag and without looking easily found the cash. She simply picked it up and stuffed it into her own travel bag, then waited five minutes, walked to her own seat two rows ahead and across the aisle. She smiled as she watched the prairie roll by.

Joe had done all he could in preparation for tomorrow's departure for Manhattan. It was getting late and he needed to get something to eat. He figured he might as well save some travel time and get a room in Chapman. He could get breakfast early in the café and be on the road by seven o'clock.

Once he made up his mind, he brought Duke, Buggy, and Silk into the barn, saddled each horse and hung the saddlebags in place, including the extra Colt. He slid the now fully loaded Winchesters into their scabbards, then fashioned a trail rope and hitched the three horses together.

He led them to the front of the house, tossed Duke's reins over the hitching post, then stepped up onto the porch and rapped on the door.

He waited for almost a minute and was preparing to knock again when Caroline opened the door and it was obvious why the door took so long to be answered.

"Joe. I wasn't expecting you," she said, breathing quickly, her clothes and hair in disarray.

"I just wanted to let you know I was leaving. I figured I could get to Chapman and cut five miles off tomorrow's ride. I've cut out the two horses I'll be taking with me. Tell Jason you can keep the other two, and all the gear I left, including the guns."

"Joe, you can stay the night. Really."

"No, Caroline. This is fine. I've got to go. I need to find Eva."

"Okay. You take care, Joe," she replied, then smiled and quickly closed the door.

Joe just shook his head. He didn't know why, but he was disappointed in Caroline.

But he didn't take time to dwell on it before he turned, stepped down from the porch quickly, mounted Duke and set off for Chapman.

He arrived in Chapman at a little after six o'clock and had dinner first. Then he dropped off the three horses and told the liveryman he'd be by at seven to pick them up.

He walked to the hotel and checked in, found his room and readied himself for tomorrow's journey. Tomorrow, he'd see Eva again and he knew sleep would be a long time coming tonight as the very thought already was making it difficult to think right.

Eva's sleep ended when she heard the conductor shouting, "Lincoln. Next stop is Lincoln."

Eva rubbed her eyes and yawned. She was very stiff from her long nap in an awkward position, then looked outside and saw Lincoln coming into view. It was a lot larger than she expected. Joe had made it sound like a nice, but not overly populous town. She was also curious about the length of the train trip because it was already dark, and she didn't think it should have taken that long.

She shrugged, picked up her travel bag and prepared to exit the train.

The only other woman in the car was the first to leave the train and Eva was allowed to exit second. If Eva had been on the platform side of the passenger car, she would have learned the shocking truth earlier by seeing the large station sign. As it was, she exited the train with a broad smile on her face, then looked around, half expecting to see Joe waiting for her.

But Joe wasn't there. In honesty, it was just a hopeful dream anyway because she knew he would be heading for Manhattan. She stepped down from the platform with her bag and saw cobbled streets. It was her first indication that something was wrong. She walked down the boardwalk, looking for the sheriff's office.

Things just didn't look right. Everything was too big, and too populated.

It was when she found the sheriff's office that she had her answer.

The sign said: William Fontaine, Sheriff, Lincoln, Nebraska.

She cursed under her breath. She had asked the clerk for the next train to Lincoln and hadn't even given a thought that he might interpret that as Lincoln, Nebraska instead of Kansas which was much closer. She took a breath and calmed down. At least she had enough money to buy a ticket back to Kansas and then onto the other Lincoln.

She walked back to the train station and to the ticket window.

“Excuse me, but I accidentally bought a ticket to Lincoln, Nebraska when I needed to go to Lincoln, Kansas. How much would a ticket be to Lincoln, Kansas and when does the next train leave?”

He checked his schedules.

“The next train that could get you there would be our 8:10 train to Topeka, then you could pick up the 1:40 train out of Topeka to Lincoln, Kansas. It would cost $36.70.”

“Alright. I’ll need one,” she said as she opened her travel bag.

She felt for the bills first but couldn’t find them and felt queasy inside, then pulled the travel bag to the shelf and opened it wider and began rummaging through her clothes and found no money at all.

“I’ve been robbed!” she exclaimed, “I had a hundred and sixty dollars in my travel bag, and it’s all gone!”

The ticket agent made no expressions of sympathy nor assistance. He felt it wasn’t his job. Besides, it was a fairly common trick. A good-looking woman comes to buy a ticket, claims she was robbed and expects the kindly ticket agent to give her a ticket gratis, but not Horace Belton, no sir. He wasn’t born yesterday.

Finally, a distraught Eva had to move away to allow other customers access to the ticket window. She calmed down, reached into her pocket and counted out the money she still had in her possession and found the $7.85 from the last ticket purchase. It wasn't much.

But Eva knew one thing that mattered. She knew how to find Joe.

She walked over to the Western Union Office and wrote out a telegram.

SHERIFF HENNESSEY LINCOLN KANSAS

TELL JOE EVA IS IN LINCOLN NEBRASKA BY MISTAKE
WAS ROBBED AND ALMOST OUT OF MONEY
CAN STAY AT RAILWAY HOTEL FOR TWO DAYS
WILL WAIT ON PLATFORM FOR HIM IF FUNDS EXPIRE
TELL JOE EVA SAID YES TO FOREVER

EVA PORTER LINCOLN NEBRASKA

The operator said, "That'll be eighty cents, ma'am."

Eva handed him the change and hoped this would work.

CHAPTER 6

Joe did hit the road at seven as he planned and found that his new pocket watch had an alarm which made getting up late no longer possible. He was moving quickly, with his two-horse entourage following and expected to be in Manhattan before noon.

———

Will looked at the telegram that he found in his office on the floor when he arrived, but it didn't make much sense to him.

Who was Eva and why would Joe want to know she was stuck in Lincoln? Besides, where was Joe?

He picked up the telegram to take it to the experts, left the office walked back to the house and was soon showing it to Clara and Josephine.

"What do you think, Clara?"

"I'm not sure, Will. Josephine?"

"Remember he said he was going back to Manhattan for a few days? If I'm right, I think Eva is the reason he was going back. Now she writes that she was in Lincoln, Nebraska by mistake. She must have wanted to come here. Then there's the line at the end. She wrote to tell Joe she said yes to forever. It sounds like Joe proposed."

Will and Clara stared at Josephine before Clara asked, "Do you think so, Josephine?"

"I'm pretty sure."

"What can we do, Jo?"

"Look. I've got tons of money. I'll wire fifty dollars to her and tell her to come back here."

"It might be a waste of money, Jo."

"I'll gamble it for Joe. It's the least I can do for my big brother."

Clara smiled and said, "You're a good sister, Josephine."

"Mama, you'll never even come close to guessing just how much I owe him."

———

Eva had lunch at the café, spending twenty-five cents of her small reserve and leaving a nickel tip. She wanted to wait until after two o'clock to get a room, so she could stay until tomorrow at check out. She was running the numbers in her head. The room was two dollars and the meals would cost her about fifty cents for dinner, but breakfast and lunch would be cheaper. She decided to stay the night and have dinner. She'd have breakfast in the morning and see what happened before she stayed another day. Her biggest hope was that the telegram to Joe's father would provide the help she needed.

She was sitting on the bench outside the hotel and noticed a man staring at her and acted as if she hadn't noticed, but she would turn her head every now and then to find him still watching her. She felt a chill and decided to go to the hotel earlier.

When she reached the desk to register, she glanced backward and noticed that he was gone, exhaled and went to her room. She'd take a longer hot bath this time knowing Mrs. Morrison wouldn't be able to find her.

———

Joe arrived in Manhattan just before noon, stopped at the livery and had all three horses unsaddled, brushed, fed and watered. He asked the liveryman to check their shoes and replace any that needed new ones and he said he'd take care of it.

He left the livery and stopped at the café for a quick lunch. After he wolfed it down, he left the eatery and was anxious to head to the boarding house to take the now-adult Eva with him to Lincoln.

He walked to the boarding house with a spring in his step, reached the boarding house and opened the door, his heart pounding. He walked inside, hoping to see those dancing blue eyes and smiling face but instead, he saw a large, stern-looking woman striding toward him.

"Who are you?" she almost growled.

Joe was taken aback by the greeting but recognized the voice.

"My name's Joe Carlisle, ma'am. I just got in from the Crown D ranch and heading to do some work at the Double C outside of Riley. I figured I'd take a day to see the town. I'll be needin' a room for the night."

"It's four dollars a night."

"Seems a might steep for a boardin' house, ma'am. Your prices always been that high?"

"If you don't like it, go to the hotel. I don't have time to argue with a dumb cowboy."

Joe dropped the cowboy act and said, "You must be Mrs. Morrison. Where's Eva, lady? Don't make me mad, either. I'm already on the edge of shooting both you and your husband for the way you treated her."

Gertrude's visage went from hostile to positively evil.

"Are you threatening me? I've squashed bigger men than you," she snarled.

"I don't doubt it. Especially if you want to be on top. And in answer to your question, yes, I'm threatening you. In the past two weeks, I've killed seven men, gotten one hanged, and left one a cripple. Every one of them was some tough bastard who thought he could take advantage of others. I'll put you in that category, despite your anatomical differences. So, snarl all you want, you bitch. If you don't tell me where Eva is, I'll do better than pound you to a pulp."

Then he flipped open his vest showing his badge and said, "I'll just head over to the sheriff's office and have him shut you down for violating the terms of the contract you signed. You and your husband will be penniless in a week."

Gertrude's wheels were churning. She knew that she had seriously violated all terms of the contract. If they investigated, they might find out about her being locked in the room.

"Alright. The truth is she left yesterday. She ran off. I really don't have an idea where she went."

As much as Joe would love to tell her she was lying, he knew she wasn't.

"You could have just said that in the beginning and saved us both a lot of insults."

She said nothing as Joe turned and left the boarding house. *Where would Eva have gone?*

He could only think of one place. She must have gone to Lincoln. She would have gotten his telegram and if she had run from the Morrisons, she would most likely been looking for him before she left town. *Why hadn't he gotten here a day earlier?*

He walked quickly to the train station, stepped up on the platform and headed for the ticket agent.

"Can I help you, young man?"

"Did you sell a ticket yesterday to a pretty young woman about five and a half feet tall with light brown hair and blue eyes. She probably wanted to go to Lincoln."

"I did. She took the 2:40 for Lincoln yesterday."

"Wait a minute. The train for Lincoln leaves Salina at 9:30, so it must leave here around 7:30."

"That's the train to Lincoln, Kansas. She took the train to Lincoln, Nebraska."

"Why would she do that? Did she specifically say Lincoln, Nebraska, or did she just ask for Lincoln?"

The ticket agent didn't want to admit his mistake, so he waffled.

"I'm not sure. It was yesterday, after all."

Joe made a snap decision and said, “Give me a ticket to Lincoln, Nebraska. When does it get in?”

“It'll arrive at Lincoln at 6:50.”

Joe paid for the ticket and figured he had an hour left, so he trotted back to the livery and paid for two more days for the horses. He had his saddlebag with his clothes over his shoulder, so he was ready to go.

He returned to the train station and checked his watch. It was 2:20.

In Lincoln, Nebraska, Eva was in her room when there was a knock on the door. She was afraid it was that man out in front of the hotel and opened the door carefully. It was a messenger.

“Ma'am, I have a telegram for you.”

Eva was amazed that she had received a response so quickly.

She reached in her pocket and pulled out a nickel and handed it to him after he had given her the telegram.

She opened it and found a fifty-dollar Western Union voucher and felt a soothing flush of warmth for her salvation, then read:

EVA PORTER RAILWAY HOTEL LINCOLN NEB

SENT MONEY FOR TICKET
HOPE MY BROTHER FINDS YOU
HE IS SPECIAL

JOSEPHINE CARLISLE LINCOLN KANSAS

Eva wiped a tear from her eye as she remembered the story Joe had told her about how he had rescued Josephine, and now his sister had rescued her. She would go to the bank, cash the voucher and buy her ticket on the 8:10 train to Topeka and then on to the correct Lincoln.

She left the hotel and walked down the boardwalk, looking for the nearest bank, found the First National Bank on the next block and walked inside. This time, she signed the voucher first, and was given the cash.

She walked out of the bank and almost ran into that man from the platform who had obviously been following her. He gave her a smile that made her shiver as she hurried on to the train station and avoided looking behind her, but could feel his eyes examining her with every step.

Eva reached the ticket window and bought her ticket for the 8:10 train to Topeka and then to Lincoln, Kansas. She put the ticket and change in her skirt's small pocket. Without turning around, she walked into the hotel and quickly into her room and locked the door behind her.

She was so close to ending this disaster that her trip had turned into. She knew she'd need to eat dinner before she left, but she'd stay in her room until then.

This was the first train that Joe had been on in three years. He hated it then, and he hated it now. He was just annoyed at the loss of freedom. He liked to be able to go where he wanted and when he wanted. With trains, everything was dependent on when they wanted to leave and where they needed to go. The only advantage was speed, which is what he needed now.

He pulled out his pocket watch. It was 5:10, and he was getting hungry, too. He spent some time checking his two pistols. It made some of the passengers nervous, so he moved his badge to his vest and they all relaxed.

Another hour and a half, then he'd get to Lincoln, Nebraska and try to find Eva. He'd stop at the ticket agent first and find out if she'd taken another train back to Kansas, then he'd check with the hotel. After that, he'd check with the local law. He grinned when he realized that his badge said: Deputy Sheriff with *LINCOLN* in the middle. He may appear to be a local lawman himself.

———

It was almost six o'clock, and Eva thought it was time to leave. She took her travel bag and walked down to the lobby, left her key and went to the hotel restaurant.

She ordered a steak and baked potato because she had enough money now. She finished her dinner and paid for her meal, picked up her travel bag and decided to check and see if the train was on time. It was almost seven o'clock when she left the hotel's restaurant.

Eva walked out onto the platform and saw the man leaning against a roof support smiling at her, then hurried past to the ticket agent to ask about the departure of the train for Topeka as a train was pulling into the station.

———

Joe was sitting on the platform side of the car looking at the station and suddenly sat up. *Was that Eva at the ticket window?*

Eva had the time confirmed and decided to wait in the lobby. She turned, and the man was standing between her and the lobby entrance. She thought she was safe, so she walked toward the lobby as the train slowed.

Joe watched her and was sure it was Eva and was ecstatic to find her so quickly.

Then he saw her hurry toward the lobby, then get intercepted by a man smiling at her and could tell she was getting ready to run and Joe needed to get out…now. But there were six people in front of him exiting the train and he had to wait in line. He kept watching helplessly through the passenger car's windows as the drama in front of the hotel continued.

The man reached over as Eva started to go past and grabbed her left arm.

He said in a low, threatening voice, "Don't make any noises, missy. I've got a pistol in my other hand. Let's go quietly. Now!"

Eva didn't protest as she could see the barrel of the revolver, and she walked more quickly than she wanted to because he was forcing the pace as he led her from the platform onto the boardwalk.

Joe had lost sight of Eva when he finally reached the end of the car, but thirty seconds later, he was off the train and trotting across the platform, weaving between departing and boarding passengers. He left the platform and stopped, looking for Eva.

The man had steered Eva onto the boardwalk and then yanked her into the first open space between buildings.

Joe had to think without panicking. He would've most likely taken her to the nearest place to walk away from the station, so he headed for the boardwalk. He looked ahead and saw no women, just a few men a twenty yards or more away. He could have ducked into a dark space, so Joe walked quickly down the boardwalk, stopped at the first space between buildings and looked into the narrow dirt corridor. There was enough light to see the fresh footprints in the dirt, so he gambled they were Eva's and her captor's and jumped off the boardwalk and followed.

Eva was desperately thinking of a way out of her predicament, and it was obvious what the man had planned for her.

He had pulled her out of the spaces into the back alley and turned right. He went another fifty feet and pulled open a door, shoved her inside, followed her into the dark room, then slammed it closed behind him.

Joe heard the door slam and moved faster. He saw the footprints turn down the alley in the late spring twilight and moved along more slowly until he spotted where the footprints entered a doorway.

He pulled his Colt and cocked the hammer.

Inside the room, the man had shoved Eva onto an old, foul-smelling bed.

"Alright, Missy. Now, you're gonna perform. Let's see those clothes come off."

Joe heard the baritone voice and its threat, took a breath and got a good grip on the door handle, then yanked it open and found a terrified Eva on a bed with the man standing over her with a pistol.

"Drop it, mister! You're under arrest!" Joe shouted.

The man turned quickly, not sure if he was really covered, but his revolver's hammer wasn't cocked, and he quickly discovered that Joe's was.

He dropped the revolver and grinned.

"Just having a little fun, Deputy."

"Not with my fiancée, you weren't. Eva, come over here behind me."

Eva was still in a state of shock. She was about to be raped and suddenly, there was Joe ready to shoot the would-be rapist. *What was Joe doing in Nebraska?* She shook her head to clear it, then stood up, buttoning her dress as she walked behind him.

"Eva, pick up his revolver."

Eva reached down and lifted the Colt from the floor.

"Give me the gun."

Eva handed Joe the gun, now wondering what he was going to do. Joe dropped his saddlebags on the floor along with his Stetson.

With his left hand, Joe cocked the Colt's hammer back one click, and opened the loading gate. He rotated the cylinder until all six chambers were empty and tossed the man's pistol aside. He then handed her his cocked revolver.

After she had it in her hand, he said, "Eva, the pistol is ready to fire. All you have to do is pull the trigger. Now, I aim to show this poor excuse for a man the error of his ways. If you want to go outside, go ahead."

"I'll stay, Joe," she said firmly.

"You're my kind of woman, Eva. The only one."

He pulled off his empty gunbelt and dropped it to the floor. He left his Webley in place for a reason.

"Okay, horse face, let's see if you can do anything but hurt women."

The man grinned. He thought he was pretty good with his fists. Joe was a little bigger, but he'd beaten bigger men before, so he moved in. As Joe took one step forward, Eva took one backward until her back was against the door jamb. She was prepared to shoot the man if he started hurting Joe.

Joe let him take the first swing, so he could judge his level of skill. He should have led with a jab, but instead tried a roundhouse right. As soon as the man's fist cleared his line of sight, Joe hammered a hard uppercut into his ribs with his right and followed immediately with a left to his kidney. Both blows did damage as the man grunted with both shots.

He turned angrily at Joe and lashed out with a swift kick to Joe's knee. It made contact, but Joe's knee was off the floor and moving backward, so his boot struck the lower thigh rather than the knee. But while his leg was extended for the kick, Joe dropped his elbow on the man's knee. It popped, and the man screamed. It wasn't nearly the level of damage he had inflicted on Wallace Gunter, but Joe knew it hurt like hell.

The man was in a crouch and warily approached Joe, weaving back and forth. He swung a hard right at Joe's chest. Joe pivoted slightly and let the blow strike the Webley. Joe heard bones crack in his hand as it crunched into the steel of the holstered pistol. He screamed again, and Joe finished him with a crushing right to his face, smashing his left cheekbone and shoving his nose more than a half an inch to his right as blood splattered across the dingy floor. He slumped over and hit the floor, sobbing.

Joe picked up his gunbelt and put it on. Eva handed him the revolver and Joe released the hammer before returning it to its holster and slipping the hammer loop into position. He picked up his Stetson and saddlebags, slung his saddlebags over his shoulder and pulled the Stetson onto his head as Eva picked up her travel bag.

"Let's go home, Eva," he said, taking Eva's arm.

They left the room and walked out of the alley, then Joe escorted Eva back between the buildings and had to assist her to step up to the boardwalk, then joined her.

"I'm sorry I lost my temper, Eva. Like I told you before, seeing someone innocent being hurt is the only thing that really makes me angry, and it was much worse this time because it was you."

"There's no need to apologize, Joe. If I had been able to, I would have done the same."

"Eva, are you okay?" he asked as he looked at her.

"I am now, Joe. How did you find me? Did Josephine tell you where I was?"

Joe cocked his head and looked at her as he asked, "Josephine?"

"I thought she might have somehow gotten word to you about what happened."

"Why would Josephine know what was going on?"

"I accidentally took the wrong train, and then I was robbed, so I sent a telegram to your father. Josephine replied and sent me money for a ticket to Lincoln."

Joe smiled and said, "No, she didn't let me know. I just found that you had gone and had been misdirected to Nebraska by that idiot ticket agent. I hopped on the first train I could so I could find you. I just happened to see you as the train pulled in. If I hadn't had to wait in line to get off the train, I could have prevented you from even being taken off the boardwalk."

"I'm just so happy that you found me. Do you know what your telegram did to me? I had convinced myself that you were going to find Caroline and forget all about me. Then I read your telegram and saw the word *forever.* I was lost. I had it held against my chest, dreaming of your return. I couldn't believe that you loved me, Joe."

"You should, Eva. I knew almost the moment I saw Caroline that she wasn't even close to you."

"Isn't she pretty?"

"No, she's very pretty. Maybe the prettiest woman I've seen. But remember what I told you about people not acting like themselves? I just got that feeling about Caroline. I may be wrong, but it doesn't matter, Eva. Now I need to get a ticket, but I need to stop in Manhattan. I have three horses there. Did you want to stay overnight and then take the next day's train?"

"Can we ride back? I'd rather do that. I'm getting tired of trains."

Joe continued to smile as he said, "I'd prefer that, too. It's a two-day ride, but we'd get to spend more time together."

"That's a real bonus, then."

“I’ll buy my ticket and then I’ve got to send a telegram to my parents.”

“Okay.”

Joe and Eva walked to the ticket window where Joe bought his ticket and then they headed for the Western Union office. Joe quickly wrote out the message, paid the fee and they headed back out to the platform to catch the train.

Thirty minutes later, they were rolling south through the dark night. For the first hour, Joe filled Eva in on all the events that had happened since he had gone to find Caroline. She had to see his bullet wound, and oddly, it looked worse after it had healed than it had when it was fresh.

She told him what Mrs. Morrison had done to her after reading Joe’s telegram, and how she had escaped. But after an hour, Eva began drifting and soon was sound asleep with her head on Joe’s shoulder. Joe had his arm around her as they left Nebraska and entered Kansas.

———

They arrived in Topeka at 1:45 in the morning. They were staying in the same train, but it had to coal and water, so they didn’t depart the station for forty-five minutes. They arrived in Manhattan at five o’clock in the morning, and Joe was as tired as Eva, but they both left the train in good spirits. They walked straight to the Railway Hotel. Joe got two rooms and carried Eva’s travel bag to her room.

He opened her door, set her bag down and looked into those beautiful, tired blue eyes. He pulled her close and kissed her tenderly. It was Eva’s first experience and as tired as she was, felt herself floating away as if she was in a dream. She kissed Joe harder and held him tighter and didn’t want it to end.

But it did when Joe looked at Eva and said, "I love you, Eva. I'll knock on your door around noon and I'll take you to lunch. Okay?"

She nodded, but as he started to leave, Eva pulled on his elbow, turned him around and kissed him again. He was happy about it, but he knew he had to leave, so he took one more look into Eva's remarkable blue eyes, then smiled, turned and headed for the door.

Joe left the room, closing the door behind him, went to his room next door and set down his saddlebags, took off his Stetson, his gunbelt and boots, then quickly stripped down and crawled under the blankets.

He didn't have to spend any more time imagining what it would be like to be with Eva but was more than pleased to be able to dwell on the memories of the short time they'd spent together.

Eva, as tired as she was, was still so excited, not only her first kiss, but by the man who'd shared it with her. She simply had no idea just how much it would awaken in her and knew she couldn't wait to spend more private time with Joe.

———

The messenger arrived at the Hennessey home at 8:45. It was late, but Joe had the telegram marked urgent.

Josephine answered the door and gave the youngster a nickel.

"Papa, I think we just got our answer from Eva," she said, walking into the kitchen.

She handed Will the telegram, expecting it to be a thank you from Eva, but it wasn't.

Will read the telegram and smiled.

"Well, Clara, it looks like we're going to have a daughter-in-law," he said as he handed the sheet to his wife.

Clara read:

WILL AND CLARA HENNESSEY LINCOLN KANSAS

FOUND MY EVA
MY THANKS TO JOSEPHINE
WILL RIDE BACK FROM MANHATTAN
ARRANGE FOR WEDDING WITH REVEREND HATFIELD
SHOULD BE BACK ON JUNE 9
LOVE TO ALL

JOE HENNESSEY LINCOLN NEB

Clara smiled as well and handed it to Josephine. After reading it, Jo smiled wider than his parents. She would have a sister now, forget the in-law nonsense. If Joe thought she was good enough to marry, Josephine was sure they would become the best of friends.

The next day, Joe woke up after ten o'clock and went down the hallway to the bathroom, took a bath and shaved, returned to his room and dressed in new clothes.

Eva was up shortly afterward and was in the bath ten minutes after Joe had left the tub.

So, when Joe tapped on her door forty minutes later, he was met by a wide awake, clean and very happy Eva. He escorted her downstairs to the hotel restaurant, where they had a big lunch, making up for the missed breakfast. Joe had also missed his dinner the evening before, but felt it was worth it.

Joe and Eva engaged in some serious visual romance while they ate but continued their conversations about what had happened and what each hoped would happen when they returned to Lincoln…Kansas.

After they finished eating, Joe needed to go to the livery to arrange for pick-up of the horses in the morning, so Eva returned to her room for a nap.

Joe was able to trade one of the saddles for a pack saddle, understanding the liveryman was getting the better part of the trade, but he needed the pack saddle. As part of the deal, the liveryman waived his fees for shoeing the gray mare and black gelding.

While Eva was napping, Joe paid a visit to the sheriff's office.

"Good afternoon, Sheriff."

"Welcome back, Deputy. What's going on?"

"Well, I finally tracked down Eva. We're heading back to Lincoln to be married."

"Well, congratulations!"

"We'll be leaving in the morning, but I don't want to leave without letting you know why Eva had to run from Manhattan. It seems that Mrs. Morrison didn't want her to leave, so she locked Eva in a room with no windows, no furniture, and only a chamber pot. What makes it interesting was that she spent her eighteenth birthday locked in the room. She was imprisoned as an adult and it appears that the Morrisons are guilty of unlawful imprisonment. They also violated almost every term of the contract they signed when they chose her from the children's train. Now I know that's a civil case, and when we get to Lincoln, I'll find a lawyer and let Eva sue them, but I did want to let you know about her being locked in the room."

"You're right, if she was in that room when she turned eighteen, it's unlawful imprisonment. They could have gotten away with it when she was under their care, but once she turned eighteen, it's against the law. Want to take a walk with me?"

Joe smiled and replied, "Wouldn't miss it."

The sheriff and Joe walked the two blocks to the Morrison's Boarding House, and when they arrived, the sheriff walked through the door with Joe trailing, as Mrs. Morrison came striding purposefully down the hallway.

"What do you want, Sheriff? And why is that irritating young man with you?"

"Mrs. Morrison, did you lock up Eva Porter in a room with no windows or furniture?"

"Yes, I did! She deserved to be punished. I can do that. And that bitch struck my husband in making her escape yesterday."

"She escaped yesterday?"

"Yes. If I ever find the bitch, I want her arrested for assault."

"Where is your husband? I need to talk to him."

"Just a moment," she replied before she walked away, glaring at Joe as she did.

She returned a minute later with her diminutive husband.

"Hello, Sheriff. Gertie said you wanted to talk to me about how that girl hit me."

"Yes, I did. When did she do this?"

"Yesterday, when I brought her lunch. She hit me in the head with a chamber pot."

The sheriff pulled out a pad and wrote a few lines.

"So, what I need you to do is for each of you to write a quick statement that says what happened. Make sure the date is correct. Yesterday was the 6th of June, I believe."

He handed them each a sheet from the notepad and a spare pencil. They wrote their statements and signed them. He took them back and read them both.

"Well, this is quite obvious that a crime has been committed."

Both Morrisons nodded vigorously.

"You're both under arrest for unlawful imprisonment. Miss Porter turned eighteen on the 5th of June."

They were both thunderstruck as the sheriff turned to Joe and said, "Deputy Hennessey, could you assist in escorting the prisoners to the jail."

"Yes, sir."

Joe and the sheriff walked the still dumbfounded Morrisons out of their boarding house and down the street to the jail.

The sheriff seemed to be enjoying himself and Joe wondered about a trial. If there was to be a trial, Eva would have to stay until the trial was over. He knew he'd stay with her, but it would delay their wedding and he suspected that Eva didn't want to see either of them again, especially the witch.

The sheriff locked the Morrisons in a cell then waved Joe over and they walked outside.

"I'm going to let them sit for a while until they realize this is serious."

"I'll take Eva shopping and then I'll stop by later."

"I'll see what they'll be willing to do to try to get out of going to jail."

Joe shook the sheriff's hand and left the office to return to the hotel. He crossed the lobby and went to Eva's room, knocked lightly and the door opened quickly. Joe stepped inside and was attacked by Eva. She grabbed him and kissed him as he kissed her back and pressed tightly against her.

Finally, their lips parted as he asked, "No nap, Eva?"

"I was too excited, Joe. You took a long time to get the horses ready."

They were still tightly bound as Joe explained, "I swapped one saddle for a pack saddle. Now, you and I are going shopping. You'll need a couple of more nice dresses, a riding outfit, a hat to keep out the sun, and then we'll stop by the dry goods store. I'll need to buy some things for our trip."

"Let's go then," she said, smiling as she finally released her grip.

Joe escorted her from the room, across the lobby, and when they reached the boardwalk, Joe slowed Eva down and said,

"Eva, after I took care of the horses, I paid a visit to the sheriff. I told him what had happened to you and we went to the boarding house. They wanted to file charges against you for assaulting Mister Morrison, so the sheriff had them write out statements about what had happened."

Eva stopped and turned to Joe with wide eyes, "They're going to put me in jail?"

Joe smiled, and replied, "No, sweetheart, not you, the Morrisons. You see, when they threw you in that room, they legally could do it as your guardians. But they left you in the room after you turned eighteen. That makes it unlawful imprisonment. That's why the sheriff had them write the statements. They actually incriminated themselves by writing out that they had locked you in the room and you escaped the day after your eighteenth birthday. Oh, happy birthday, by the way."

"You mean they're going to go to jail?" she asked, her eyes still wide.

"I'm not sure. I think the sheriff's purpose is to wrangle some sort of settlement out of them if you say you'll drop the charges."

"Really?" she asked.

"Really. Now, let's go do our shopping and we'll stop by the jail on the way back."

A buoyant Eva walked with Joe to the clothing store where she bought three dresses, two nightdresses, a riding skirt and blouse, a Stetson and some Western boots. She added some more socks and some other things whose purpose left Joe a bit mystified. Joe paid for the order and checked his remaining cash. It was down to a hundred and seventy-eight dollars and some change, which wasn't too bad, considering. They arranged to have the order sent to the hotel.

Before going to the dry goods store, Joe took Eva to the jewelry store to buy a wedding band set. Eva was fighting back the tears and losing as she looked at the selection. They chose a traditional pair of gold bands that were sized properly, then Joe paid for the rings and slid them into his vest pocket.

Next was the dry goods store, where Joe bought four panniers for Eva's clothing and whatever else they bought. They didn't buy much in the way of food, but they did buy some basics like toothbrushes, tooth powder, and some privacy paper. Joe added some cord to lash the panniers down for the trip, and he also added another box of the .45 caliber cartridges for his Winchester. They took this order with them as they walked to the sheriff's office.

Joe held the door for Eva and followed her inside. The sheriff saw them coming and was wearing a big grin.

"Welcome back. It turns out that the Morrisons also admitted to violating their contract when I mentioned that you were planning on suing them. I suggested, not incorrectly, that they would probably lose the boarding house. Anyway, they've offered a settlement of fifteen-hundred-dollars if Eva drops the charges. They'll write out a draft that you can take to the bank directly."

Joe replied, "Tell them it'll be sixteen-hundred, because they still owe Eva the money that the contract called for."

"I'll be right back."

After the sheriff left, Eva looked up at Joe, her smiling eyes gleaming and Joe knew it wasn't about the money. It was about justice for all the years she had worked for nothing, or that's what he thought. She was really that way because she was with Joe and would be marrying him when they returned to his hometown.

She still had a difficult time digesting it since he'd casually mentioned what he'd written in the telegram he'd sent to his parents. It had been an unusual proposal, and after he told her of the Western Union message content, had formally proposed and she had pretended to think about her answer before he tickled her into submission.

The sheriff returned with a bank draft and handed it to Eva.

"I'll hold them here for another thirty minutes. If the draft clears, then don't come back and I'll let them go. If it doesn't, come on back."

Joe shook his hand and Eva gave him a kiss on the cheek, then the young couple left the office and walked down one block and across the street to the Morrisons' bank. They cashed the draft and Eva handed the large wad of cash to Joe.

"The last time I had any money I was robbed. You hang onto it, Joe."

"Alright, but this is your money, Eva."

"No, Joe. It's our money. It'll be our house, Joe."

"I can afford a house, Eva."

"Well, it really doesn't matter, does it, Joe? If we're together, that's all that matters."

"You're right, Eva."

They reached the hotel, found that Eva's order had been delivered and Joe had them take it to her room. Joe opened the panniers in Eva's room and put all the items they wouldn't need for tomorrow inside. There was still plenty of room.

Eva picked out her riding outfit, boots, socks, undergarments, and Stetson and set them aside. When they finished, all that Eva had on her bed was what she needed to dress in the morning. When they were all done, Joe and Eva closed the door and went down to the restaurant for dinner. They completely enjoyed each other's company, well beyond just being a betrothed couple. They were best friends after all.

After dinner, Joe and Eva stayed in the lobby's sitting area and just talked about what they would be doing tomorrow.

"Eva, did you want to take a side trip? After we reach Chapman, we can take a short swing south to see Caroline and her daughter Joanne."

"I'd love to meet Caroline. I feel like I owe something to her. If you hadn't been looking for her, you never would have found me. Did she name her daughter after you?"

"That's what she says."

"This ought to be interesting."

"There was something unsettling about Caroline that may just be me thinking too much."

Eve didn't answer, but just waited until Joe continued.

"When I arrived at the Crown D, I met with the foreman of the ranch, Jason Arbuckle. I told you how he and the hands rescued Joanne from the Drapers. Anyway, when he saw the adult Caroline, he was smitten. I thought it would be good for Caroline because Jason is a good man. Anyway, we left the Crown D for Abilene later that day, so she could meet Danny and his family, then we left two days later and returned to the ranch.

"I was going to leave in the morning for Manhattan, so I picked out all the stuff I was going to take with me, then returned to the house because I had decided to spend the night in Chapman and get an early start. We hadn't been back to the ranch more than an hour, and when the door opened a very disheveled Caroline answered the door. When I said I was going to leave, she wished me luck and closed the door."

Eva's eyebrows raised as she said, "That was quick."

"I know. I was kind of disappointed in Caroline, but I don't know why. Maybe she got so used to being with men she needed it. I was thrown off seeing her that way. So, now I don't know what to expect after a few more days."

"Did you want to skip going down there?"

"No, I want you to meet her, but more importantly, I want her to meet you."

"Why?"

"Because, soon-to-be Mrs. Hennessey, I want to her to see just how special you are."

Eva smiled and said, "Okay. Maybe everything will have returned to normal."

"I hope so. Maybe they really are right for each other and knew it right away, like we did."

Eva didn't reply. She may only have just turned eighteen but working in a boarding house for all those years gave her a better appreciation of the whole man-woman relationship experience, and she'd had to fend off quite a few advances in her time based on her looks, but it was only when she met Joe that she realized the enormous difference between being smitten and being in love.

"Anyway, we'll stay in Abilene tomorrow night and be in Lincoln the next day."

Eva asked, "We don't need to visit Danny, do we? I think that might be awkward."

"I was going to suggest we don't. He asked me not to tell his wife about how he came on to you, and I told him I wouldn't."

"I think it's for the best."

"Now, tomorrow morning, we'll have breakfast in the hotel. You pack your things in the pannier after breakfast while I'm getting the horses. I'll bring the horses around front and I'll come in, take the panniers and load the gelding. Then we'll check out and be off. How's that sound?"

"Very well thought out. Joe, what about the cash? That's a lot of money to have while we're riding to Lincoln."

"I know. When we leave here, I'll put most of it in one of your clothing boxes. You take a hundred dollars and I already have about a hundred and fifty left of my original cache. Besides, we have enough weapons to scare off most evil doers."

"I should learn how to shoot, shouldn't I?"

"Only if you want to."

"I think you'll have to show me one of these days."

"I can do that. So, are we ready to get packing?"

"Yes, sir."

Joe escorted Eva to her room and opened her door, then closed it behind him, so no one could see the money transfer, or at least that was the excuse he gave himself.

Eva didn't give him a chance to even take out the cash, when, as soon as the door closed, she wrapped her arms around his neck and kissed him passionately. Joe dropped his saddlebags and responded in kind. Eva poured everything into that kiss: her heart, soul, mind and body and Joe did the same. Then Eva experienced something new and more exciting when Joe slipped down and began kissing her neck. Eva felt her toes curl and a chill run down her spine and held onto Joe's head as he continued kissing her.

She whispered hoarsely, "Joe, do you have to go to your room tonight?"

Joe kissed her once more and answered, "I'd love to spend the night in your bed, my almost wife, but I think we can wait three or four more days. The anticipation will make it that much better."

"I want you so badly, Joe. I suppose that makes me an immoral hussy."

Joe laughed softly and said, "Hardly. You're a healthy young woman and have needs and desires just like I do. It's the way God made us, Eva. Without those desires, there would be no children. It'll be my job to satisfy your desires and make you happy. I'll do that, sweetheart. I promise."

"And you always keep your promises," she said as she smiled.

He kissed her once more on the lips before she released him, so they could find the appropriate box for the cash. He gave her the hundred dollars and one more kiss before leaving the room. It would be a difficult night for them both as they lay awake for two hours before succumbing to sleep.

CHAPTER 7

Joe's alarm woke him at six o'clock, and he was dressed and ready to go thirty minutes later. As he left the room, he ran into Eva in the hallway, heading for the bathroom. Joe scanned the empty hallway quickly and gave her a good morning kiss before she padded down the hallway.

After having been through too many bad circumstances the past two weeks, Joe didn't want to leave anything to chance, so he leaned against the door jamb, waiting for her to finish her morning toilet. It took a while, so Joe filled the time imagining life with Eva. He surprised himself, pleasantly, when he realized that he spent most of the time imagining the day-to-day life with her: having meals, talking about daily events, taking her to church, and even waiting for her to bring him his lunch at the office like his mother did. He only spent part of the time imagining the private time with Eva, but it was more than enough.

Joe was almost startled when Eva suddenly popped out of the bathroom and waltzed down the hallway to Joe, kissed him and smiled as she went into her room. Joe checked his watch and was surprised to find he had been standing there for a half an hour. Imagination is good.

He returned to the room and strapped on his gunbelt, put on his Stetson, and threw the two saddlebags over his shoulders. He felt like a pack mule as he left the room.

He had to wait another ten minutes for Eva to make her grand appearance, for that's what it was. She was wearing her riding skirt, Western boots, a white blouse, her Stetson, and a dazzling smile. Joe was speechless as he looked at her.

"Are we going downstairs, Joe?" Eva finally asked, breaking him out of his reverie.

"Oh…right. Let's go, Eva. You just threw me. You look incredibly beautiful in that outfit."

Eva thought she was getting accustomed to Joe's compliments, but this one made her blush as she took his arm and the couple went down the stairs to the restaurant.

When they were finished with their breakfast, Joe paid the check and took Eva's arm as they crossed to the lobby.

"I'll be back in ten minutes with the horses. I'll load the gelding and we'll be on our way."

Eva nodded and sat in one of the lobby chairs.

Forty minutes later, they were walking the horses out of Manhattan heading west.

Joe and Eva rode side by side, so they could talk easily. The horses were moving at a fast walk, so Joe estimated their arrival in Chapman to be around noon. They'd have lunch at the café and drop down to the Crown D but would only stay for thirty minutes or so if they wanted to reach Abilene at a decent time for dinner.

Joe didn't drift on this trip. Aside from having Eva there to engage in stimulating conversation, Eva's presence demanded vigilance against any danger.

It was a noisy ride, punctuated by frequent bouts of laughter. Eva was pleased with Silk, even her name. She hadn't any opportunities to ride in years and was very grateful for Silk's smooth gait. Even with that, her backside was getting sore and was happy when she was finally able to see Chapman in the distance.

Joe said, "We're going to make a short stop at the sheriff's office, so I can introduce you to Hank. He was a big help in fixing Caroline's mess and I'm sure he'll be happy to meet you."

"I'll be happy just to walk again."

"We could have taken the train, Eva. We still can if you'd rather wait until the morning."

"Could we do that, Joe? My bottom is ready to fall off."

"That would be a terrible loss, ma'am. We'll spend the night here in Chapman and then pick up the train early. It should leave around eight o'clock, I think."

"Thank you, Joe. But having the sore behind was worth it. It was a wonderful ride."

"I enjoyed every second, Eva."

They reached Chapman before noon and Joe stopped at the sheriff's office, dismounted and loosely looped Duke's reins around the rail. He helped Eva down from Silk and tied her off.

Eva walked gingerly onto the boardwalk, then stopped, put her hands on her hips and arched her back as she smiled at Joe. Joe almost missed the smile as he was too busy watching other things as Eva had arched her back.

"Entertained, are you, Mister Hennessey?" she asked.

"Very much so, soon-to-be Mrs. Hennessey," he replied honestly.

She grinned and took his arm as Joe opened the door to the office.

Hank saw Joe enter and stood, saying, "Welcome back, Joe. And who is this handsome young lady?"

"In a few days, Eva will be my wife, Hank. We're heading back to Lincoln tomorrow."

"Well, congratulations to you both! Pleased to meet you, Eva. Joe is a very lucky man."

"Oh, I don't know. I think I'm getting the better part of the deal."

"We're going down to the Crown D to pay a visit to Caroline and Jason, then we'll be back here and get a couple of rooms at the hotel."

"Then I'll be seeing you later. I've got to make my rounds here shortly."

Joe shook his hand and Hank tipped his hat to Eva, who smiled at him.

They returned to the horses and Joe helped Eva up onto Silk. Giving her sore behind a very short massage on the way. Eva looked down from her perch and smiled, "Getting fresh, are you?"

"Just practicing, my love," he grinned back.

"Why don't we get lunch when we get back. That big breakfast is holding on."

"Same here. I'll go along with that plan."

Joe mounted Duke and they headed south to the Crown D.

They had a very pleasant ride for the first three miles, despite Eva's continuing discomfort. She knew she'd need a hot bath to sooth her soreness.

After that, however, things began to change. Eva noticed it first.

"Joe, is that gunfire?"

Joe stopped the horses. Eva was right. It was gunfire. A lot of gunfire.

"Eva, I'm going to hitch Buggy to Silk. I want you to ride at a trot back to Chapman and tell Hank what you heard and that I'm going to investigate. You stay in his office until I return. Don't forget. You've got our house in those panniers."

Eva knew she'd be useless in a gun battle, so she just nodded. Joe hopped down and transferred the trail rope to Silk. Luckily, all his spare ammunition was in his saddlebags, so he didn't have to transfer anything.

"Go, Eva! Tell Hank it sounds like it's coming from the Crown D."

Eva said, "Please stay safe, Joe. I'm not going to lose you so close to our wedding."

"You won't, sweetheart. Now go!"

Eva set Silk off at a trot and Buggy followed.

Joe stepped back onto Duke and set him at a fast trot toward the Crown D. He had wondered if shooting those two from the Happy House would have repercussions and was surprised that they waited this long. He just didn't know who was behind it.

He moved his badge to his vest and kept going. The shooting was getting louder and more sporadic. He'd have to slow down and get an idea of the situation he was facing before he stuck his nose in the hornet's nest.

He came around the final bend and saw six horses hitched near the access road on the signposts. So, there were six attackers, and they were still shooting Winchesters, so they must not be close to the house yet.

He stopped Duke and stepped down, took out the box of .45 cartridges and filled his vest and pants pockets with the entire box. He let Duke just stand and grabbed his Winchester after leaving his Stetson on his saddle horn.

He began jogging toward the sound of the gunfire and it took five minutes to get a good view of the situation. He spotted several locations with gunsmoke clouds hovering overhead, and two were in the barn. Joe knew that Jason probably had limited ammunition and hoped he had moved the two extra Winchesters with their hot loads into the house, but he doubted it.

It was another five minutes, when he was two hundred yards out that he spotted the first shooter. He was behind the trough at the front of the house, so Joe took a knee and began looking for others that might be covering for the trough man. He saw another bloom of gun smoke to the man's right and found a second man standing behind the barn. That gave him two targets if he shifted to his right.

Joe began jogging to his right as he moved closer to the house and barn. Fire from the house was sporadic which meant they were saving ammunition, and they were using pistols by the sounds of their reports. He wondered why they were shooting at all as the attackers were all well out of pistol range.

Joe closed to within a hundred yards and stopped. He had both men in range and in clear sight. This was no gentleman's fight. This was war.

Joe levered in a fresh round, catching the expelled cartridge and shoving it back into the loading gate, then aimed at the barn shooter first. He would be able to find cover faster if he saw the trough shooter fall. The trough shooter had nowhere else to hide.

Joe took aim and squeezed the trigger. The Winchester '76 belched a large cloud of gunsmoke and flame as the .45 caliber round blasted from the muzzle toward its target and didn't take long to find it. The man threw up his hands and fell face first into the barn, but Joe didn't waste time as he quickly turned to the trough shooter. The man hadn't seen the barn shooter get hit, which probably wouldn't matter much as he was so exposed.

Joe levered in a new round and aimed, held his breath and fired. The second man must have been hit a little low, because he grabbed the side of his abdomen and rolled onto the dirt in pain. Joe didn't sympathize, as he began jogging for the barn.

One of the two loft shooters had seen the trough shooter get hit and didn't know how it was possible at the angle the defenders had available to them.

He turned to his loft partner and said, "Hey, Jim. Take a look at Orville. He's been hit. How'd they get him?"

Jim peered down from the loft doors and saw Orville squirming.

“Maybe a splinter hit him from the trough. They’ve been aiming his way.”

“Yeah. That’s probably it. Figure they’re almost out of ammo?”

“Gotta be. They’re only firing once or twice a minute now.”

“Pretty soon, they’ll be out. Who gets first shot at Carol?”

“I think Billie does, but we’ll all get her at least once for what she did.”

“We’ll get that cowboy first, though. I wanna see her face when we gut him right in front of her.”

While they were imagining gutting Joe, Joe had opened the back door to the barn and stepped inside, his Winchester fully loaded again and cocked. He could hear them talking from the loft and debated climbing the ladder or shooting through the loft floor. If he climbed the ladder, he could be heard. If he shot through the loft floor, it would more than likely be a miss, but if he peppered the loft floor with six rapid shots, it was unlikely the two shooters would escape damage, so he opted for the loft floor shots.

Joe kept moving forward as Jim and Earl resumed firing at the house, which helped him locate their positions above his head.

He stopped in the middle of the barn and looked up and caught a break. Both men were in kneeling positions and they blocked the light coming through the loft floor gaps, giving him a much more precise location. He aimed at the shooter on the right first.

Earl had just fired and was levering a new round when the floor beneath him exploded and the powerful .45 caliber round traveled through his calf, shattering his tibia before passing through his left kidney, lung and exiting under his left clavicle, dropping him to the wooden loft floor.

Jim pivoted rapidly, shocked at the sudden trauma four feet away, but wasn't shocked long as Joe's second round crashed through the board under him. The bullet missed Jim's lower extremities but because he had turned to look at Earl, hit him in the right abdomen, making a mess of his liver before destroying his right lung. The bullet exited almost at the same location as Earl's fatal bullet had departed, but on the opposite side. Jim hit the floor, his head smacking into Earl's side, but felt nothing.

Joe didn't wait to see if they were dead. They were surely out of action as their blood began to drip through the holes in the loft floor. He trotted to the front of the barn to find the last two shooters.

Jack Ritter, the bartender from the Happy House and the instigator of the raid, had seen both Jim and Earl die and was confused. *How had they been shot?* It didn't take long for him to realize that it had to be from inside the barn. *But how did one of them get out of the house and into the barn?* He was debating about heading to the barn and find out what was going on, but knew he'd lose the protection that he and Jasper had behind the bunkhouse.

He turned to Jasper and asked, "Jasper! Did you see any of them get out of the house?"

"Nah. We've got 'em penned up real good, Jack."

“Somebody just took out Jim and Earl. And if he got them, he probably got Bob in the back of the barn too.”

“What about Orville? I haven’t heard anything from him lately.”

“I don’t like this, Jasper. If we make a break to get back to the horses, we might get hit from the house. We have an unknown shooter in the barn. If he killed everybody else, he’s probably a better shot than anyone in the house. Tell you what, let’s head east about fifty yards and then circle the house fast about a hundred yards out so they can’t hit us. We get on our horses and head back to Alta Vista. They can’t touch us there.”

“Sounds like a good idea, Jack. Let’s go on three.”

As they were counting to three, Joe figured out that the last two shooters had to be behind the bunkhouse. It was within Winchester range of the house and provided cover. But they had stopped firing and Joe guessed they had seen the two barn shooters go down. Maybe they were planning on running, and if they reached their horses, they’d be back to their Hell Hole Hideaway before they could be run down, and he didn’t want them to make it off the ranch alive.

Joe decided to gamble, so he ran to the back of the barn and after he was out, began running for their horses that he could still see tied to the ranch sign three hundred yards away.

Inside the house, Jason and the other four men were still hunkered down. Jason was next to Caroline with Joanne in between, and none of them had rifles. They had tossed out sporadic pistol fire, but now they were all empty except for two or three rounds in their chambers and were waiting for the inevitable.

They had been caught flat-footed enjoying a pleasant lunch when the first rifle shots had blasted through the house. It had been going on for almost forty minutes now. Miraculously, no one had suffered a serious hit. One of the hands, Jerome Whitfield, had been punctured by a large splinter which lodged in his neck, but hadn't hit anything serious.

Suddenly, they noticed the cessation of gunfire, which could only mean one thing.

"I think they're coming in," said Jason. "Let's all sit in a circle, backs toward Caroline and Joanne. If they come in the house, we start shooting our last rounds."

"Okay, boss," answered Charlie Davis.

But the only two survivors weren't going in, they were running away. They had already arced across the yard and were only sixty yards from their horses and were beginning to think they'd get away.

Joe was still breathing hard after his sprint from the barn to their horses and knew they'd probably see Duke just standing by his lonesome a few hundred yards away, but that couldn't be helped now.

He was bent over at the waist, not because of his lack of breath, but to keep most of his body hidden behind their horses. He had heard the last two shooters running, but not so much because of their boot steps, but from their labored breathing, which meant they were close, less than fifty yards out. So, he quickly stood up and stepped out in front of the horses, his Winchester already cocked and leveled.

"Drop the rifles! Now!" he shouted.

Jack recognized him, but didn't hesitate and pulled his Winchester to bear and Joe fired. The powerful round struck the stock of Jack's Winchester, shattering the wood and taking off most of Jack's left shoulder that had been supporting it, the mangled bullet expanding into a lead plug as it struck.

Jasper had already dropped his rifle when Joe's shot hit the stock, sending large splinters of walnut into his face and neck. He was in a lot of pain, but he would survive.

Joe jogged over to the two men finding that Jack was obviously dead with the huge hole where his shoulder had been.

Joe didn't show a lot of mercy as he bound Jasper's wrists and ankles without pulling any of the splinters, dropped him to the ground, then fast-walked toward the house. He didn't know if they'd shoot him, so he stopped when he got within fifty yards.

He cupped his hands around his mouth and yelled, "Hello the house! Caroline! Jason! It's Joe Hennessey. You can come out now!"

Inside the house, they heard his shout but didn't believe it at first. Joe was back in Lincoln. *Wasn't he?*

"Think it's a trick, boss?"

Jason replied, "I'm not sure. Caroline, did they know Joe's name?"

"I don't think so."

Outside, Joe figured they might be too afraid, so he tried again.

"Caroline! I promised to come and find you, but I didn't think I'd have to do it twice!"

Caroline smiled and said, “It’s Joe.”

They all stood quickly, and Jason helped Caroline to her feet. She picked up Joanne and they walked toward the door.

Jason opened the door and saw Joe standing there with his Winchester ’76 on his hip. It was the most welcoming sight that they could imagine.

Joe saw them exit and began walking closer, his Winchester now in his hand.

“Joe, you are a sight for sore eyes!” shouted Jason.

“We need to go and make sure that the two in the loft are both dead. I’m pretty sure they are. One of them surrendered. He’s tied up near their horses. I sent Eva back to Chapman for the sheriff, so he should be here shortly. Is anyone hurt?”

“Jerome took a splinter, but we already removed it and bandaged it. Joe, we only had twelve rounds in our pistols left. If you hadn’t arrived when you did…” Jason said, then shuddered.

“Jason, I can’t tell you how much I need to get back to Lincoln where I don’t get into gunfights every twenty minutes.”

Caroline asked, “Did I hear you say you sent Eva to get the sheriff?”

Joe turned to her and said, “Yes, ma’am. I had to track her all the way to Lincoln, Nebraska. Some yahoo ticket agent assumed she meant Lincoln, Nebraska instead of Kansas. As soon as we get home, we’re getting married.”

Caroline didn’t smile, but asked, “Will she be coming down with the sheriff?”

"I told her to wait there, but I have a suspicion she'll be trailing along. She left about an hour ago, so the sheriff should be showing up shortly. Did someone want to check on the two in the loft? I've got to go and pull those splinters out of the one up front. Caroline, I'll need you to come along and tell me who he is if he doesn't feel like talking."

"I'll come, too," said Jason, which was no surprise to Joe.

They walked up front to the shivering, bound Jasper and Caroline immediately identified him.

"That's Jasper Brock. He's one of Phil's lackeys."

Joe crouched in front of him. "Jasper, I'm going to start pulling these splinters. Whose idea was this, anyway?"

Jasper was in pain and needed no incentive to talk.

"It was Jack's. He said we owed it to Phil and that we could get the operation going again by ourselves, but only if we made an example of Carol."

Joe didn't comment as there was no point. He began pulling out the large splinters, and Jasper winced whenever one came out. Joe had all the large and medium ones out, but it would take a doctor to get the myriad smaller ones pulled free.

"That's the best I can do, Jasper. The rest will have to be removed by a doctor."

The sound of hooves turned Joe around, and he spotted Eva trailing Buggy as they rode behind the sheriff.

They pulled up and both stepped down, Eva holding onto Silk's reins.

Joe passed Hank holding up his index finger to delay questions as he said, “Just a second, Hank. I need to chew out my fiancée for disobeying orders.”

Eva thought she might be in trouble for coming back, but she had to know if Joe was safe.

Joe stepped up to Eva, her blue eyes filled with apologies, but Joe didn’t want to hear them. He just picked her up and kissed her.

He then whispered in her ear, “I love you, Eva.”

That was the sum of his admonitions, which she readily accepted. Eva was so relieved and happy to see Joe without a scratch all she could do was smile.

Joe set her down and turned to the sheriff.

“Hank, near as I can tell from what Jasper over there on the ground told me, Jack, the bartender at the Happy House Saloon convinced these other clowns to attack the ranch to prove to the whores that there was no escape, then they’d reopen under his management. They surrounded the house while everyone was at lunch and opened fire from protected locations. Jason told me all they had was pistols, so there was no chance of returning effective fire.

“When we got close, Eva heard the gunfire and I sent her back for you. Even though they had numbers, I had a real advantage. I was behind them and they didn’t notice my firing because they were all shooting. It wasn’t until I had taken out four of them that Jack and Jasper noticed and made a break for the horses, but I was already there waiting. I told them to drop their rifles. Jasper did, but Jack leveled his Winchester, so I shot him. Looks like my shot hit his stock and then blew through his shoulder. Jasper caught a lot of splinters, so he needs to see a doctor to get all the small ones removed."

"Jesus, Joe! Do you have to find these things everywhere you go? This is just crazy!"

"You don't know how crazy it is, Hank. I've only been in four or five gunfights before I left to attend what should have been a pleasant reunion, and I surely don't want to get into any more for a while. Do we send one of the boys to fetch the doc and the undertaker?"

"Good idea. I'll go and check out the dead ones."

"Hank, if it's all right with you, let's leave the horses and guns with the boys. They should have had Winchesters in the house. Any money they find on these jerks can fund their burial and repairs to the house."

"That works for me. Less paperwork."

Jason sent Jerome to Chapman, so the doctor could look at his neck wound before coming to the Crown D. The other men began consolidating the bodies and checking pockets and saddlebags. The six men had a total of $218.45 which was more than enough to cover putting them in the ground and fixing the holes in the house.

Caroline and Jason returned to the house with Hank and the hands to do some writing and Joe knew he'd have to submit his report as well.

But now, he and Eva were alone in the front yard under the hot Kansas sun.

"I've got to go and get Duke. Will you walk with me, Eva?"

She didn't answer, but just took his hand and they stepped off.

"How bad was it, Joe?"

"Not too bad, Eva. This one was almost unfair. They were all concentrating on shooting the house and they never even saw me. The others were worse. The worst of them was the drygulch attempt by those two highwaymen. They almost got me twice and had me in a bad situation. If they had spread further apart, it would probably had ended very differently. The others were all amateurs. They made too many mistakes. Now, Big Jim Anderson and Snake Jones were professional criminals, so I was lucky then. But I'm getting tired, Eva. I want to take you home, get married and live a nice life and come home to you every night."

"I can live with you being a lawman and even getting into shootouts, but I really don't like not getting to help. When I was riding back to get the sheriff, I promised myself that I would learn to shoot well, and I'd never be sent away again. And, like you, I never break promises."

Joe looked at Eva and said with a big smile, "You'll do."

Eva grinned back at him.

They retrieved Duke and brought him and the other two horses to the trough on the other side, away from the dead man.

After they had finished, they led them to the crowded hitch rail and tied off Duke and Silk then walked inside.

It was well past lunch time, so Eva asked Caroline if she could use the kitchen to make lunch for her and Joe. Caroline joined her in the kitchen as her report already written. It wasn't very long. In fact, none of the defenders had long reports, only Joe's was lengthy.

While Joe wrote, Caroline and Eva became better acquainted. Eva had to admit that Caroline was prettier than she was and had a fuller figure, but it didn't bother her for a second. She had Joe and Caroline didn't, and there was a reason for her feeling that way. She'd tell Joe later.

Joe spent twenty minutes writing and as he finished, Eva came out with two plates of food for her and Joe while Caroline brought two glasses of water, then quickly turned and left.

Joe and Eva had their lunch, and Eva would occasionally give him knowing glances with sly smiles. Joe didn't understand what she had found out, but it must be interesting. He was sure it had something to do with Caroline as she'd been more distant since Eva's arrival.

After the reports were done, the sheriff collected them all and went back out to his horse with everyone following.

Out front, the doctor was helping Jasper into his buggy.

"Joe, are you and Eva coming back to Chapman today?" Hank asked.

"Yes, sir. We'll be leaving here shortly and checking into the hotel. I'll probably stop at the dry goods store before we check in though. I need to pick up a couple of things."

"Good enough. I'll see you when you get back. I imagine Carl will be by in a bit to collect those five bodies. I gotta tell you, Joe. That '76 really packs a wallop. That was some nasty damage."

"I was pretty close for most of them."

"I may have to have the city splurge for one of them."

Joe walked to Duke and pulled out his '76, then walked back and handed it to Hank.

"You keep this one. I have a few '73s I can use until I get a new '76."

"Thanks, Joe. I'll remember how this one was used, too."

They shook hands and Hank mounted with his new rifle in his hand.

He waved, then headed out and passed the undertaker as he drove his wagon onto the ranch.

"Eva, I think we should be headed back, too. It's already after two o'clock."

"That's fine with me. Let's go and make our farewells."

Eva and Joe walked with linked arms as they climbed the steps to the front porch and walked through the still open door.

Caroline and Jason were talking when they entered but stopped and looked their way.

Joe said, "Caroline, we're going to get back to Chapman. We need to do some things before we leave on the early train tomorrow."

Caroline and Jason stood and stepped over.

"Are you sure you've got to go?" she asked as she looked into Joe's eyes.

"We do. We need to buy some things before the store closes, and I need to see the sheriff and send a telegram."

“We understand. You have a nice trip back and be sure to tell Josephine that I wish I could meet her again.”

“You’re always welcome to visit, Caroline. It’s only a two-hour train ride.”

“Maybe we will.”

She gave Eva a hug and Joe a kiss on the cheek, then Jason shook Joe’s hand and that was the end of their visit to the Crown D.

Joe was secretly glad to leave, and it wasn’t anything to do with the gunfight. There was an uneasiness he felt when talking to Caroline. Everything she said sounded as if it was from some etiquette manual. He’d talk to Eva about it later, maybe on the ride back to Chapman.

They stepped down from the porch and Joe was tempted to help Eva up onto her horse again but didn’t. Eva was disappointed that he hadn’t because she really wanted to let Caroline see him do it.

They turned their horses back to the access road and rode past the undertaker as he and his assistant were loading the bodies into their wagon. There were too many for a hearse.

Once they were on the road, Joe turned to Eva.

“All right, Eva. What were you dying to tell me?”

Eva grinned and replied, “I was talking to Caroline in the kitchen. She said some interesting things about you.”

“What in God’s name could she say about me?”

“When you first found Caroline, where was it?”

"In the Happy House Saloon."

"And what happened when you went to her room?"

"She kissed me before I had a chance to tell her who I was."

"Exactly. She told me that when you did, her toes curled. It had never happened to her before."

"I'm surprised about that."

"I'm not. Remember, I've been on the receiving end."

"Well, you've had the same effect on me, Eva."

"Really?" she asked with an unbelieving smile.

"Trust me. You do."

"Well, anyway, it seems that when you were leaving the ranch to come and find me, you interrupted a private moment between her and Jason."

"I am well aware of that."

"Well, it started because Caroline wanted to feel her toes curl again. Jason took that as a go signal and, well, he went. The problem was that Caroline said she didn't get to feel her toes curl again and was disappointed. Now, she feels like she might have made a bad decision in telling you that she thought of you as a big brother."

Joe let loose with a long laugh, feeling as if he had dodged a bullet. It explained her using stilted language when they were there and that long look that she gave him when he said that they'd be leaving.

"She'll be all right after a while, Eva. Jason's a good man. When she figures it out that marriage involves a lot more than having your toes curled, she'll be fine."

"I'm glad I'm going to get the toe curling as a bonus, though."

"So, am I, Eva."

They reached Chapman fifteen minutes later and stopped at the sheriff's office first. Hank told them that everything looked good and he notified the county sheriff that he might want to head down to Alta Vista and let the citizens know that they might be able to hire a lawman now.

Joe and Eva then went to the dry goods store. Joe bought a money belt and a thick envelope. Their last stop before the hotel was the Western Union office where Joe sent a telegram to his parents.

WILL AND CLARA HENNESSEY LINCOLN KANSAS

**WILL BE ARRIVING ON TRAIN TOMORROW WITH EVA
GLAD TO BE COMING HOME
LOVE**

JOE HENNESSEY CHAPMAN KANSAS

Joe paid his forty cents and they crossed back to the hotel. Joe unloaded the panniers from Buggy, including the one with the cash, brought them into the hotel and engaged two rooms. Joe brought the panniers into Eva's room and then took out the cash, put the money in the thick envelope and initialed the sealed edge and signed the front. He stopped at the front desk and asked that the envelope be placed in the hotel safe, was given a receipt and returned to Eva's room.

“Eva, I’m going to take the horses down to the livery for the night. What will you be doing?”

“I am going to take a bath, a long, hot bath. I need to get my backside feeling normal again.”

“I’d be willing to provide massage services later,” he said as he grinned.

“I have no objections. It’s you, oh prude of a fiancé, who seems to have concerns.”

“Now, I’ve been called many things, but never a prude.”

“The truth hurts, doesn’t it?” she said as she smiled as she began collecting things for her bath.

Joe laughed, knowing how much he was going to enjoy having Eva around all the time.

He went back outside, led the horses down to the livery and told the liveryman that they’d be taking the 8:10 train in the morning and he agreed to have them ready to go.

He was going to go directly to his room but changed his mind and returned to the dry goods store, made one more purchase and then returned to the hotel and his room.

Eva must have waited until the bathwater was room temperature, because she finally returned to her room an hour later with prune toes and fingers. Joe gave her twenty minutes to dress, then walked to her room and tapped on the door.

Eva opened the door wearing one of her new dresses. As usual, Joe was impressed. He kept having to remind himself that Eva had just turned eighteen and couldn’t imagine how even more amazing she would be in two or three years when she physically matured.

He offered Eva his arm, then they left the hotel and crossed the boardwalk to the café. After an unremarkable dinner, except for the company, they returned to the hotel and sat in the lobby talking. Eva asked what had happened at the Crown D and Joe gave her a detailed description. Like Joe himself, she wondered why in the past few weeks, he had been involved in so many gunfights, not to mention two fistfights. Part of the reason was that he was so busy getting his friends out of trouble, but three were totally unrelated and just seemed to happen.

"Joe, I think you need to go and lock yourself in the office when you get back."

"Somebody would probably just break in and start shooting."

"Joe, I have to admit I'm a bit nervous about meeting your parents tomorrow."

"Eva, look at it this way. You met the Morrisons and survived that horrible situation. I met my parents ten years ago and have loved them ever since, and you'll find the same thing. You'll be loved by them and Josephine almost as much as you are by me."

Eva smiled and said, "You sure know how to make a girl feel wanted."

"You have no idea how much you're wanted, Eva."

"I think I do," she replied before she sighed.

He just looked into her expressive eyes and smiled.

After an hour of innuendo and suggestive conversation, they finally called it a night and headed to their rooms.

Joe opened her door, followed her inside, then just as the door clicked shut, Eva renewed her assault as the sexual inferences over the past hour inspired her recently discovered lust.

Joe finally risked being called a prude again and gave her one more long, passionate kiss and a final fondle before struggling out of her room into the hallway.

Eva was sad to see him go, but knew he was right. They could wait a few more days, and tomorrow she'd be meeting his family, and she was still a bit nervous, but she was excited, too. Having a family that cares about you would be a new experience just as much as having a man love her for her and not for the pretty package on the outside.

Joe reached his room and even after undressing and getting in bed was still uncomfortable. Eva had him so excited, he thought he wouldn't be able to stop. It had been very close and now he was paying the price, but felt it was well worth the discomfort. Tomorrow, he'd be taking her home and was absolutely sure that his parents would welcome her just as they had welcomed him, and maybe more because she would be arriving happy and not sullen as he had been when he first arrived in Lincoln. He knew that Josephine would be ecstatic to have a true sister to share experiences.

As he thought about Jo, he knew that, of the four, she had the worst experience. Caroline's was marginally better in that she wasn't about to be beaten to death. Then there was Eva's circumstances which while not as bad as either Jo's or Caroline's, wasn't exactly pleasant.

His and Danny's were positively benign experiences and he wondered if most girls had problems as bad but found it hard to believe. He thought it was more because they had been the last ones chosen, and suspected that it was true for Eva as well because it was so far away.

He had no real idea why it had worked out the way that it did, but he knew that he had helped the three women he cared about to have better lives and felt better about that than anything else. It was worth all the death and mayhem to free the three of them from their miserable lives, and he'd be spending the rest of his life with one of them, just not the one he had thought he would when he'd left Lincoln. But that decision to keep his promise had resulted the greatest reward he could imagine.

CHAPTER 8

Joe and Eva's morning was hectic. Joe was up and dressed and outfitted by six o'clock. While Eva slept, he walked to the livery and took the three horses to the railroad stock corral, bought two tickets and three horse transports to Lincoln…Kansas this time. He felt he should write a letter to the railroad about the ticket agent who worked for the Atchison, Topeka and Santa Fe, the same railroad he had saved from having a train scattered all over the prairie.

He returned to the corral and took Buggy, with his pack saddle and walked him back to the hotel, then tied his reins to the hitching rail.

He walked quickly into the hotel, tapped on Eva's door as he passed, went into his room and picked up his saddlebags, hung them over his shoulders and picked up yesterday's last purchase. He double-checked the room and found it clean of his possessions then left the room and waited outside Eva's room, putting down the last item against the wall. She opened the door just a few seconds later, seemingly ready to go.

"Good morning, Eva. You look your usual stunningly beautiful self."

She smiled and curtsied as she said, "Thank you, sir."

"I'll go and load the panniers and get Buggy back to the corral. Then we'll go and get some breakfast. As we have a reasonably long ride to Lincoln on rather hard seats, I picked this up for you."

Joe reached down and picked up the pillow he had bought and handed it to her.

She laughed, took the small pillow and said, “I thank you from the bottom of my bottom.”

Joe laughed and gave her a chaste hug, entered the room and began hefting the panniers out to the street. He had Buggy packed and ready to go fifteen minutes later, then returned to the hotel, checked out and recovered the envelope from the safe. He walked down the hallway, slipped the cash into the new money belt he bought the day before, then returned and escorted Eva out of the hotel. They led Buggy to the café and tied him off before entering, and after their breakfast, they led the loaded gelding to the train station where Joe took him into the corral and tagged all three horses.

As they waited for the train, Joe and Eva sat on one of the benches near the tracks holding hands.

“One adventure is almost over, Eva, and a much more wonderful one is about to begin.”

Eva took his arm and held on tight knowing that nothing more needed to be said.

The train’s whistle was heard in the distance and Joe squeezed Eva’s hand. It was time to go home.

There was a party-like atmosphere in Lincoln, and Will, Clara and Josephine were preparing the house for their arrival. It was as clean as it ever had been, the larder had been stocked and Josephine made sure that all the female things that Eva would need were available.

"Do you think it'll be all right, Jo?" Will asked.

"I hope so. It'll be wonderful to have a sister."

"We're excited, too. Maybe we'll have a grandbaby next year," added Clara.

Will smiled at his wife. She had never had a baby and now, their wonderful son would give her the joy of holding her grandchild.

"Well, they'll be arriving in less than an hour. Is everything ready?" Will asked.

Both women said things were as well-prepared as it would ever be before they left the house for the train station.

The train had just passed through Tescott, and they were ten miles out of Lincoln and Eva was a cauldron of emotions as the train neared her new home. Joe was aware of most of them just by looking at her face, so he just held her hand.

Will, Clara and Josephine were on the platform and could see the smoke from the coal-burning locomotive in the distance and Jo was even more anxious to see Joe and Eva than his parents were. It would be the real reunion that she had missed just a few days ago.

The train began slowing as it neared Lincoln's station, and excitement was building both on the platform and in the last passenger car that held Joe and Eva.

The locomotive finally began belching plumes of steam as it released unnecessary power and rolled to a hissing halt.

Joe picked up his saddlebags, hung them over his shoulders, pulled on his Stetson, rose from their seat, then helped Eva to stand. She left the pillow for some other sore-bottomed passenger.

Eva let Joe take the lead as her nerves were still singing loudly. Joe stepped out onto the passenger car steps and saw three people on the platform awaiting the only two passengers to be disembarking.

Joe stepped down onto the platform and put out a hand for Eva. She held his hand as if it was a life preserver and stepped down beside him, then both took two steps forward, and Eva soon discovered that she had a family.

Clara was the first to embrace Eva as Joe gave Josephine a big hug and a kiss on the cheek. He shook his father's hand and then pulled him into a bear hug. By then, Josephine had managed to get hold of her soon to be sister-in-law and hugged her as well.

Eva was overwhelmed, these weren't perfunctory acts of welcome, they were genuine acts of love and affection. Her nervous state was washed away, and she gladly returned the same feelings to her new family.

Joe was beaming as he said, "Papa, Mama, Josephine, I'd like you all to meet Eva. Eva, I'm sure you can figure out who is who."

His father said, "Joe, you're going to have to tell us what happened after you found Josephine. We received two five-hundred-dollar vouchers and a letter from the railroad. Then we read all these stories in the newspaper."

"It was an eventful time, Papa. But the most eventful was finding Eva."

“I can see that, son. She’s a beautiful girl.”

Joe looked at Eva who was smiling at him and said, “She’s so much more than that, Papa. She’s my best friend.”

“Just like my Clara is mine,” he replied as he smiled at his wife.

“You’ve taught me well, Papa.”

“Now, let’s head home and get everything settled.”

“Papa, I have to go and get the horses.”

“You go ahead. We’ll all escort Eva to the house and make her feel at home.”

“You already have, Papa. I’ll be back soon,” Joe said before glancing at Eva.

Eva gave a finger wave and a smile to Joe as Josephine and Clara took her arms and Will took Clara’s other arm before they paraded off the platform while Joe left the other side to get the horses.

Joe walked to the corral, picked up the three animals, then led them across the street to the Hennessey house. He needed to visit the bank today to deposit the money and the almost two thousand dollars in vouchers. He knew he and Eva could buy a nice house and furnish it as well with the voucher money alone.

He led the horses to the hitching post and tied them off, then stepped up onto the familiar porch and felt an overwhelming sense of relief. It was all over: the shootouts, the fighting, the anxiety. He was home with his parents, his sister, and his Eva.

He walked inside and set his saddlebags down, knowing that everyone must be in the kitchen when he heard laughter from the other end of the hallway. It was good to be home.

When he reached the kitchen, Clara already had coffee prepared and some of her wonderful cinnamon rolls.

“Mama, you’re going to make me fat,” he said as he entered.

“I’ve been trying for ten years and all you keep doing is getting taller.”

Joe laughed along with the rest of the family before he took a seat and they all enjoyed coffee and cinnamon rolls while talking about the many escapades that Joe had been through since he left Lincoln two weeks earlier which took a while and Eva added her parts of the stories as well.

After they had finally finished, Joe asked the question that Eva wanted answered as badly as he did.

“Papa, when will Reverend Hatfield be able to marry us?”

“We set it up for the 12th of June. Is that all right?”

“I suppose Eva and I can wait another three days. Is it all right with you, Eva?”

“It’ll be difficult, but I can suffer three more days,” she replied with a smile.

“We need to get to the bank and deposit the vouchers and the cash I have in a money belt and I want to add Eva to the account as well. Even though we’re not married, it won’t matter to the bank. She’ll just sign her name as Eva Hennessey.”

“Why don’t you do that before lunch?” asked Clara.

“We’ll do that, and while we’re there, we can talk to Henry about buying a house. We’ll have more than enough to buy a house now,” said Joe as he looked into Eva’s smiling eyes.

“Remember the Wilson house?” asked Will.

Joe looked back at his father and replied, “Sure. Pete Wilson lives three houses down.”

“Well, after you left, he and his wife moved to Salina, so it should be available.”

Joe turned his eyes back to Eva and said, “It’s a big house, but very nice. Can we go and see it later, do you think, Papa?”

“I think so. I have the key. I’m supposed to check on it every now and then.”

“Is it furnished, Papa?”

“Yes. Very nicely, I might add.”

“Eva, did you want to go and look at it after we make the trip to the bank?”

“I’d love to,” she answered with excitement in her voice.

“Here are those vouchers and the letter from the railroad. You might want to read it first. Maybe they sent you a reward for saving the train,” suggested Will.

“The Atchison, Topeka and Santa Fe isn’t on my list of appreciated firms right now. Their ticket agent sent Eva to the wrong state.”

Everyone smiled as he opened the envelope, and to his surprise, it did contain a reward; a substantial reward of a thousand dollars. There were also two lifetime passes on the railroad. The letter was a well-written thank you from the president of the railroad, which meant it was probably written by his secretary.

"Well, I guess they've moved up on the list after all," he said as he smiled and slid the letter and everything else to Eva.

Eva looked at the passes, then smiled at Josephine and said, "I wish I'd had this when I was stranded in Nebraska, but I did get a wonderful telegram from my future sister instead."

They finished their coffee, then they stood, Joe took Eva's arm and the envelope with the draft, then slid the four vouchers into the envelope as well.

"We'll be back in a little while and we can all head over to the Wilson house."

"It sounds like a sound plan to me," replied his father.

Joe and Eva left the house and walked to the bank. It was only two blocks away, so it didn't take long.

Joe found Richard Stacey, one of the clerks.

"Richard, we need to take care of some things. Can you help us?"

"Sure thing, Joe. The whole town is glad to see you back. It sounds like you've been living a dime novel life since you've been gone."

"That's one way to describe it. Richard, this is Eva. We're going to be married in three days and I'd like to add her to my account, and we have some deposits to make as well."

"Sure. Let me get the forms and your account balance."

Joe took out the envelope and the money belt. He signed the vouchers and the bank draft from the railroad.

Richard returned with the forms and Eva wrote her name as Eva Hennessey for the first time, smiling as she did, then when she finished, she took Joe's hand as he began handing Richard the vouchers and the draft, and let him count the cash.

When all was said and done, Joe and Eva had a balance of $6,328.65. Joe slid the balance sheet to Eva, and she was taken aback by the amount. It was more than enough to buy three or even four houses.

Richard also gave them five blank drafts with the account number already on them. Joe folded them and put them in the money belt.

Richard congratulated them on their upcoming nuptials and shook Joe's hand.

They left the bank and headed back to the Hennessey house.

"Eva, this is going to be the longest three days in my life," Joe said as he walked with Eva on his arm.

"I know. I wanted it to be today, but we'll survive, Joe."

"That's easy for you to say," he said as he grinned at her.

They reached the house and found the family waiting outside.

"All done at the bank, Joe?" Will asked.

"Yes, sir. Shall we go and see the Wilson house?"

"Let's do that," he replied and stood up gingerly. His knees weren't happy.

The group turned left at the Hennessey house entrance and walked past two houses until they approached the Wilson house.

"Joe, it's beautiful!" gushed Eva.

"I always thought so. Pete Wilson had good taste."

They walked up the steps to the porch and Will unlocked the door.

The first one in was Eva, then Joe let Josephine and his mother in followed by his father before he entered.

It was a very nice house. The rooms were large and well furnished. There was a lot of light and none of that dark wood that was so popular in the East. Eva was bouncing from room to room excitedly, almost giddy mostly because she knew she would be living in this house with Joe. Everything about it was perfect, just like her future husband.

Joe watched his fiancée and had a permanent smile on his face. The house even had a full dining room and a library. The books were still there, too.

But when he reached the kitchen, he was confused, but Eva hadn't noticed what Joe had. She was too wrapped up in the beautiful stove and all the kitchenware, dishes and glassware. The kitchen was complete, much more complete than it should have been, and his trained investigative instincts noticed the anomaly.

He turned to his father and said, "Papa, there is fresh food in here. How could Peter leave two weeks ago, and all this food be here?"

Josephine answered, "Because we put it here, big brother. Papa, Mama and I made sure it was ready for you and Eva."

"But how did you know I'd want to buy it?"

"We didn't. I bought it for you and Eva. When we received the telegram three days ago saying you were bringing Eva with you, we knew you were going to need a home. Now, I had all this money and nothing to spend it on. I have a wonderful place to live and new parents that love me. You did this all for me, Joe. Buying this house for you and Eva is just a small way of telling you that I love you and will love Eva as the sister I know she'll be. So, don't fall into any manly protesting. This is a wedding gift from me to you and your beautiful bride."

Joe didn't protest, he just stepped to Josephine, hugged his sister and said softly, "Thank you, Jo."

Eva was a bit more demonstrative. She hugged Josephine, then looked at her almost-sister-in-law for three seconds before they both squealed and started bouncing. Josephine felt the money was well spent after Eva's reaction.

"Well, now that we don't have to spend the money on a house, Eva. We could add a small barn for the horses."

"That's an excellent idea," said Will.

"Papa, that reminds me. I have Duke and Eva has Silk. Did you want Buggy?"

"Buggy? Does he have fleas?"

"He's the horse I used to smash into the buggy when Mrs. Draper was going to shoot Caroline. He's a very good horse. Handsome, too."

“Do you know I’ve never had my own horse? I’ve always had what the town had bought for my use, and if you have a barn and corral, it would be easy to come over and ride. Thanks, Joe. I won’t even change his name. It’s one of those names that begs a question and a story.”

“How about if I fix lunch in our new home?” asked Eva.

“We’ll help,” added Josephine.

“We’re going to go outside and see where to put the barn,” said Will.

With assignments made, Will and Joe headed out the back door. The property itself wasn’t large by western standards, three acres, but it was more than enough for a barn big enough to house four to six horses with an accompanying corral.

While they were choosing a location, Will asked, “How bad was it, Joe?”

“Close on two occasions, Papa. Other than that, not too bad. I really wouldn’t want to take that kind of risk again now that I have Eva, but if I have to, I will.”

“So, you’re going to stay in Lincoln as my deputy?”

“Of course, Papa. I love it here. We have good people and I feel it’s an honor to protect them.”

“The reason I’m asking is that I’m retiring, Joe. I’ve already talked to the mayor and council. They agreed, but only if you’ll take over as sheriff. We struck a rather unusual agreement. Because of your proven skills, they’re not going to hire a deputy. What they’re going to do is pay me a deputy’s salary for the rest of my life and I’ll serve as an advisor to you. Your pay, now that you’re getting married and they don’t have to pay for food or boarding, will be seventy-five dollars a month. I'll get thirty-five dollars a month, which is plenty for me and your mother. We have a healthy bank account. You know we don't buy things we don't need. I just can't get around well enough to do the job right anymore, Joe."

"Okay, Papa. I'll do it. Having you as an advisor will be important. You've been my advisor since the day you and Mama picked me."

Father and son embraced and made a show of measuring off the site of the new barn.

They returned to the house and Clara asked, "Did you tell him?"

"Yes, Clara. The town of Lincoln will continue to have a sheriff named Hennessey for years to come."

Eva looked over at Joe with a big smile on her face. She had been told by Clara after Joe and Will had gone outside.

"Did you find a good place for the barn?" Eva asked.

Joe replied, "We did. I'll talk to Lee Enders about getting it built tomorrow. I suppose I've got to go and buy a suit tomorrow, too."

"You'd better. I don't expect to marry a man wearing the suit that God provided," Eva replied as she smiled.

"Why not? We could make it a natural wedding. Everyone wearing the same suits."

"Including the reverend?" asked Eva with arched eyebrows.

That instigated a lively, and often off-color discussion as they all settled down to lunch.

The afternoon was spent moving the panniers of clothing into the new house. Josephine had thought of everything else. Eva was surprised to see all the soaps and shampoos that were obviously for her and not Joe.

They had dinner at the older Hennessey's house and afterwards the awkward question of sleeping arrangements hung over the young couple. Neither wanted to ask, so the five talked about everything else as the sun began to set, and the answer came, surprisingly, from Joe's mother.

"Well," said Clara, "it's been an exciting day. As much as we'd love to have you stay longer, I'm already getting a bit tired. So, we'll say goodnight to you both. Enjoy your new home."

Joe hesitated, "Mama, we're not married yet. I don't want anyone thinking badly of Eva. I can sleep here, and Jo can stay with Eva until the wedding."

Josephine interrupted, saying, "I'm not giving up my comfortable bed for a strange bed. You two just behave yourselves. I'm sure you will behave perfectly."

Eva glanced over at Joe and blushed slightly.

"Goodnight, Joe and Eva. We'll see you in the morning," said Will with finality.

"Goodnight, then," said Joe, taking Eva's hand.

Joe gave his mother and sister a hug and kiss and his father a hug as well. Eva followed suit but added a kiss to Papa Hennessey.

The young couple walked slowly in the twilight toward their new home.

"I can't believe what Josephine did for us, Joe. She even has scented soaps and shampoo for me."

"Jo was always like that when we were little. We didn't have much, but she was always willing to share."

She glanced at him, and asked, "And you weren't?"

"I would have died for Jo," he replied quietly.

Eva knew it wasn't some offhand remark as she could see the bonds when they were together and didn't doubt for a moment that he would do the same for her, because she knew she would for him.

The mood was much lighter by the time they climbed the steps to the porch of their new home. Joe opened the door and let Eva enter. After shutting the door, Joe lit some lamps and closed the curtains as Eva watched with a smile.

They didn't say a word as Joe led Eva to their new bedroom, although Eva wasn't being led as much as she was pushing him to a faster pace. Once they cleared the bedroom's threshold, things grew frantic, as kissing, grabbing and disrobing all occurred simultaneously. Built up passions were released in a mayhem of love and unbridled lust. It was a powerful combination.

Joe regretted that he wasn't able to restrain himself as long as he'd wished he could, but Eva didn't mind. She wanted Joe as much as Joe wanted her.

They were lying in bed thirty minutes later, Joe still overwhelmed by Eva's enthusiastic responses to their lovemaking.

"Eva, for one who was new to all this, I've always wondered how you seemed to understand so much. I mean, Caroline, who was in a similar situation, didn't even know what was going on. Did someone explain it all to you? I can't see Mrs. Morrison doing that."

Eva, her head resting on Joe's chest, replied, "No. No one told me anything at all, but I did work in a boarding house for seven years. I heard a lot of things and a lot of the women would take me aside and confide in me or explain what had happened. You know the odd thing? So many of them expressed disappointment in their husbands' performances. They wanted more but received less. The husbands would feel satisfied and roll over and go to sleep, but trust me, my husband, I was not disappointed in the least."

"I was disappointed in my own performance, Eva. I wanted to take longer to make you feel more excited. I just couldn't hold back," he said as he slid his fingers on his left hand softly across her skin.

"I couldn't exactly restrain myself, either. Does this mean that we didn't behave ourselves as Josephine knew we would?"

Joe continued to feel Eva and answered, "I think we behaved exactly as Josephine expected us to behave. But still, Eva, the next time will be slower, and I will make you feel more love than you could ever imagine."

Eva smiled and slid even closer up on Joe's chest.

"Will you be ready again tomorrow night, Joe?" she asked quietly.

"Why, are you already too tired tonight?"

"But, Joe, all those women said…"

Joe began to kiss her, and as she felt her excitement rising, she whispered, "But they all said that…"

Joe rolled Eva onto her back and she knew that what those women had said was…wrong.

An hour later, a thoroughly exhausted Joe and Eva were cuddled under the blanket. Eva acknowledged to Joe just how much she had enjoyed the second time even more than the first…much, much more. Joe was pleased that he had made Eva happy.

"It's because I love you so very much, Eva."

"And I love you that much, Joe. You own my heart, soul, mind and body. I'm yours forever."

Joe kissed his Eva softly, feeling so content, so unbelievably happy. This was the only proper way to christen a new home.

The next morning, Joe and Eva walked to the family home for breakfast after seven o'clock and entered the back door when Josephine caught Eva's eyes and winked. Eva just grinned at her and wished she could have a few private minutes with her.

After breakfast, Eva and Josephine did spend a few minutes together and whatever Eva said had Josephine giggling.

Joe heard her as he sat at the table drinking his coffee and thought he was mistaken at first because he had never heard Jo giggle before. When she and Eva returned to the kitchen,

Josephine caught Joe's eyes and held up three fingers, raised her eyebrows and giggled again, then Joe knew that there would be no secrets between the two women, so he'd have to watch himself.

Later that morning, Joe and Eva left the house and met with builder Lee Enders about the barn and corral. He told them it would only take ten days or so and would cost two-hundred-and-fifty dollars. Joe wrote out the draft and Lee said they'd start work on the 14th of June. He and the rest of the town knew what was happening on the twelfth of the month.

After the meeting with the builders, they headed for the church to see Reverend Ike Hatfield of the Methodist church. The wedding was set noon on the 12th of June and Reverend Hatfield explained the later time was because he had already made plans for earlier in the day.

The rest of the day, Eva spent with Josephine and Clara as Will and Joe transferred the sheriff position to Joe. It wasn't a big ceremony, just a simple exchanging of badges and a handshake from his father. Joe stocked the gun rack with the Winchesters he had obtained from the trip and hung the excess gunbelts and Colts from pegs nearby.

While the men were engaging in manly pursuits, Clara and Josephine helped Eva fit the dress she had chosen to wear for the wedding. When Eva had picked the dress, it was for that purpose, and hadn't worn it yet. It was a royal blue with slightly lighter blue highlights. Clara and Josephine thought it was perfect.

Joe made his first rounds as sheriff later the next day, and it took almost two hours as everyone wanted to shake his hand and ask about the trip or offer congratulations for his upcoming marriage, and usually both, but Joe thoroughly enjoyed meeting everyone again as the two weeks he had been gone had seemed more like two months.

When he returned to the office, he went through the wanted posters and set them aside. Twenty minutes later, the door opened, and Eva entered carrying a tray with his lunch wearing a big smile on her face.

"Lunchtime, Sheriff Hennessey."

"Thank you, ma'am. Your civic mindedness will be entered in my daily log."

"I'm just trying to keep your energy levels up for later tonight," she said, with the hint of a grin.

"Then you'd better eat a lot as well, my love."

"I already have. I feel stuffed," she replied, then held up a finger and said, "Don't go there!"

Joe had his mouth open and snapped it shut after her admonition before they shared a good laugh.

Eva sat as he ate and asked, "Did everything go well on your first day?"

"Very. Everyone was happy about the wedding and are looking forward to meeting you."

Eva was already so comfortable in Lincoln and with her new family because it felt as if she belonged.

"It seems that everyone knew about the date before we did."

"It does, doesn't it. Eva, this may sound a bit different, but I want my father as my best man. Is that okay, do you think?"

"I think he'll be ecstatic. I was going to ask Josephine to be my witness, but what about Mama?"

"We'll let Mama escort you down the aisle, that way the entire family will be participating in the ceremony."

"Did you want me to tell them, or can you come over?"

"I'll carry the tray back and we'll tell them together."

"That will be perfect."

So, after he finished eating, Joe and Eva walked to the house and informed Will, Clara and Josephine of their decision. Each was happy with the details and set about making their preparations. They all met with the reverend later that afternoon and he smiled at their exotic choices but said it was perfectly acceptable. He reviewed the entire program before they went home for dinner and chatter about their roles.

Joe and Eva adjourned to their home for a second night of unabashed lovemaking, and the more often they pleasured each other, the better it was. Joe, and Eva even more so, believing that to be impossible.

———

The day before the wedding was one of an odd mixture of mundane and frenzy. Joe did his rounds and had a minor altercation to handle that took three minutes with no damage to either party. The frenzy was at the house, finalizing alterations, preparing food for tomorrow's festivities, and handling last minute details that were missed.

The night before their wedding, Joe and Eva lay together, covered in a light layer of perspiration.

"Shouldn't a bride be nervous on the night before her wedding?" Eva asked.

"That's what I hear. And the groom is supposed to get a case of cold feet, wondering if he is ready to give up his bachelorhood, but my feet are warm and toasty, just like the rest of me."

"And I'm as content as I've ever been in my life. I want this for the rest of my days, Joe."

"And I promise to make them that way, Eva."

She sighed, rested her head on Joe's chest, closed her eyes, then they both slipped into a peaceful sleep.

The morning of the 12th of June was as perfect as possible. Joe made his morning rounds as preparations were made for the wedding, while food was transported to the church basement where a post wedding luncheon would be served. Josephine had arranged for a photographer and other details as well. It was the other details that were the most difficult, but Josephine was adamant that they be done.

At nine o'clock, Eva was escorted to the family home by Clara and Josephine took Joe to their new home to dress for the wedding. Joe asked her why she needed to help him dress and why she insisted he take so long. She replied that men just didn't understand the significance of the ceremony to women, which he admitted was probably true, but still didn't seem to be much of an answer.

Joe thought Eva wouldn't have cared if they had been married by a traveling judge in a privy, but he acquiesced to Josephine, as she knew he would. She was confident in her ability to get Joe to do as she asked, and in this case, it was important.

At 10:50, the train arrived, and six passengers exited, then went directly to the church. Other guests began filtering in later, and soon the church was filled with a good portion of the town.

Finally, Josephine took Joe to the family home where he and Will were subjected to final brushing and lint removal by Clara and Josephine. At 11:40, they were sent to the church, entering the side door.

When Joe and Will reached the altar, Joe looked at the large crowd and was startled. Sitting in the front row were Caroline and Joanne, Jason, Danny, Elizabeth and their son, David. He couldn't react much more than a slight wave of acknowledgement as they all smiled back, but Caroline was practically beaming at him.

Joe knew how they had arrived, and he knew who had talked them into coming. Only Josephine could have pulled it all off.

Josephine, Clara and Eva left the house five minutes after Joe and Will and used the boardwalk most of the way but had to lift their skirts to avoid the dust for the last hundred yards to the church.

When they arrived in the back of the church, Reverend Hatfield spied them at the doorway and waited until Josephine gave him the sign that they were ready. The reverend then nodded to the organist to begin playing and everyone stood. Josephine hurried down the side aisle and took her place at the altar, waiting for Eva.

Clara and Eva stepped off and Joe watched as his bride approached. He was surprised how his heart was pounding in his chest just looking at her. He had heard the phrase 'radiant bride' so often that he put it in the myth category, but not any longer. It seemed that she was bathed in sunlight and everyone else was in the shadows as she neared the altar.

Finally, he took her hand and the formal ceremony began.

To Joe and Eva, the wedding flew past. Their vows were exchanged, the rings placed on fingers, and suddenly, the reverend was pronouncing them man and wife. Joe kissed Eva like they had never kissed before, curling twenty curled toes on the altar.

When they separated, they ignored the applause coming from the assembled crowd as they just smiled into each other's eyes.

After thirty eventful seconds, they finally turned and smiled at the assembly before walking back down the aisle with arms linked.

The newlyweds left the church, and everyone was invited to share a festive luncheon in the basement. More than half the crowd had to return to work so there would be plenty for everyone.

Joe and Eva sat at the head table with the family as well as Caroline, Jason, Danny and Elizabeth. When asked, Josephine admitted to inviting and arranging the trip for everyone. She said it was as much for her own curiosity as to surprise Joe.

Eva paid just a casual amount of attention to Danny, who appreciated her tact.

While they were all eating, Caroline got everyone's attention and stood.

She smiled at everyone and said, "I'd like to thank Josephine for bringing us to this joyous event. For those of you who don't know me, my name is Caroline Stevens. My brother, Danny, Joe and his sister Josephine were the last four children on the children's train ten years ago.

"We made a pact to meet at the end of May in Salina, but circumstances not of our own choosing prevented that reunion. Only Joe was able to make it. He could have just returned to Lincoln and forgotten about all of us, but he didn't because he had promised a nine-year-old girl that he would return and find her if she didn't show up.

"He did just that and saved me not once but twice. I am so happy to see him with Eva and wish them the most happiness. Thank you, Joe. You are and will always be my hero."

She took a seat to a hearty round of applause.

Danny then stood, glanced down at Joe, then back to the room.

"My situation was a bit different from my sister, Caroline's. I had made a mistake and thought I had murdered a man. I was running from the law, but Joe found me and convinced me that I needed to do the right thing. I listened to him and it turned out that I hadn't murdered him at all.

"If Joe hadn't found me and talked to me, I wouldn't have been able to return to my beloved wife and son. As all of you here, I wish only the best for Joe and Eva. And just like Caroline, I regard Joe as a true hero."

Danny sat amid more applause before Josephine rose.

"Most of you already know me as Joe's sister. Since we were small children, Joe was always my big brother and my protector.

When no one else cared. He did. When I was chosen and taken away from Joe, I thought I would die. But Joe searched for me and my protector arrived in time to save me.

“All those years we were apart, I dreamt of his return. I envisioned a strong young man with a star on his chest and justice in his eyes. Those last few days when I had been hoping to see him again at our reunion, I was living in that fantasy. When Joe did arrive, I thought it was just a continuation of that dream, until he meted out justice on my behalf. He did more than just rescue me.

“He brought me back here and gave me a family that loves me and one that I could love. And now, he’s brought me a wonderful sister to love as well. Joe has always been my hero and nothing he has ever done has changed that. I love you, Joe.”

Josephine sat to applause and a lot of damp eyes.

Will then stood, looked down at Joe and kept his eyes there rather than on the assembly.

“Ten years ago, my Clara and I went to the church and found a young man who needed a home. My wife and I had hoped to find a small child, but there was something in Joe’s eyes that talked to us. We chose him and a year later, we adopted him.

“Since he has come into our lives, he has brought us nothing but happiness and pride. All of you are familiar with his exploits over the past month. Everything he did was just to protect the innocent, which is the mark of a good man, a man a father could be proud of, and Clara and I are so very proud of him, as many of you are.

“My son has brought his wonderful wife into our family and we couldn’t be happier. Eva is every bit as good a person as

Joe is, and I consider him to be the best man I've ever known. He is a real hero."

Will sat down to more applause.

Finally, Joe slowly rose to his feet and the room was silent as he spoke.

"I've heard all this talk about my being a hero for doing things that had to be done. But, to me, the greatest heroes are those who do things that don't have to be done, but they do them because they believe it's the right thing to do.

"Winning gunfights or fistfights is all well and good, but ten years ago, two kind and generous people took an angry young man who no one else wanted and brought him into their home. They gave him love and understanding. They gave him a place in their hearts. It took a while for him to adjust to the change because he didn't understand their motive at first. Why would they give so much for nothing in return?

"But then I finally did understand. It was simply because they were good people. They wanted to share what they had, but not just the material things. They wanted to share the love that they already had in abundance. Once I understood that, I accepted them as my true parents.

"So, to me, the true heroes, the ones most worthy of respect and admiration, are my wonderful parents, my beloved mama and papa."

Joe sat down and there was a moment of silence before the room was filled with applause. Joe looked at his mother and father as they looked at him.

There were tears in each of their eyes as they recalled that day ten years earlier when they stood in the church, one angry boy and a childless couple. Each needing the other, and each finding what they needed.

Love.

EPILOGUE

After the wedding, there were photographs made of the newlyweds and the families. There were also photographs taken of the last four children from the train ten years earlier.

At the train station as they were leaving, they vowed to meet each year in Lincoln.

Eva became pregnant in September, and the following June, she gave birth to their daughter, Clara. Clara's grandmother was given the honor of holding the baby before Joe did, at his insistence. The adult Clara looked down at her squirming namesake and openly wept. She was so completely happy as Will stood behind her and smiled at Joe. Eva looked up from her bed and smiled at all of them. They were her family.

Clara was a permanent fixture at Joe and Eva's house after the birth, spoiling her granddaughter horribly.

Caroline and Jason were married in January of that year. She was already pregnant at the time and had a little boy in October, not surprisingly, they named him Joe.

Danny's wife Elizabeth gave birth to another boy the next month, and also named Joe.

But when Eva gave birth to a son the following year, they agreed to name him Will. Grandpa Will was popping buttons over the honor.

Each year, they had their reunions. The photographs showed the changes. Caroline was putting on weight and Danny was losing his hair.

After Joe had rescued Josephine and Caroline, he had remarked that he had been amazed that neither woman showed any signs of serious emotional damage, but over the years, he began to realize that he had been wrong.

Josephine would never marry. She just couldn't trust being with a man again and many young suitors were turned away, not knowing the reason. But Josephine was content with her life. She had her new parents, her brother, and she had Eva. She and Eva became true sisters, and she never regretted her decision to not marry.

Caroline's troubles had just the opposite impact on her. She couldn't sleep without having a man with her. It took a lot of understanding and love from Jason to keep her from wandering, but their marriage survived a few indiscretions.

But Eva flourished in her marriage. Joe had shown her how to shoot and she became very adept. They would ride whenever they could as well. The passion that they felt for each other never waned. It only grew.

Ironically, Joe would never get into another gunfight. His reputation seemed to provide a protective blanket over Lincoln. Bad men didn't want to risk going into the town.

Will continued to advise Joe, not that he needed it.

Joe received frequent offers to work at bigger cities for more money but stayed in Lincoln. It was where he had his family and considered the entire town his extended family. He would never leave his family when they needed his protection.

Eva knew she had his protection even before they had been married, and she had three beautiful children now with the birth of Josephine. She had a family, a sister, and a husband who worshipped her. The same man she regarded as her best friend. She smiled when she thought of how her heart would still skip a beat when she saw Joe each day. Joe had often told her that he felt a rush when he saw her.

At the tenth reunion, they agreed to call an end to them. It seemed the right time. One last photograph was taken, farewells were made, and they returned to their homes.

That night, Eva was curled up with Joe after all the children were asleep. Eva may have filled out some, but she still had a beautiful figure, as Joe told her often.

“Joe, are you sorry that the reunions are over?” she asked softly.

“No, Eva. It was time. We made the vows to meet ten years after we first were separated, and we did meet for ten more years. It was time.”

“Won’t you miss them?”

“I will. But we all miss someone, sooner or later.”

Joe pulled Eva closer and kissed her and said, “But I will never miss you, my love. Because I will never let you go.”

So, Joe and Eva slept. Each once a forgotten child. One of the thousands that crossed the land hopefully to find a family that wanted them. Some were unfortunate, like Josephine, Caroline, and Eva. Others were blessed, like Danny and especially Joe.

As they slept, just three houses down slept the two compassionate adults who had seen more than just an angry young boy standing in front of them. They saw a son they could love and would love them in return and had been rewarded for their faith many times over.

Joe was indeed the most fortunate of the last four on the train.

THE LAST FOUR

1	Rock Creek	12/26/2016
2	North of Denton	01/02/2017
3	Fort Selden	01/07/2017
4	Scotts Bluff	01/14/2017
5	South of Denver	01/22/2017
6	Miles City	01/28/2017
7	Hopewell	02/04/2017
8	Nueva Luz	02/12/2017
9	The Witch of Dakota	02/19/2017
10	Baker City	03/13/2017
11	The Gun Smith	03/21/2017
12	Gus	03/24/2017
13	Wilmore	04/06/2017
14	Mister Thor	04/20/2017
15	Nora	04/26/2017
16	Max	05/09/2017
17	Hunting Pearl	05/14/2017
18	Bessie	05/25/2017
19	The Last Four	05/29/2017
20	Zack	06/12/2017
21	Finding Bucky	06/21/2017
22	The Debt	06/30/2017
23	The Scalawags	07/11/2017
24	The Stampede	07/20/2017
25	The Wake of the Bertrand	07/31/2017
26	Cole	08/09/2017
27	Luke	09/05/2017
28	The Eclipse	09/21/2017
29	A.J. Smith	10/03/2017
30	Slow John	11/05/2017
31	The Second Star	11/15/2017
32	Tate	12/03/2017
33	Virgil's Herd	12/14/2017
34	Marsh's Valley	01/01/2018
35	Alex Paine	01/18/2018
36	Ben Gray	02/05/2018

37	War Adams	03/05/2018
38	Mac's Cabin	03/21/2018
39	Will Scott	04/13/2018
40	Sheriff Joe	04/22/2018
41	Chance	05/17/2018
42	Doc Holt	06/17/2018
43	Ted Shepard	07/13/2018
44	Haven	07/30/2018
45	Sam's County	08/15/2018
46	Matt Dunne	09/10/2018
47	Conn Jackson	10/05/2018
48	Gabe Owens	10/27/2018
49	Abandoned	11/19/2018
50	Retribution	12/21/2018
51	Inevitable	02/04/2019
52	Scandal in Topeka	03/18/2019
53	Return to Hardeman County	04/10/2019
54	Deception	06/02/2019
55	The Silver Widows	06/27/2019
56	Hitch	08/21/2019
57	Dylan's Journey	09/10/2019
58	Bryn's War	11/06/2019
59	Huw's Legacy	11/30/2019
60	Lynn's Search	12/22/2019
61	Bethan's Choice	02/10/2020
62	Rhody Jones	03/11/2020